STIFF PENALTY

"You claim to be Paul Niccolo Rénard?" Chiang challenged.

The figure on the screen tilted his head with the grave irony familiar from so many news clips. "No," he said. "I claim to be Brother Benedict. However, I was, years ago, Paul Niccolo Rénard."

"96.7 percent correlation, based on voiceprint and body mannerisms," Kirsten informed Chiang. "After ten years, that's as close to unity as you'll get."

Chiang shook his head. "Whatever you call yourself, I have need of your talents. I am sending down a life pod. You will enter it and be taken up to my craft."

Benedict pursed his lips. "If I refuse?"

"I shall destroy every installation on or orbiting this planet."

THE GAME OF
FOX AND LION

Robert R. Chase

A Del Rey Book

BALLANTINE BOOKS • NEW YORK

A Del Rey Book
Published by Ballantine Books
Copyright © 1986 by Robert R. Chase

Library of Congress Catalog Card Number: 86-90869

ISBN 0-345-33384-5

Manufactured in the United States of America

First Edition: September 1986

Cover Art by Darrell K. Sweet

To my father,
for his love, friendship, and constant support

A prince being thus obliged to know well how to act as a beast must imitate the fox and the lion, for the lion cannot protect himself from traps, and the fox cannot defend himself from wolves.

—Machiavelli, *The Prince*

Where lion's skin will not reach, you must patch it out with the fox's.

—Plutarch, *Lives*

I

CRASHING DOWN THE QUANTUM LADDER, SPLASHING
out a halo wake of Cerenkov radiation, the *Gryffon's
Pride* fell into normal space. New sets of physical con-
stants grasped the frame of the cruiser, slowing and
compressing it.

A shock of coldness washed through Chiang's fevered
body. Chemjets embedded in the commchair pinpricked
his neck, injecting stimulants, but his exhaustion overwhelmed the drugs. Sleep swept through his body, attempting to claim the due too long denied it.

No! Chiang thought violently, willing his eyes to open.
His hands clenched the arms of the commchair as if he
could literally pull himself up from that dark, comforting
well. *I cannot afford to be unconscious at the doorstep of
our goal.* The fact that once asleep he might never be
allowed to waken spurred his production of adrenaline.

"Navigation." He grimaced at the hoarse quaver in his
voice. A fit of shivering seized him, making further
speech momentarily impossible.

"Altair is at thirty by forty-two," Kirsten reported,
her voice sliding falsetto through half a dozen micro-

1

tones. Chiang grinned involuntarily. She must be in even worse shape than he was.

The star was close enough that even with the view-screen's compensators reducing the glare, it was far too bright to look at directly. Certainly too bright for Chiang's eyes, so long used to the gentler yellow-orange of Centaurus B.

Kirsten tapped out a series of figures, causing them to appear simultaneously on Chiang's and the captain's screens.

"We are fifty-five degrees above the ecliptic and ap-proximately four light-minutes away from Ariel," Cap-tain MacAndrews announced. "I am programming deceleration to have us in orbit in approximately—two hours."

The pause was for a quick glance at Chiang. They both knew it was possible to program more violent deceleration and so advance the ETO one hour. But after thirty-six hours of consciousness in Space$_4$, Chiang needed the recovery time.

"Very good," Chiang said.

At that, it was not easy. Timed bursts of intensive deceleration made the inertial compensators whine and strain beyond their limits. At those times, Chiang would be pressed more and more firmly into his commchair until his vision blurred and his breath came in short, forced pants. During one of the worst periods, Chiang lost consciousness. He was sure he had been out no longer than a few minutes. The crew pretended not to have noticed.

"We have Ariel on visual," MacAndrews said.

A sickle of light appeared on the screen before Chiang.

"Lemnos," he murmured. The reference meant noth-ing to anybody but Chiang, now that Herter was dead. Herter, who had been his expert on the Rénard. Herter, whose scorched body was floating in emptiness more than a light-year behind them.

"That dot off to port is the Stewards' main station," the captain said. "According to our reports, it coordinates what little freighter traffic they have and also monitors their terraforming progress."

"Have they noticed us?" Chiang asked. "Our Cerenkov wake has preceded us by nearly two hours."

"No sign of it," MacAndrews replied. "Given our surfacing distance, they would need a full wartime alert with a seven hundred twenty intruder watch. Monks generally aren't set up for that."

"Perhaps," Chiang said, withholding judgment. "Gunners," he requested, irritated that he had not asked for their input before now. And he'd made a double mistake. They had only one gunner now.

"No problem on my scopes." Younger's voice was as easygoing as always. "All emissions consistent with the settlement being as advertised. Not even any screening. No bogies in a full seven twenty."

"What's transmission delay?" Chiang asked.

"Approximately ninety seconds," Kirsten replied.

"Set to transmit and record." Chiang waited. When a new light winked green before him, he spoke formally.

"This is John Lei Chiang, Centauran Councilor, master of Chiang Biosynthetics, commander of the battle-cruiser *Gryffon's Pride*, calling Ariel. This is a Priority Mission of the Human Alliance. You are ordered to locate and surrender to me one Paul Niccolo Rénard. Failure to do so will be considered treason and will be dealt with accordingly."

Chiang relaxed as the green light vanished and the recorder began rebroadcasting his message. In a very few minutes, there would be chaos in the Stewards' headquarters.

For the first time in months, his desperation-fueled anger drained away. The Stewards would not be able to withstand him. Nonetheless, they might not be able to help him, either. The trail was ten years cold. It led to Ariel only on the slimmest of conjectures. And the Fox, who had duped a dozen planetary governments, could certainly have done the same to a group of monks.

Considered realistically, the odds were absurdly long. Only certainty of defeat, otherwise, made the game worth playing at all.

A face materialized on his screen: close-clipped white hair; a beefy, lined face; chest and arms clothed in some anonymous brown fabric. Only the pendant cross, of some finely polished wood, rescued the figure from complete drabness.

"I am Abbot Tsintolas," the figure stated. "For the record, I protest your uncalled for and peremptory tone. I reminded you that Ariel is far beyond your jurisdiction. Despite this, out of respect for the authority you do have, I have run a thorough memory check of our computer. We have no record of any Paul Niccolo Rénard."

Chiang touched the squelch button. "Targets."

"The main orbital station," Younger replied. "There are also two weather satellites over this hemisphere."

"Manned?"

"Unlikely. They are less than two meters across."

"Lock on one." He released the squelch button. "Abbot Tsintolas, the Rénard came to Ariel ten years ago on the freighter *Gypsy Dancer*, out of 61 Cygni V. He may have been using the name Philip Head or Philip Archer. He never returned.

"I must also inform you that your legal analysis is faulty. Under wartime emergency powers, the jurisdiction of officers of the Alliance is defined not by territory but by subject. Put simply, where humans are, there is our jurisdiction."

Unexpectedly, the feigned anger became real, rising out of nowhere to master him. "And since you wish to force the matter, I shall demonstrate the punishment for foot-dragging. If you do not cooperate, my next target will be your main orbital station. If still you balk, I will then destroy, one by one, your ground installations until none are left. You have exactly one half hour.

"Cut transmission." Then he gave the order. "Fire."

The laser pulse leapt from the battlecruiser. Chiang found himself holding his breath, waiting for the returning photons to bring their tardy message.

Over the planet, a new, small star blinked into existence, grew, then dimmed as the vaporized metal expanded into the vacuum.

"That was almost directly over their main ground installation," Younger remarked. "It should have made a good show from the ground."

Chiang collapsed back into his commchair, his anger suddenly gone. Another fit of shivering shook him. For most of his adult life he had realized that his fellow humans were not to be trusted. Now his own body was betraying him.

Firing on that satellite might have been an irrevocable mistake. Perhaps the Stewards truly knew nothing of the Rénard under any name. How, then, could he keep from destroying their base without disastrous loss of face? Yet that would gain him nothing but the dead end of the one trail that might have led to safety. Worse, the Stewards were far from the weakest Order in the Church. Once news of his apparently unprovoked attack reached Chiron, even those who hated the Church would use it to tear him down.

Give me an excuse to spare you, he thought. For both our sakes.

The planet grew before them, the light of Altair sweeping across its surface. Red lights glowed mysteriously in the half that was still in darkness. Chiang frowned. There were no large cities on this planet. Then, as they swung fully over the dayside, he saw the source of the red glow. In a mountain range fringing the western edge of a large continent, no fewer than six volcanoes were erupting simultaneously, spewing clouds of ash that wreathed the continent until broken up by a frontal system. Innumerable shades of gray and brown textured the land. A dust storm a thousand kilometers long, like a snake writhing sideways, raced across a desert. Rings stretched across the plains, intersecting and encircling each other. Even much of the coastline seemed scalloped.

"I have moved us into synchronous orbit," MacAndrews announced. "We are thirty degrees away from the main orbital station."

"I have it locked on my scopes," Younger confirmed.

They waited.

If the Rénard was down there, he would know that all he need do was sit tight in some suitably deep hole, and his pursuers would rage vainly from the sky.

At twenty-seven minutes, Chiang's screen glowed to life. It was a split image, apparently originating from two separate locations. One half was Abbot Tsintolas; the other was a taller, thinner figure dressed in the same drab clothing.

"—is a full member of our Order and so is entitled to sanctuary of Holy Mother Church," Tsintolas was saying. "He speaks to you because he wishes to, and to keep you from grave sin."

Chiang felt torn between anger and derisive laughter. "You claim to be Paul Niccolo Rénard?" he challenged.

The figure tilted his head with the grave irony familiar from so many news clips. "No," he said. "I claim to be Brother Benedict. However, I was, years ago, Paul Niccolo Rénard."

"Herter's program gives a ninety-six point seven percent correlation, based on voiceprint and body mannerisms," Kirsten said in Chiang's earphones. "After ten years, that's as close to unity as you'll get."

Chiang shook his head, fascinated yet unsure. "Whatever you call yourself, I have need of your talents. I am sending down a life pod. You will enter it and be taken up to my craft."

Brother Benedict pursed his lips. "If I refuse?"

"I shall destroy every manmade installation on or orbiting this planet."

Abbot Tsintolas apparently said something not picked up by the microphones. Benedict listened intently, then shook his head.

"No," he murmured. "That would be poor repayment for your hospitality. Please grant me permission to leave Ariel and the immediate discipline of the order."

Tsintolas was silent for a long minute. "Granted," he said, most unwillingly.

Benedict looked directly at Chiang. His whole manner had changed so that he brought to mind a fencer, excited yet supple with forced relaxation.

"I capitulate," he said. "Is indenture still legal in the Centauran system?"

"Yes," Chiang replied.

"Then set your recorders going." The monk seemed to draw himself up. "I, Brother Benedict of the Order of Stewards, formerly known as Paul Niccolo Rénard, in sound mind and of my own free will, by the laws of Centaurus and with the witness of the Church, do hereby indenture myself for the customary term of seven years to John Lei Chiang, to serve him faithfully and well and to obey his every legal and moral command, so help me God."

"I accept your bond," Chiang replied, sealing the contract.

"I am pleased you find that acceptable."

It was more than acceptable; it was much more than Chiang had dared hope for. In a breath, what might otherwise have been construed to be piracy and kidnapping had been transformed into a legally binding transaction.

"I will send the life pod down for you."

"No," Benedict said. "You will come down. We must talk."

Chiang laughed. "And play fly to your spider, just like that? Fox, you have been among simpletons too long if you think to catch me that easily."

Benedict assumed an air of pained innocence. "You don't trust me?"

"Given your initial reluctance, I would be a fool to."

"Then you have an insoluble problem. For you to have come so far and to behave so violently argues that you need me very much."

Chiang was silent.

"You are a proud man," Benedict continued. "You would not seek help for a problem you could handle yourself. Finding yourself overmatched, you reasoned that a Multi-Neural Capacitant could evaluate more data, see connections and relationships you could not, and perhaps find a solution.

"Therefore, at some point you will ask me for advice, and I will give it to you. You will then be faced with a dilemma. Perhaps I have given you the solution you have been seeking, in which case you should follow my advice. On the other hand, what appears to be a solution may be a time bomb, conceived by the vengeful Fox to gain his freedom while destroying you.

"Either you can trust me or you cannot. If you cannot, you will not follow my counsel. That will make me useless to you, and in that case I may just as well be left here. Or you can trust me. In which case you will come down now. Alone."

"What will that gain me?" Chiang asked after a pause.

"My counsel. For your ears."

"This has gone on long enough," MacAndrews decided. "Younger, prepare to fire on the orbital station."

"No!" Chiang countermanded. Benedict had convinced him by an argument he had *not* made. Because, as they both understood, it was not an argument that could be made over an open communications link.

"Ready the life pod. I'm going down."

II

THE LIFE POD WAS DIM AND QUIET. LIGHT GLOWED softly from the simplified instrument panel with its one viewscreen. Not that either were necessary for this trip: The pod's computer was homing in on a radio beam that would guide him straight down. There was plenty of time to reflect on his conversation with MacAndrews.

It had been clear that she was near open rebellion. Normally, Chiang would have let her fume. Now, however, anxious to confirm his reasoning, he had given her an opening. They had been checking out the life pod.

"You doubt my decision, Captain." It was not a question.

"They will take you hostage," MacAndrews said.

"No. Abbot Tsintolas would never do anything so foolish. There are too many interests still smarting from the loss of New Eden. Taking a Centauran Councilor hostage would give them the perfect pretext to go grabbing real estate."

"Rénard will, then, on his own."

"He won't, because he realizes it would do him no good." Seeing her expression, he activated the communicator.

"Kirsten, this is Chiang. Are you receiving?"

"Loud and clear, sir."

"Patch in Younger. This is for everyone."

"Younger on."

"Good. I want you all to hear the orders I am giving Captain MacAndrews so there will be no argument if she has to execute them.

"In the event I am taken hostage, you are to *immediately* destroy the orbital station. You shall then locate and destroy the surface installations at the rate of one each thirty minutes until the pod returns with both myself and Rénard.

"Should I be returned dead, you are to return to Chiron by the safest route and make a report of these happenings to the Citizens' attorney. Under no circumstances will you pay any heed to threats on my life. Understood?"

There was a chorus of affirmatives.

"Good. Out." He turned back to MacAndrews. "The thing about hostages is that they are useful only so long as they are unused. Rénard knows that. I think he also knows enough about me already to realize I am not about to beg for my life."

Surprising, he thought now, the exhilarating freedom of action one had when utterly desperate.

There was a slight jar as the pod touched down. Telltales blazed green. Chiang thumbed the transmit button. "This is Chiang. I have landed. Will get back to you per schedule."

Without waiting for a response, he flicked both airlock switches. Part of the wall next to him sank into itself. Brilliant white sunlight slanted into the cabin, turning the dust motes into minute, dancing diamonds. Cool, thin air drifted inside smelling of ozone and other, more subtle fragrances.

Chiang swung himself out of the cabin and stood, squinting against the sunlight. Two silhouetted figures were approaching. Nausea, sudden and unexpected, made him lean against the side of the pod.

Gentle pressure supported him beneath both arms. "Master Chiang, you have had a difficult voyage. I'm doubly glad I brought Brother Dimitri with me."

Chiang looked at the speaker. Benedict's eyes appeared open and guileless, their only emotion a faint concern. Brother Dimitri, on his other side, was a younger man with narrow, dark eyes and a large hook nose that vaguely resembled a pelican's bill.

"I am as well as can be expected," Chiang said, straightening himself. He did not yet feel strong enough to shake off their arms. "What is this counsel of yours that is worth this inconvenience?"

"In a moment, sir. We must first take you through in-processing."

Chiang looked sharply at Benedict. "I am to report to my ship at irregularly timed intervals," he said, gesturing at the transmitter slung over his shoulder. "Failure to adhere to schedule will cause immediate retribution."

Both of his companions nodded politely, as if he had made no more than a comment on the weather.

They walked across the dusty, leveled plain that served as a spaceport. Three sides of it were enclosed by rows of scrub pines that tried futilely to serve as windbreaks against the sudden gusts that whirled dust about their knees. There was in the distance another roaring distinct from the wind. They were, Chiang remembered, right on the coast.

The fourth side of the field was flanked by a building three stories high and quarried from a light native granite. Looking at it, Chiang thought of a series of intersecting, squat, truncated cones. Or, incongruously, of A-frame houses he had seen high in the ski country of the Rocky Mountains on Earth. Whatever had been the main architectural plan had long ago been swallowed up in a baroque assemblage of added wings and extensions.

A large porch extended across the face and around the sides. Small groups of monks walked sedately about their business, seemingly oblivious to his arrival.

Benedict led him up a short ramp into the building. "We have visitors and novices from every settled system. A distressingly large number have masters who do not want to let them go. These methods of bondage can sometimes be quite ingenious. For this reason, Brother Dimitri had our Clean Room constructed."

They entered a long, carpeted hallway and stopped before an open doorway. Chiang became aware of a distinct electronic hum.

"Perhaps you should leave your transmitter here," Brother Dimitri suggested, indicating a chair by the doorway. "What's going to happen is absolutely harmless to humans, but it just might damage some circuitry. We should hate"—he glanced up involuntarily—"to do that."

Reluctantly, Chiang unshouldered the transmitter and laid it on the chair. He stepped through the doorway.

The Clean Room was no more than four meters by four meters and slightly over two meters high. It was lit by standard glow panels on the ceiling, the walls, and the floor. In the left wall, in the ceiling, and directly in front of him were transparent panels behind which crouched what looked like cameras.

"Hold on, now," Benedict murmured. "This can be disconcerting."

The light began to increase. Chiang shut his eyes—futilely. The light seemed to penetrate right through his lids.

At the same time, a hum, barely within his range of hearing, became more and more insistent. The sonics became tangible, like little cat claws gently raking every centimeter of his body—and suddenly all converging on the back of his neck. Dimitri, his face a skull-shaped black blur, reached behind Chiang and plucked something from his collar.

The light and the sonics ceased simultaneously. Guided by Benedict, Chiang staggered into an adjacent room and sat down heavily, waiting for his eyes to readjust.

Brother Dimitri bent over a table and peered through a magnifying glass. "Beautiful," he said. "Smaller than the ones I used and even more versatile."

He passed the magnifying glass and the object of his admiration over to Chiang. A mechanical insect, Chiang thought as it came into focus. The egg-shaped body was no larger than a millimeter. Two threadlike legs, each fifteen millimeters long, protruded from opposite sides of the body.

"What is it, exactly?" Benedict asked.

"Eavesdropping device," Dimitri said. "One of the cute things about it is that it not only picks up conversation but also transmits the subject's pulse rate and perspiration, giving an experienced operator a reasonably good indication of when the subject is lying."

"Range?" Benedict asked, a shade of urgency in his voice.

"One kilometer in the city. Maybe up to five kilometers in the country, depending upon terrain and atmospheric conditions."

"Power source?"

"Well, that is another clever thing. These legs not only anchor the device and serve as antennae *and* sensors, they are also formed of thermoelectric couples. The subject's own body heat powers it."

There was a momentary silence.

"We used to use these all the time," Brother Dimitri continued. "Had thousands of people bugged. That's no exaggeration. In fact, the bottleneck was transcribing the data and trying to make some sense of it all. We used to run out of recording disks quite regularly. The only thing to do then was dummy up the log. When the Inspector caught on, we were all canned."

What, Chiang wondered, is a man like this doing in a monastery? With an effort, he focused on a more immediate problem. "How did you know I carried such a device?"

"I didn't," Benedict admitted. "I mean, never having seen you before, knowing nothing except the self-evident about you, how could anyone possibly know that?

"But when I was in the world, my patrons were generally targets of such devices. It seemed only a sensible precaution to resolve the matter. Our discovery, however, raises an inevitable question: Who placed it on you? Do you have a spy on your ship, Master Chiang?"

"I did," Chiang said. "He's dead."

"Tell me about it."

Gustav Herter had been a professor of political philosophy at the University of Munich. He had won awards for his three-volume study *Florentine Brotherhood: A Study of the Multi-Neural Capacitants and Their Effect on the Polity*. He had been the greatest living expert on Paul Niccolo Rénard. Chiang had managed, at great expense, to free him from his university commitments and take him on as an adviser. When the trail had led to Ariel, Chiang had brought him along to aid in negotiating for Rénard's services.

They had all been in the cold-sleep cubicles in the aft of the ship, metabolisms almost halted in an effort to minimize the distorting effects of Space$_4$ as the *Gryffon's Pride* sped through the quantaverse at 250 times lightspeed, aimed at Altair.

What happened was necessarily conjecture, but this was the best reconstruction: A light-year from their goal, the ship's computer, responding to an unauthorized program change, had awakened Herter. His first act on reaching consciousness had been to inject himself with tranquilizers from his kit to minimize the stress of Space$_4$

on his nervous system. His second act had been to start down the row of cubicles, ripping out their life stabilization circuitry. James, a gunner, and Faisal, the ship's engineer, had died that way.

Then he had arrived at Chiang's cubicle, flipped open the cartridge, and reached in. Ten thousand volts had arced through his body and left him floating in the walkway.

"Very nice," Benedict said approvingly. "Such foresight is as commendable as it is rare."

Brother Dimitri looked at him reprovingly.

"Did Herter have access to the ship's computer?" Benedict continued.

"No," Chiang said. "He was brought on board just before lift-off and immediately conducted to his cold-sleep cubicle."

"So he must have had a confederate. Someone in your dock or on board. Of the ship's crew, who had access to that program?"

"Every one of them. There are consoles at each station. Each has general access."

The electrical discharge had kicked in an automatic awakening program for the rest of the crew. Chiang had ordered the bodies jettisoned. Then, telling the crew that he feared further tampering with the ship's computer, he had ordered manual control for the rest of the flight. MacAndrews, Kirsten, and Younger had stood staggered eight-hour shifts. Chiang himself had stayed awake for the entire thirty-six-hour period until they surfaced in Space$_1$, within the Altair system.

"Thirty-six hours conscious in Space$_4$," Benedict murmured in astonishment. "That has to be six times the previous record. You are blessed to be alive, even more blessed to be still sane. You must have a constitution of iron."

"The difficulties," Chiang said, "are much exaggerated. We had damper fields on, of course. And we had tranquilizers to deal with the most serious effects."

"The shirt you have on," Brother Dimitri said. "Is it the same shirt you were wearing when Herter arrived on board?"

Chiang shook his head. "I carried it on board in my flight bag and stowed it in my locker. Both have locks keyed to my thumb only."

"So it was either in place when the shirt was packed, or one of your crew placed it in the last few hours," Benedict concluded.

"We can do better than that," Brother Dimitri said. "Anyone who had access to this shirt before it was packed would have placed it inside the collar, both to lessen chances of detection and to increase the efficiency of the thermoelectric coupling effect.

"This, however, was snagged on the outside threads of the collar as if someone in the close confines of the ship had just brushed past, leaving it behind."

"So Herter's accomplice was definitely one of my crew." Chiang sighed. "I suspected as much. That was the real reason I kept myself awake: I did not want to leave the spy with only one other member of the crew conscious.

"But with this device we have our clue. We will now go back to the *Gryffon's Pride* and conduct a surprise search. Somewhere there will be a receiver and a recorder. They will identify the spy.

"And with that out of the way, we will return to Centaurus."

"No," Benedict said. "You are a sick man, Master Chiang! You have been putting off the debt you owe your body far too long; it will soon be claimed with a vengeance. The only place you or your crew should be headed is to our infirmary."

"I am quite able—" Chiang began heatedly.

"And even if you and your crew *are* superhuman,"

Benedict continued, "there is still your ship to consider. Your computer data base has to be checked and justified. Space$_4$ stresses have almost certainly introduced random factors into the memory. The main drive itself *must* be recalibrated. Otherwise, even odds that you will jump into Space$_5$ and be vaporized. You know these things!"

"I have already been away too long," Chiang objected.

"Perhaps so," Benedict agreed. "I have no idea what situation you left behind. But if you leave immediately, you shall be in no condition to influence anything in the unlikely event you actually arrive. Much better to recuperate and overhaul your ship. Even if the entire Centauran system is out after your blood, with a healthy crew and a sound ship, I can help you wheel and deal, feint, attack, plead for mercy, whatever is most likely to shift the odds. But I am not going with you now. If that displeases you, then shoot me. That death, at least, will be clean and quick."

The other man was right, Chiang realized. Whatever his motivation, whether in good faith or not, Benedict had the facts on his side. In the last few minutes, chills and nausea had followed each other with increasing frequency. He feared suddenly that he had very little time remaining to him.

"Very well," he said heavily. "Let's go outside. I will call the ship down."

They guided him back to the corridor. Dimitri handed him the transmitter.

"This is Chiang sending true blue to *Gryffon's Pride*. Bring the ship down for recalibration and justification, Captain. The situation here seems secure."

After a pause, the answer came: "Acknowledged."

He let the transmitter fall. The roaring of the wind and the unseen sea seemed much louder now. Benedict was asking him something, but Chiang could not distinguish the words. He took a step forward.

And the wind and the dust and the bright white star whirled above his head faster and faster and shrank to an eye-searing point.

And vanished.

III

HE EXISTED IN JAGGED, DISCONNECTED LIGHTNING strokes.

—Being supported above the tiles as tension grew in his abdomen to crest in convulsions that jackknifed him forward in waves of vomiting so severe that he had hardly time to gasp for breath. Again. And again.

—Cool wetness as a cloth was laid across his forehead, as it gently cleaned his lips.

—The fist seemed to fall from his stomach to his bowels and squeeze spasmodically. The pain was unprecedented. Even when he was completely voided, the spasms continued, as if trying to excrete the essence of pain itself.

—Sheets fresh and crisp from the wind. He drowsed, savoring their white cleanliness.

—Inside the *Gryffon's Pride*, decelerating as it came out of Space$_4$. Decelerating too quickly. The ship began to shudder. He held his breath, trying vainly to control the shivering. Hands tucked a blanket about him.

"Not another one. The main thing is to get that temperature down! If it goes any higher, I will authorize ice packs."

—Timeless moments between one breath and another, rest as deep as if he were floating in zero gravity.

Shreds of self-awareness returned. He was Chiang. He was here for the Rénard.

As if triggered by that thought, his point of view fled through the walls down long, dim corridors to where one figure dressed in the Stewards' coverall and hiking shoes walked alone. Although the face was in shadows, Chiang knew he was looking at Benedict.

The figure walked slowly and silently. Sudden tongues of fire, blinding in brilliance, leapt upward from the floor. The figure strode right through, unconcerned. Not a line of his face was changed.

Yet Chiang was absolutely certain that this was a different person.

It happened again, times without number. Each time the flames seemed to have no effect. Each time Chiang sensed profound change.

Then Benedict was by his bedside, sponging his brow, arranging his bedclothes to make him more comfortable. Each movement was both gentle and impersonal. There was no hint of anger or threat. Yet something unidentified about him was terrifying.

Shamed, Chiang levered himself up from the bed to confront the object of his irrational fear. The night-light showed him only the ghostly outline of an image. He lurched across to it.

This time the face itself shifted. The hair became dark and thick, framing the skull like a mane. The eyes deepened to brown flecked with gold. Skin color darkened, cheekbones lifted, yet the whole face seemed to become flatter.

Chiang staggered back from the mirror in confusion. He collapsed across the bed and slept peacefully for twelve hours.

* * *

"Very pleased to see you well again, sir," MacAndrews said.

Chiang regarded her over the rim of his teacup. She was standing at ease, legs slightly spread, hands clasped behind her. The tea was hot and soothing; he excused himself from reply by taking another swallow.

Only a slit of sunlight spilled onto the floor; he guessed the time to be near the local noon. Propped up on pillows, Chiang found the silence almost sensuous. It was only accentuated by the tread of passing footsteps, the murmur of voices outside his window.

"Thank you," he said at last. "I trust the other crew members have recovered."

"Pretty well for the last two days," MacAndrews said. "Of course, none of us had more than twenty-four hours' consciousness in Space$_4$, and that was split up."

Chiang grunted. "How are you being treated?"

"All things considered, extremely well." Inexplicably, MacAndrews's face became an even deeper red than her sunburn could account for. Chiang raised an eyebrow and waited patiently.

"We were surprised by your order to land," she explained. "As soon as the drive was shut off, we looked for you. When you didn't appear at the ship, our fears of treachery seemed well founded. Benedict shouted up at us that you were suffering from reaction to Space$_4$. Given the way we were all feeling, that should have sounded plausible enough. It didn't, though. I had Younger keep Benedict hostage while I followed Brother Dimitri to the infirmary. I interrogated the medical staff at gunpoint for twenty minutes before I was completely convinced."

Chiang smiled grimly. "Have our high-handed methods made us unpopular?"

"No." MacAndrews seemed to search for words. "Oddly enough, they seem to regard us as—heroes!

Everyone seems to know that we survived an assassination attempt and then made the last part of our
voyage without cold sleep. With a few exceptions, they
have given us the deference due explorers like Cook or
Armstrong."

"They must lead very dull lives," Chiang said drily. "I
see you have taken advantage of your ascent to stardom
by spending most of your time on the beach, sunbathing.
I can smell the lotion from here."

"What—oh, no, sir. We have all been issued sun-
screen and been told to wear it if we spend more than a
few minutes outside. Altair is an A-type star with much
more ultraviolet than any of us are used to." She looked
down at her reddened hands. "You can fry before you
know it," she added ruefully.

She looked up again. "You will notice it on the monks
when you dine in the refectory. Their hands and faces
are nut-brown. But then one reaches across the table for
salt, and a sleeve pulls back exposing dead white flesh.
The effect is so startling, you catch yourself thinking that
you are looking at a patchwork of two different people."

That called forth an uneasy echo in Chiang's mind.
"Captain, I suppose you have spent some time with this
man who calls himself Brother Benedict. Are you absolutely sure that he is the Rénard?"

"One of the first things I did," MacAndrews said,
"was to take a skin sample from his index finger. The
readout was positive. Brother Benedict is genetically
identical to Paul Niccolo Rénard."

"Do you have some special reason for asking?"

Chiang had no intention of recounting his bizarre
dream to her. "Only that it would fit very nicely what we
know of the Rénard's humor to leave on his trail a decoy
to be picked up as himself by any searchers, a decoy that
would protest another identity in an unconvincing manner."

"The genetic pattern is the same," she repeated, "and Snowden made no MNC clones."

"None," Chiang corrected, "that we know of."

The hallway twisted and twisted again. Kirsten stopped, trying to regain her bearings. There was absolute silence. Light blazed from narrow horizontal slits near the ceiling. The effect, paradoxically, was to increase the gloom of the corridor.

The problem, Kirsten told herself, was that each building had been designed and added on individually. The atmosphere apparently had not been breathable during most of the construction, so each building was self-contained, save for one or two locks that led into adjoining buildings. The locks were on different levels in different buildings. Not being able to discern any plan, Kirsten had had to travel the length and back of several floors to get from one building to the next. To make it worse, each hallway had become deserted as soon as she had realized she was lost. The only faces were those of obscure bearded men and dull-eyed Virgins staring down from paintings or occasional woolen tapestries.

"May I help you, Navigator Kirsten?"

Kirsten turned around, startled. "Yes, you may, Brother Timothy. I have been looking for you for over an hour, stumbling around in this disordered maze you call a monastery. I would have asked directions, but I couldn't find anyone. Where have you all been?"

Brother Timothy looked a bit surprised himself. "Forgive me, please. We were just at sexts, in the chapel."

She followed him to his office. Brother Timothy was just out of the novitiate and had been assigned to the ship's crew as guide, Kirsten suspected, only to keep some more senior and important monk from that task.

Brother Timothy sat down at his desk, picked up a stylus, and began sketching directly on his terminal's cathode tube. When he finished, he touched a button, and several sheets tumbled out of a slot.

"Here is a rough map of the entire complex. It's a bit crude, I'm afraid, but it should prevent you or your companions from getting lost again.

"Now, what were you coming to see me about?"

"Our quarters," Kirsten answered. "Captain MacAndrews and I are lodged in the extreme northern corner of this complex, at great remove from both our spacecraft and from Master Chiang and Younger, our gunner. This is very inconvenient."

"Your quarters are those set aside by the Abbot for female visitors," Timothy explained. "I think you would appreciate the privacy, especially as regards sanitary facilities."

"We are crew members," Kirsten said indifferently. "We are used to close quarters with little or no privacy."

"There is also the emotional tranquility of the brothers to consider," Timothy said slowly. "They would almost certainly find your, uh, intimate presence disruptive."

Kirsten stared at him, uncertain whether to laugh or take offense. "I assure you, Brother Timothy, that however little your order thinks of women, whatever defects we have are not catching."

"Oh, no, Navigator! Please don't take offense at my poor phrasing. There is nothing wrong with you. Indeed, were you and Captain MacAndrews less vibrant examples of the full flowering of young womanhood, the difficulty would be less.

"The problem is, precisely, with us. If we were perfect monks, we could treat you as our sisters, with perfect love and perfect detachment. However, most of us are far from perfect. Vows of celibacy, which cause only minor difficulty most of the time—when, after all, there are no women for light-years—become suddenly very sticky in close proximity to an attractive blonde and," he added with a nod, "an equally attractive brunette."

Kirsten was touched by Timothy's evident sincerity and his anxiety about having offended her. "If your vows of celibacy are so difficult, why not join another order? I mean, I know little about your Church; my own background is Baptist. But my understanding is that since the Reunification the Catholic church has allowed several communities and orders of married religious. Why not join one of those?"

Timothy shook his head decisively. "That is very well for them. For us, given our mission, it is impossible.

"Look, rather than have me lecture, why don't you accompany me on a tour? I can show you what we are doing. It should also help you find your way about."

Caught up in his enthusiasm, Kirsten followed him down a flight of stone steps. To her surprise, she recognized the main entry hall of the monastery. Timothy indicated a large oil painting hanging above the hallway. A young man in a habit somewhat different from that of the Stewards seemed to be arguing with three other men, evidently superiors of some kind. Their expressions respectively ranged from skepticism to amusement to frank appraisal.

"What do you know of Dom Diego Cervantes?" Timothy asked.

Kirsten ransacked her memory. "He...was one of the major figures in the Ecological Reconstruction of Earth following the Tri-Planet War. And wasn't he also the founder of your order?"

Timothy nodded. "Not everyone remembers how important a part the monastic orders, particularly the Benedictines, of which Dom Diego was then a member, played in the Reconstruction. Actually, it was a reprise and extension of their role in the Middle Ages when they had founded towns in the wilderness and were the first to use technology—in waterwheels and windmills, mostly —to free men from repetitive, backbreaking toil.

"Dom Diego realized sooner than most that the Reconstruction would be successful. Yet that was not enough. Meditating on the command in Genesis to replenish and subdue the Earth, he became convinced that "Earth" meant not one planet but all of natural creation.

"This grant of dominion, however, was balanced by an equally large imposition of responsibility. The parable of the Stewards in Matthew was the natural complement to Genesis. Simply safeguarding the ecology of the Earth was no more than hiding the Master's gold pieces in the ground. God, he came to realize, wanted humanity to spread life throughout the universe.

"As you can see from their expressions, his superiors found these plans somewhat grandiose. He was eventually allowed to implement his ideas, but only after founding the Stewards."

A door below the painting led to a low, narrow corridor. At the far end, Brother Timothy opened a massive metal double door, which, Kirsten recognized, had once functioned as an airlock.

They stepped down into a courtyard garden. Large trees lessened the sun's glare, protecting hedges and paths lined with flowers. Several monks were working, taking snippets of leaves, hammering unidentified items into the soil, or performing other functions even less comprehensible. Other monks strolled silently down the paths, engaged in prayer or, Kirsten thought with surprise, perhaps just enjoying themselves.

"We do a lot of experimenting here," Timothy explained. "We get an idea how various species will adapt to the soil and the sun. We also do a fair amount of crossbreeding."

Kirsten stopped by a small bush ablaze with trumpet-shaped blossoms. She was suddenly aware of a not-unpleasant hum that seemed to approach, then recede, then do both at once.

"What purpose do these beautiful colors serve?" she asked.

"Well, they help attract the attention of the bees to fertilize the bush. Of course, we could have done that in the ultraviolet only. But since God made flowers beautiful to humans as well as bees, we felt we should return the compliment."

They took a diagonal path to a building at the edge of the courtyard. Timothy descended five steps and led Kirsten into the basement.

Passing between the doorsill and the corridor, they seemed to move forward several centuries. The ceiling and walk were soundproofed. There was an almost subaural but constant *whoosh* of air-conditioning.

Two rows of back-to-back consoles ran down the center of the first room to the right. The walls were lined with readout screens, several of which Kirsten recognized as electronic maps of portions of the planet. Monks sat at the consoles punching in figures, examining the results, occasionally requesting a printout. A large raised console, semicircular and covered with screens and keyboards, occupied the very center of the room.

"This is the heart of our mission here on Ariel," Timothy explained. "All the data from our weather satellites" —Of which you are missing one, Kirsten thought with a guilty start—"as well as sensors we have scattered throughout the ocean, on the continents, and even in weather balloons, funnel in here. We are trying to condense millions of years of evolution into two generations, so we need to monitor everything very carefully. Under these pressures, the ecology could easily unbalance and collapse.

"We also do our computer modeling here, trying to extrapolate the effect of introducing a new variety of nitrogen-fixing bacteria into the soil or of seeding the oceans with a species of plankton that give off more oxygen than current types do. That is where Brother Benedict has been such a godsend. Watching him at that central keyboard, I get some inkling of what it must have been like to listen to Bach playing the organ. It's not so much that he is a better programmer than anyone else on the planet. Rather, his understanding of the entire planetary ecology is so deep and comprehensive that he asks questions of the computer that simply haven't occurred to anyone else yet. He has been in charge of monitoring and modeling for only four years, but in that time we have moved twenty years ahead of schedule."

Timothy sighed. "He will be sorely missed. He has been up late with three assistants ever since you arrived, training them to take control.

"I suppose it was both selfish and shortsighted of us to suppose that we could keep his talents here when they have such obvious use in the war against the Bestials."

So that's the story they have given out, Kirsten thought. She knew little enough of Chiang's inner counsels. Still, it was clear that any use of Benedict against the Bestials would be incidental. Chiang's stakes were both more immediate and more personal. But if it helped the monks reconcile themselves to their loss, that small deception would at least make the remainder of their stay more pleasant.

They left through a different exit. A plain stretched away to mountains gray with distance. From one, a plume of smoke rose silently, a child's pencil scrawl on blue paper. Thin wisps of clouds raced through the bright vastness of the sky. Wind rushed down from the heights, making the grasses wave like a storm-tossed sea. A bleat drew Kirsten's attention to small white shapes grazing in the field. There was a sudden blur of brown, and one sheep, which had strayed too far, was chased back into the herd.

"Why do you have dogs?" Kirsten asked. "Surely there are no predators here."

"Their main job is to keep the sheep from straying over the cliffs, and herding them into shelter before storms," Timothy replied. "In a few years, though, they will be needed for protection, as well. Once sufficient vegetation is established, the plan calls for setting out groups of herbivores and carnivores simultaneously."

"Why?" Kirsten asked, obscurely troubled by the idea. "You certainly don't seem to need predators here!"

"That is because here we are the predators," Timothy answered frankly. "Oh, we care for them, feed them, try to make sure they are healthy and contented, but when their numbers increase beyond a certain point, we weed out the oldest and weakest and dine on mutton. The alternative would be for the herd to outgrow the grazing area and for them all to starve.

"Actually, you touch a continuing controversy within the order. Some of our members believe we have both the power and the responsibility to undo Original Sin. If you can't make the lion lie down with the lamb, then eliminate the lion. They have even created some computer models of genetic modifications that might make predators unnecessary, such as having fertility automatically decrease with population density. So far, none of these models have withstood scrutiny: They all destabilize after about three generations.

"The proponents insist that we have to keep trying, that to consider predation a necessary means of population control is the same as considering evil a necessary counterpoint to good. I myself am not convinced, since that equates flesh eating with evil, which seems theologically dubious."

"Has Brother Benedict taken part in the controversy?" Kirsten asked.

"Yes. He is on the side of the predators."

"He would be," Kirsten muttered. Timothy shot her a sharp glance but said nothing.

They walked for a few minutes in silence. Kirsten felt all her muscles relaxing under Altair's heat. Her thoughts melted away in a sensuous enjoyment of light and air.

"You wondered back in my office why we must be celibate," Timothy said finally. "Maybe now I can answer you. It takes generations to bring a world to flower. During that time, the world must be served with a disinterested love. You cannot look for a return in your day or in that of your children.

"Yet a man with a family must do that. It is his duty. And that is the reason the terraforming of Venus was such a disaster: The investor states needed a return in twenty-five years. They pushed too hard in the initial stages with too little data. As a result, the planet became a financial black hole that never paid off.

"The Stewards don't need a planet to pay off. Our celibacy is really part of our vow of poverty. It means that what we do is not for us or for our children. We seed a planet for the sake of life itself and for the glory of God."

Rain rattled off the storm shutters like machine-gun fire. Thunder cannonaded close at hand in a concatenation of reports that vibrated even through the stone. Younger stopped as the porch lights dimmed to darkness. Lightning, almost continuous, peeked through the slits in the storm shutters to provide the only illumination. These storms were not infrequent, Younger had been told. The ground heated up rapidly, creating strong updrafts that boiled into thunderheads in the cold upper atmosphere. It was the extreme temperature gradient that powered the violence of the tempests. Fronts would form almost too rapidly for the satellites to record them and would sweep out from the mountains, spewing tornadoes all over the plain.

The lights flickered weakly. Younger could just discern the entry to the hallway he sought and, beyond it, the stairway, a deeper blackness carved in the dark.

He descended one flight. The lights died again. As he paused, he became aware of candlelight gleaming down the hallway. A chant echoed off the stone, a plaintive sound that might have been torn from the heart of the universe.

How do they know when to pray? Younger wondered irrelevantly. They were apparently following the seven prayer times established on Earth nearly two millennia before. But how was that schedule divided up on a planet where the day was only nineteen hours long?

Younger considered the Stewards. On the one hand, a more practical group of men did not exist in the universe. As a practical man himself, Younger appreciated that. Yet their motivation was far from practical: It was mystical.

The frightening thing, Younger thought, was that that aspect of the Stewards was beginning to appeal to him as well.

The lights surged back into existence. He continued his descent, quickly losing count of the landings. There must be a freight elevator somewhere, he thought. I just wasn't smart enough to ask about it.

He finally reached the bottom. Stepping through a doorway, he found himself in the underground hangar, which reverberated with the drumming of the rain on the large metal hatch high above.

Small orbiters crouched silently in the shadows. Towering above them was the silvered form of the *Gryffon's Pride*. Monks were working in busy silence about its base. Wire ran from their portable banks of instruments up into the guts of the ship.

"Good evening, Mr. Younger. Very pleased to see

you." The speaker was a small black man, his curly hair salted with white. I should know him, Younger thought. He runs their shipyard here and recalibrates the drives of the quantaships that put in.

"I am surprised to see all of you," Younger replied. "Shouldn't you be at prayers now?"

"Normally, yes," Father Nsbugu—*that* was his name —agreed. "Abbot Tsintolas has excused us from vespers and compline this evening to work on your ship. We want it ready to go in thirty-six hours." He talked easily while watching the readouts, his face illuminated by the dancing lights.

"What's the rush? You've had the ship for nearly two weeks."

"Had it physically here," Nsbugu said. "Considering the fate of Herr Herter, we thought it advisable to wait for Councilor Chiang's permission before we entered the craft. That was given only this morning."

Touché, Younger thought. He looked up at the gleaming reflective surface. "So what sort of shape is the old girl in?"

"The superstructure is excellent—these Vesta hulls are nearly indestructible. The computer data base is being reviewed separately by Councilor Chiang and Father Wiener, so I know nothing save for what I heard from Father Wiener this evening. Were you planning a flight to Sirius soon?"

Younger blinked at the seeming non sequitur. "Not that I know of. Why?"

"Father Wiener informs me that a few digits slipped in the navigational program. The coordinates of Sirius were shifted somewhere outside the local group of galaxies.

"Physically, the computer is in reasonable condition. We replaced a few boards, degaussed where necessary, and balanced the electrical flow.

"The quantum drive is another matter. We started charting variance points and correcting them this morning. By midafternoon we had found so many that I gave the order to yank and replace modules. That has just been completed. Now, of course, we need to integrate the modules with the main drive. That will take most of the rest of our time."

"What about fire control?" Younger asked.

"In excellent condition, sir," said an eager-faced man who had just stepped out of the shadows. "Tracking and aiming are fully synchronized. All the power leads are solid. Swivel mounts are clean and functionally frictionless."

"Brother Sean," Father Nsbugu said, introducing the youthful monk.

"Your ship could take on most anything," Sean said. "Have you seen much battle action?"

"Next to nothing," Younger admitted. "We go on alert regularly: The Bestials send out raiding parties about once every two weeks. However, we have never been in the vicinity of an attack. The main reason is that the attacks have clustered around manufacturing centers orbiting Centauri A. We are normally based on Neoptolemus, which is in the B system. Do you fellows out here follow the war closely?"

"Oh, yes, sir," Brother Sean answered. "We were all —almost all—outraged at their unprovoked sneak attack on Sol and Centaurus. We pray regularly for an Alliance victory."

"We pray for peace," Father Nsbugu said sternly.

Suddenly there was the slightest of tensions. Even though all the other monks kept working, Younger sensed that they were listening closely—that they had, in fact, already chosen sides.

Younger's eyes shifted from the monk to the priest. "Is there much Defenders of Humanity sentiment here?" he asked, breaking a silence that would in another second have become embarrassing.

"Some," Brother Sean said. "However, Father

Nsbugu and Brother Benedict have scored some good points against them. The Defenders *are* a bit simplistic: Their biblical exegesis is overly literal and their understandings of biology and genetics inexact. Still, they have some good points of their own."

Brother Sean paused, his eyes darting to Father Nsbugu as if gauging how much he could try his superior's patience. Apparently he decided that he had pushed as far as he dared, for he abruptly changed the subject.

"I suppose arguing policy would be boring for a man of action like yourself. The news that gets here says that Councilor Chiang is one of those pushing for a more aggressive war policy. Is that why you joined up with him?"

Younger allowed a wry smile. "Councilor Chiang pays extremely well for those who meet his standards. I find that sufficient excitement."

MacAndrews had been attempting to see Chiang all day. During the morning, he had been closeted with Benedict.

"He says he is not to be disturbed," Brother Timothy said apologetically, "but perhaps for you . . ."

Perhaps nothing. The prohibition extended as much to her as to anyone. Maybe to her most of all.

While waiting, she had a few words with Younger. She was already familiar with most of his update on the refitting of the *Gryffon's Pride*. One item, though, was especially interesting.

"All the cold-sleep cubicles, except his own, have been detached from the main computer. They will be operated manually." That meant that only Chiang would be awakened automatically. He would then awaken the others. Or fail to do so.

Younger was watching her reaction closely. "I don't like that," she admitted, "but it is understandable."

"Understandable, hell! The bastard doesn't trust any-one." There was a perverse admiration in Younger's voice.

MacAndrews withheld further comment.

After lunch, Benedict was gone. But now Chiang was with Father Wiener. MacAndrews summoned her resolu-tion, knocked, and entered without awaiting an answer.

Chiang and Wiener sat in a small room adjacent to the computer control center, cross-checking program print-outs. MacAndrews recognized *Gryffon's Pride* cassettes in the comp station input slots.

Father Wiener looked up at her entrance, his round face beaming geniality. He did not at all look the part of a brilliant programmer.

"Captain MacAndrews," Chiang said. His face was expressionless.

"Sir. I understand that you and Father Wiener are re-viewing the basic operation programs of the *Gryffon's Pride*."

"You understand correctly."

"Those programs are my responsibility, sir. With all due respect to Father Wiener's expertise, I am charged with the duty of maintaining those programs and of cor-recting any errors."

"Enjoy what small vacation you may get, Captain," Chiang said mildly. "I assure you that Father Wiener and I have this operation well in hand."

"My responsibility as captain—"

"You are relieved, Captain . . . of that responsibility. I shall make an official record of that in the log."

His eyes were still emotionless—and utterly implac-able. They both knew exactly what he would do if she pushed him one centimeter further.

"Sir," she said, pivoted, and left the room.

Her face flushed with anger, she stalked down the corridor and up to the outside. The palpability of his sus-picion gnawed at her pride.

Damn it, she thought. If he can't trust me, why doesn't he just pull me from command?

It took a few minutes for her to cool down enough to admit that most of her anger was directed not at Chiang but at herself. And at Herter, that white-haired little German with the avuncular manner, the charming accent, and the long, amusing anecdotes about the cathedral town on the Rhine where he had grown up. He had sucked her in completely. She had not even been aware of how fully she had trusted him. And now, because of that trust, two of her shipmates were dead.

Without thinking, she had come around to the cliffs. The sky was covered with high gray clouds that had moved in after the storm of the night before. A cold, stiff wind gusted off the water. She turned her face into it, pitting her strength against its force. The wind seemed to blow straight through her flesh, chilling the bone beneath. Her lips drew back from her teeth.

The ground fell away in a series of jagged slanting steps. Feeling reckless, she jumped down, knees flexed to absorb the shock. She jumped again, grabbing an outcropping with one hand to swing over to a foothold. And then again.

Gray waves crashed beneath her. Spray exploded into the air, was caught by the gusts and blown up to her. The bay was a welter of waves colliding with one another in uncertain heaves and dips. Farther out into the bay, small, rocky islets thrust themselves above the surging waters.

She stood there for a while, letting the wind and spray wash rage and resentment from her. After a time, she began to shiver. Turning, she scanned the rock face for a way up.

After a few minutes of study, she began edging her way to the left. The rocks were smooth and slick with spray. Her half boots, which served well on shipboard, provided little traction. Cautiously, testing her weight before she dared put each foot in a new position, she began to move along a narrow, upward-slanting crack.

When you consider it, she thought, trying to keep her mind off the straight fall beneath her, the Stewards' garb was much more pragmatic than ceremonial. The hiking shoes provided traction while being tough enough to protect against stone fragments and volcanic shards. Trousers and pullovers were as strong and warm as they were nondescript. Robe and cowl provided almost complete shelter from sun and wind.

Much better than her synthetic uniform, which was already beginning to fray at knees and elbows.

The crack ended abruptly, just a short distance below a ledge. Unfortunately, it had no sharply defined edge she could grab to pull herself up. Instead, the rock face gradually curved inward, eventually becoming horizontal. She would have to put her weight on the upper part of her body and hope that friction and decreasing slope would give her purchase.

Arms extended with fingers spread to give her maximum surface area in contact with the rock, she began ascending inchworm fashion. Her breathing became labored. Aches spread swiftly from arms to shoulders, down her back to her thighs and calves.

Still, she made slow progress up the nearly vertical wall. One more good heave and—

Her knees slipped. In desperation, she threw herself flat. The fall slowed, stopped. She could not feel any contact with stone below her hips. Her hands were numbed by the cold spray. The rock face had abraded her arms, making them slippery with blood. If she did not begin moving up in the next few seconds, her fall would resume, and this time there would be no stopping.

Part of the rock above the ledge appeared to detach itself and move forward. The gray mass resolved itself into the robe and cowl of a Steward. Without a word, he lay down on the ledge and extended a hand toward her. She recognized him: Brother Benedict.

He had no reason to like any of them. Ten years before he had gone to considerable effort to fade into obscurity. Now, whatever legal niceties disguised the fact, he was being kidnapped and thrown onto the board as Chiang's pawn. He could wish none of them well.

His hand came even with hers. Fumbling, it hit her fingers. The jar was enough to loosen her grip. She began sliding again.

Then, suddenly confident, he reached his hand down, grabbed her wrist, and lifted with surprising strength. With her legs and free arm, she scrambled up the rock face. In a matter of seconds, she was standing next to him on the ledge.

Benedict's eyes impersonally examined her ragged, bloody form. "Not what they train you for in the Space Force."

"No," she agreed, still gasping with exertion.

"Follow me. There are a few trails that are relatively safe, but you have to know your way."

He turned and strode along the ledge, not waiting for a response. Less than ten meters on, the path dropped into a cut filled with loose, eroded rock. He waited and had her precede him up the cleft. As she climbed, he called handholds to her attention. The rubble shifted uneasily beneath her weight. She felt a rock dislodge, heard it bounce and clatter into sudden silence.

Suddenly she was at the top of the cliffs. Benedict came up behind her, not even breathing heavily.

"Thank you," she said, momentarily more grateful for his silence than for her life. She had no wish to explain how her headstrong emotionalism had nearly killed her. "Surely you and Councilor Chiang did not spend all day discussing my past career."

"We did not discuss it at all." Seeing the question in her face, he continued. "There was no need. Your bearing and regulation hairstyling speak for themselves. Space Force. Probably Academy as well."

She nodded, disturbed that he could read her so easily.

"What is not obvious is why an Academy officer would resign her commission during wartime to become a glorified chauffeur. War is, after all, the time for action, promotions, and reputation!"

Fear tightened her chest, and she felt an upwelling of the same confusion she had experienced upon awakening in Space, to learn that Herter had nearly killed them all. Truth, incomplete truth, was the only weapon she dared use on this fabled stranger whose voice was like a playfully wielded scalpel.

"Action," she said bitterly. "This war has been going on for two years with next to no action—on our side. The Allies bicker over protocol and precedence. The generals refuse to attack without ten-to-one superiority. The one commander they have with guts and intelligence they have nearly cashiered for making them look like fools. And the Bestials raid where they will, taking out our docks and shipyards, making assembly of an Allied fleet next to impossible.

"I got tired of polishing chrome. Aside from Defenders of Humanity bigots, Councilor Chiang was one of the few in power to consistently promote a more offensive effort. I thought if there were any action, it would be with him."

She braced for his challenge to her story. His attention was elsewhere, though. "Master Chiang has many talents. He earned my admiration a decade ago when I had my inoculations."

He made a wide gesture, encompassing everything about them. "This planet has a much higher proportion of heavy metals than Earth. If you live off the land, these metals will build up and poison you in a matter of months.

"The Stewards were initially quite concerned about this. About the time I arrived on Ariel, the newly formed Chiang Biosynthetics began marketing a novel variant of *Escherichia coli* bacteria. *E. coli,* as I am sure you know, lives naturally in the human intestinal system and has been one of the main workhorses of genetic engineering for the past three hundred years. Chiang had created a strain which, after inoculation, would take up its accustomed intestinal residence. There it would ingest heavy metals, and both would be excreted. Specific forms could be tailored for the gut of almost every animal.

"Simple, elegant, effective. No one else had thought of anything like it. I thought then that I might like to meet the inventor someday."

MacAndrews's joints stiffened as they walked back to the abbey. She had to force herself to keep up with Benedict.

"It's hard for me to remember that you are not as isolated here as you appear," she said. "I guess my mind still has the image of hermits fleeing civilization to seek holiness—"

His laughter was as hard and cold as the rocks. She stared at him, startled. The face deep within the hood was in shadowed relief. Of his expression, she could make out only a disturbing wildness.

"Excuse me," he said, sobering. "There are some holy men here. There are even more who could be. I, however, coming to Ariel, considered transubstantiation and the Parousia one with phlogiston and the houses of the zodiac. 'Holiness' was a meaningless word."

"Then why did you come here?" she asked.

"For the best reason in the world," he said lightly. "To keep on breathing."

IV

WEIGHTLESS, CHIANG PULLED HIMSELF INTO HIS COMM-chair. He was still groggy from cold sleep. He grabbed a bulb of hot coffee from the overhead locker and sucked on the nipple, trying to clear his brain.

All the telltales were green. The rest of the crew seemed to have come through well. Kirsten was guiding Benedict into James's gunnery station—the armament activation part of which Chiang had prudently disconnected. Chiang frowned. Benedict appeared to be little better than semiconscious.

The viewscreen showed Centaurus B, with the brighter A component above and twenty-three astronomical units more distant. Radio chatter was sparse and uninformative.

Chiang punched in his personal code, pressing his thumb against the ID plate to gain access to those programs restricted to him alone. He then called up his signal recognition and decoding program.

Orbiting Neoptolemus there was a communications satellite owned by Chiang Biosynthetics. Besides handling the data passing between his freighters and factories, it would, at seemingly irregular intervals, emit a coded pulse for no longer than a microsecond. The pulse was almost indistinguishable from the other messages—but Chiang had the key.

The message flashed across the board.

DECLINATION SLOPE LESSENED. EST. STRENGTH 87 PERCENT OPTIMUM.

Chiang sighed with relief. The situation was still bad, but it could have been far worse. Although the message was necessarily several hours old, nothing much could have changed in that time.

"Captain, set a course for—"

"Sir," Younger interrupted, "I have three blips converging on us. Estimate ninety seconds to firing range."

"Damn!" MacAndrews exclaimed. "The Allies didn't have patrols out this far when we left."

"Alliance scouts to intruder," the intercom crackled. "Identify yourself or be fired upon."

Chiang nodded to MacAndrews.

"This is *Gryffon's Pride* registered to Chiang Biosynthetics," she announced.

"Is John Lei Chiang aboard?"

Again MacAndrews looked over to him for instructions.

Chiang pressed his own transmit button. "I am."

"Follow us." A string of course coordinates appeared on the screen. "Acknowledge."

"I am on Council business," Chiang replied. "I claim Inner Council priority."

"Your apprehension has been ordered by the Inner Council. Acknowledge."

"'Apprehension,' crap!" MacAndrews muttered. "It's really hit the fan if there's a warrant out on you." She looked up at Chiang. "Shall we fight? *Gryffon* has the edge in both speed and armament."

"I'm locked on all three," Younger confirmed. "Say the word and they'll be ionized gas."

"No!" Chiang commanded. "Unless—" He looked

back. All that was visible of Benedict was his head, leaning back out of the gunnery station. His eyes were closed. He appeared asleep.

"Rénard."

The eyes opened. "The armament of the *Gryffon's Pride* is generally known?"

"Most of the armament has been declared to the Space Force under the Merchant Defense Act," Chiang said.

"Then your instincts are sound. Comply with their demands."

Chiang had MacAndrews send the acknowledgment.

"I would like to know," MacAndrews asked no one in particular, "what is so terribly clever about going docilely to the slaughterhouse."

Chiang opened his mouth to reprimand her. Benedict's dry voice cut in before he could start.

"Captain, the Inner Council and the lieutenants in those scouts are surely as aware as you are of the relative strengths of these vessels. If they really wanted to arrest Master Chiang, they would have come at us with sufficient force. That they issue their challenge while so clearly understrength leads to an obvious conclusion."

He paused. MacAndrews was stubbornly silent.

"They wish to provoke us. Were this vessel to fire on an Alliance craft, that would be sufficient cause for the issuance of a writ of outlawry. On issuance of that writ, all of Master Chiang's financial holdings would immediately escheat to the Centauran state. The game would be over, and they would have won."

He paused again. "At the moment, I don't know how to outmaneuver Master Chiang's enemies. But, Christ, Captain, let's not hand the game to them on a platter. Let's make them goddamn fight for it!"

Chiang restrained a smile. Even seated as he was, above and behind MacAndrews, he could see that her ears were burning.

At the predetermined instant, all four ships jumped into Space$_2$. Damper fields hummed on automatically as the viewscreen showed a shifting textured whiteness. There was a groan from Benedict. So it was true that Multi-Neural Capacitants were more susceptible than most to quantum drive stresses. Chiang watched with distant sympathy as Benedict fumbled with a pain pill.

For Chiang, most effects of being in Space$_2$ were canceled by the damper fields. Only by the slightest tension at the back of his head did his body respond to the forces that tried to impose normal physical laws where they did not belong. After a few minutes, Benedict recovered enough to punch in queries to the general computer memory. Curious, Chiang had his own screen display Benedict's readout. Lines of print appeared and vanished too quickly for Chiang to discern more than that the general subject appeared to be biographical data on the members of the Inner Council.

Ninety minutes later they surfaced in normal space. Chiron lay below them, its thin, curving clouds reflecting the yellow radiance of Centaurus A. Through rifts in the clouds, Chiang could see the huge continents embracing landlocked seas.

He shifted the field of view. Huge icebergs swam in orbit like a school of malformed fish, the detritus of a diverted comet. The plan was to add enough water to Chiron's budget to ameliorate the climatic extremes. The project seemed to be progressing well, as if there were no war.

He had to search harder for the heavy industrial satellites. Then, shifting magnification, he saw why. They had all bunched themselves into clumps where they could be protected by the battlestars that orbited twenty degrees ahead of and behind them. There was extensive construction around one of the long, tubular factories. Turning the magnification higher yet, Chiang could see blackened blast scars, evidence of a successful raid.

They spiraled down through the upper atmosphere, sped across the Sea of Good Hope, and descended on the capital city of Pierpont. On the hills overlooking the river Alice, the new government center had been built. The ships floated down with ponderous solemnity and were swallowed by the underground hangars.

"I will try to make this short," Chiang told MacAndrews. "Be ready to move quickly."

He turned and regarded Benedict. He paused for a breath, weighing dangers and advantages. Benedict returned the stare impassively.

"You will come with me," Chiang decided. Benedict nodded acquiescence and followed him through the lock.

The captain of the honor guard saluted, which was something of a relief to Chiang. They marched quickly across the hangar, boots banging loudly on the ceramic flooring. A moving walkway took them in seconds to the chamber of the Inner Council. The guards remained outside.

A huge stone relief of Chiron the Centaur dominated the far wall. His eyes were slightly different colors: the A and B components of the system. Far to the side, the dull ruby of Proxima adorned his tail. Five years before, his equine parts had been covered by a large Centauran flag, in deference to the objections of the Defenders of Humanity. Only recently had the flag come down.

The human figures suffered by comparison. All twelve other members were in attendance. Directly across from Chiang sat Pierpont of Industrial Microbiotics and Gould of Flying Mountains Mining, representing the oldest and most powerful of the First Families. Flanking them were those who had bought in later: Fiertag of Vesta Spacecraft, Sankla of the Chiron Hydroponicists, Ronan of Astral Engines, and Sorabji of TRANSCENDATRAN. The unions had fought their way in against great resistance. Currently, Kondrashin held the seat allotted to the United Crafts Union, while Epstein represented the spacers.

Other members had been added to the Inner Council as their economic might grew and they became desirable allies to those already members. Chiang had gained his own seat that way. So had Gulkis of the Small Businessmen's Guild, Couteau of the Freeholders, and Cowan of the Saviour of Humanity Churches.

Too often, the twelve became deadlocked. The First Families had created the position of First Councilor, which was filled by Pierpont's son-in-law. It was hard to say which faction was more disconcerted at the way he had used his position.

Chiang's gaze swept over them all as he strode to his seat and thumbed his microphone on. "For what crime have I been brought here under arrest?"

First Councilor Rascavia's laughter bounced harshly off the stone walls. Several of the Councilors fidgeted in their seats.

"My dear Chiang," he said. "Your sarcasm is more than usually refreshing."

"What Inner Council order demanded my immediate apprehension?" Chiang demanded.

"Oh, that. Councilor, you have no idea how disturbed we have been by your recent absence. There were rumors that you had fled to Earth, that you were assassinated, even that you had fallen to the Bestials. All our ships were alerted to find you and convey you back safely. If you were headed elsewhere at the time, you must blame overzealous interpretation of our orders. The patrol commander shall be suitably punished.

"In the meantime, let me speak for the entire Council in expressing delight at your safe return. By the way, I forgot to mention that one of the more absurd rumors had you chasing after Paul Niccolo Rénard, who died years ago. Don't mind those guards coming up behind you. I'm sure you remember the security measures we have had to impose, allowing only Councilors or members of their retinue into this chamber. Since your companion is unregistered, he must be identified and logged into our data banks."

Seeing no signal from Chiang, Benedict stood placidly as the guards approached him from both sides. His thumb was pressed and electronically recorded on a fingerprint register. A small apparatus was brought up close to his head, behind his range of vision. His earlobe felt cool metal and then a prick. The guards moved back.

Rascavia was watching his desk monitor intently. "How fascinating! You actually have found the Rénard. And masquerading as a Steward, at that. This promises to be a most diverting session."

"Diverting is hardly the word for it," Cowan said. "If we have here one of Snowden's Satanspawn, it has much to answer for."

"In that case," Councilor Fiertag responded, "why not let him do some answering?" He turned to Benedict. "Sir, if you are the Rénard, will you tell us where you have been and what you have been doing for the last ten years?"

"I must request a ruling from the chair." Benedict was standing out of range of Chiang's microphone, but his voice carried easily to the corners of the room.

Rascavia frowned in irritation. "Councilor Fiertag's question is simple and in order. There is no subject matter for a ruling."

"Nonetheless, I must repeat my request. I admit that for many years I used the name Paul Niccolo Rénard. As Councilor Cowan implied, I am a genetic variant usually referred to as a Multi-Neural Capacitant, developed by the late Dr. Snowden.

"Before I can answer any further questions, my legal status must be defined. Title 10, Section 1505 of the

Combined Centauran Code provides that: 'No simulacrum may be allowed to testify before any court, any
executive tribunal, or any legislative committee.... The
penalty for any such testimony...is...death.' If I
understand your constitution rightly, the Inner Council
partakes of both legislative and executive functions. It is
therefore necessary to determine whether or not I fit the
definition of a simulacrum to know if I may lawfully answer your questions."

"That is an old law," Rascavia said. "It has not been
enforced for years."

"Seven years ago, a genetic variant named Buffy
Highsinger was executed for giving testimony in court
that was subsequently confirmed by four human witnesses. Her sole crime was being judged a simulacrum."

"That was at the height of the Defenders of Humanity
reaction," Councilor Pierpont pointed out. "Political
passions have cooled since then."

"Perhaps," Benedict agreed. "But not all have re-
pented their past acts." Cowan glared at him. "In any
event, both statute and court decision stand as good
law."

Rascavia shrugged. "Your request is well-taken. I will
hear argument."

"What is there to argue?" Cowan asked. "The Rénard
has himself admitted that he was 'developed' by Snowden. We all know that it was Snowden and his associates
who loosed upon humanity the swarm of genetic mon-
strosities that nearly destroyed us."

"More to the point," Epstein said, "is the fact that the
Rénard, and all Multi-Neural Capacitants, appear
human. The purpose of the statute cited was to prevent
confusion between human and nonhuman beings. By
forcing mutations and combining human and animal genetic material, Snowden made the line indistinguishable.
A simulacrum is precisely a creature that masquerades
as a human."

"Multi-Neural Capacitants have never been so defined," Benedict said. "The cases and the legislative history speak of Succubae, Cyborgs, Savants, Satyrs, and, most recently, Bestials."

Gould laughed. "At the time the law was passed, all Multi-Neural Capacitants were believed dead. No law was necessary to deal with them."

"It was certainly not law that dealt with my sister Allele," Benedict said sharply. "Not law that inflamed the mob that broke into her study and tore her limb from limb. Even now scholars estimate that they have only begun to skim the surface of her work in sociobiology. Think of how much good she would have done our race if the law had only protected her like a human being."

"Don't try to gain our sympathy with sob stories," Cowan snapped. "What about your brother Valentino? Before he was assassinated, he was trying to turn humanity into a slave race. That's not paranoia: We have his diary, his recorded conversations, the testimony of his associates."

"He was evil," Benedict replied. "Caligula and Hitler were both evil. They were nonetheless human."

"Why can't we solve this scientifically?" Ronan asked. "The genetic code of Rénard is a matter of record. We can call it up onto our screens. When we do, we see that although the human genetic material has been altered and reamplified, it has not been adulterated with nonhuman genes. In fact, Snowden's notes indicate that the most crucial part of MNC formation was nongenetic—a series of surgical operations on the brain.

"Now, the law seems clear that humanity or nonhumanity is determined at the moment of conception, as soon as the genetic identity is complete. Rénard's genetic makeup is novel, but there is nothing you can point to as being nonhuman."

"He came out of Snowden's laboratories," Cowan said, "like all the other simulacra—"

"Not only simulacra came out of those laboratories," Benedict said. "He also developed new techniques of spotting and correcting birth defects. In fact, it was his technique that was used three years ago to prevent your niece from being born a mongoloid. Is your niece therefore inhuman?"

"That is different!" Cowan said, his face darkening with rage.

"Ah." The mockery was light, unanswerable.

"But you are specifically an MNC—" Epstein began.

"So I am." Benedict's gaze swept over Epstein with such intensity that Epstein flinched.

"So I am. Have not MNCs eyes? Do I not have hands, organs, dimensions, senses, affections, passions? Am I not fed with the same food, hurt with the same weapons, subject to the same diseases, healed by the same means, warmed and cooled by the same winter and summer as a human is? If you prick me, shall I not bleed? If tickled, will I not laugh? If you poison me, will I not die?"

There were suddenly currents Chiang did not understand. Some, like Cowan, looked merely irritated, unaware that anything important was happening. But others were noticing. Fiertag was nodding slowly in what looked like admiration. Rascavia was still as a bird before a snake. And Epstein—Epstein had gone quite pale, his breathing ragged.

"Affections and passions," Epstein said. "I am sure you have those, and to spare. It is our duty to protect our race from the natural result of those passions. As it is written: 'Whoever lieth with a beast shall surely be put to death.'"

"And two verses on it is written: 'Thou shalt neither vex a stranger nor oppress him: for ye were strangers in the land of Egypt.'" Benedict's words were like a whip crack.

There was a moment's silence. "Gentlemen," Rascavia said. "Long experience has taught me that where debate degenerates into theology, the time of reason is long past. If I may summarize, the main points seem to be the following: Simulacra have never yet been legally defined so as to include Multi-Neural Capacitants. Rowan reminds us that while MNCs are genetic variants, the variations are on human genetic material and that the main differences are surgically induced. Councilors Cowan and Epstein, on the other hand, emphasize Valentino's coup, the actual past danger from MNCs, and the fact that MNCs are indistinguishable from humans unless subject to close medical examination, which they aver makes MNCs all the more dangerous.

"Are there any more points of substance?"

No one spoke up. Chiang grimaced in frustration. He had wanted to take Benedict directly to Neoptolemus to avoid exactly this situation. Benedict, however, had deliberately forced the issue.

"Since this is a matter of first impression," Rascavia said, "on which the statute is ambiguous and the membership of the Council is clearly divided, I shall put it to a vote. The question for your resolution is: Are Multi-Neural Capacitants simulacra within the meaning of 10 CCC 1505?"

"Yes," Cowan said immediately.

"No," Chiang countered.

Pierpont, Gould, and Sankla all voted yes.

Not, Chiang thought, because the First Families believe any of that Defenders of Humanity garbage. Solely for the purpose of hurting the competition: Chiang.

Then Fiertag, Gulkis, and Ronan voted no. Chiang nodded, pleased to see that he could count on some of his allies. Sorabji's no vote was more surprising, but

TRANSCENDATRAN had for several years been distancing itself from the other First Families.

"I abstain," Couteau said.

"Perhaps Councilor Couteau would like to reconsider his abstention," Chiang suggested. Perhaps, he thought, Councilor Couteau should remember his indebtedness to Chiang Biosynthetics and what will result if I call those debts in.

Couteau's bald, plump head was shiny with perspiration. He ducked, smiling apologetically as he mopped his brow with a handkerchief. "Councilor Chiang, these matters are quite beyond me. I am sure whatever action you have taken has been for the good of the Commonwealth. But as for uh—" he nodded at Benedict. "I just don't know!" His gaze slid fearfully over to Pierpont and Sankla.

Kondrashin's yes was at least reasonably sincere. Defenders' sentiment ran strong within the United Crafts Union.

Which left Epstein, representative of the Spacers' Union. "I—" he began, then stopped. He cleared his throat. "I abstain also," he said, avoiding eye contact with anyone. There was a startled muttering, which quickly subsided.

"Well," Rascavia said. "This appears to be one of those few occasions when the duties of the First Councilor are more than ornamental. The vote is tied at five affirmative, five negative, two abstentions. I am therefore obliged to break the tie.

"I vote no. I find Councilor Ronan's argument compelling, and I further believe it dangerous to strip individuals of their humanity lightly. Beyond that, I am very curious to question Paul Niccolo Rénard, and an affirmative vote will make that impossible.

"Finally, I would like to point out, for the sake of those Council members displeased with this vote, that this matter may be reconsidered any time appropriate new evidence can be presented."

He turned to Benedict. "You may now answer Councilor Fiertag's question."

"For the past ten years, I have been on the planet Ariel, in the Altair system," Benedict said. "It is a planet being terraformed by the Order of Stewards. Four years ago I entered the Order."

"And you have been doing what?"

"Data correlation on the terraforming."

"A surprisingly innocuous activity given the past mischief you and your brother have worked," Kondrashin commented.

"If the Councilor will examine the dates," Benedict said, "he will see that I left for Ariel a full year before Valentino's attempted takeover."

"However, your connections with your brother's schemes are well documented," Epstein said. "Dr. Herter—"

"By the way," Rascavia interposed smoothly, "where *is* Dr. Herter? The presence of the foremost authority on MNCs would be extremely helpful. Rumor has it that he has recently taken a position as an adviser to Councilor Chiang."

"Dr. Herter is dead," Chiang said. "He apparently became deranged and murdered my engineer and one of my gunners before he was stopped. I have prepared a full report." He inserted the cassette into the slot, entering his report into the Council data bank.

Several faces betrayed perversely satisfying mixtures of fear and confusion. Chiang allowed himself a thin smile.

"Let's not become sidetracked," Kondrashin said. "We are to believe that the Rénard, former adviser to the great and puppeteer of prime ministers, had been for years content to program a computer for monks?"

Benedict shrugged. "Yes."

"Then what lured you away from this paradisiacal existence?"

"Master Chiang requested Abbot Tsintolas to release me temporarily from my duties with the Order so that I might be able to aid the Alliance. As a loyal human, the Abbot readily complied."

Rascavia raised an eyebrow. "Then you are a gift to us from Councilor Chiang?"

"I am sure all will reap the benefits of the Rénard's presence," Chiang said. "However, he is, at his own suggestion, under indenture to me for the duration. I will therefore control his use for the common benefit."

"That is very unlikely to be for the common benefit," Pierpont objected. "We have no reason to trust him."

"Then banish me from the system," Benedict suggested. "My indenture binds me to obey Master Chiang's every legal command. If I were under banishment, my mere presence would become illegal. I would return to Ariel and bother you no more."

"How near complete is the terraforming of Ariel?" Gould asked.

"Current projections are that it will be substantially complete in five years."

"A terraformed planet is an extremely powerful and tempting asset, which can cause difficult and dangerous complications," Gould observed. "Most of us are still smarting from the New Eden affair—in which, if my memory serves me, you were involved before your 'conversion.'"

He let the implications of that remark sink in before continuing. "Ariel is presently too far removed to be important to us. That will not be the situation once this war is over. I would feel more at ease if the Stewards finish their work there free from the Rénard's supervision. I also believe that an investigation of the situation on Ariel is called for and should be initiated soon as practical."

Gulkis seemed to catch a signal from Chiang. "That can wait. Since we have established the Rénard's legal status and have decided not to banish him, I believe we can allow him and Councilor Chiang to take their leave if they wish. They have had a long and tiring journey."

Chiang stood and made a fractional bow in Rascavia's direction. "With your permission, First Councilor."

"Certainly," Rascavia said. "I am sure we will all be seeing much more of you in the near future."

Benedict followed Chiang back into the corridor and around two corners to Chiang's office. The guards stayed outside. Chiang scanned the messages that had accumulated in his computer in the months just past.

"That was very clever," he said, not looking up as he pressed the printout button. "You very nearly succeeded."

"Master?"

"I didn't at first understand your simulacrum ploy. Only a few minutes ago did it become clear that you *wanted* to be declared a simulacrum, for if you were not human, then your oath of indenture was void."

"You mistake me. You saw the hostility my mere presence created. It was imperative that I establish my legal humanity. Else Cowan or one of his friends would have been tempted to kill me and pay you tort damages, as for the death of a horse. I doubt you would have found any monetary settlement satisfactory."

"And I suppose your suggestion to Pierpont that you be banished only coincidentally would have had the same effect?"

"That is what we used to call the briar patch gambit," Benedict said tartly. "It was going to occur to them in any event. Now that I have it planted in their minds that I desire to leave, they will make certain that I am not allowed to, for fear that I will raise an army on Ariel or some fool thing. Instead, they will want me where they can keep an eye on me.

"In any event, the legal maneuverings would have only tangential effect on my indenture. I swore, as you remember, not only by the laws of Centaurus but also with the witness of the Church. Even without legal enforceability, the moral obligation would remain."

Chiang stared at him for some seconds. "Forgive my forgetting your 'moral obligation,'" he said drily. "Come, let us go to Gryffon House. I am sure you will want to catechize me on the way."

V

GRYFFON HOUSE WAS A STONE SHOEBOX OF A BUILDING three stories high and a block long. Tall, narrow, beveled-glass windows glinted from the walls of locally quarried rose marble. It was set in the heart of the commercial district of Pierpont, midway between the docks and warehouses of the waterfront and the government center on the slopes of the hills. Buildings of the other major houses surrounded it: Industrial Microbiotics, Chiang's largest rival; Flying Mountain Mining, whose spacers were exploiting two asteroid belts, innumerable comets, and the very Oort clouds of the Centauran system; TRANSCENDATRAN, the news network that was close to being a de facto monopoly; Chironian Hydroponicists, the lobby for the great agricultural families. And many more

From his room on the third floor, Benedict could see Chiang's flag, a golden gryffon on a crimson field, snapping in the breeze that blew from the Sea of Good Hope. He had spent the morning calling up data on Chiang Biosynthetics, trying to translate financial statements into a map of strategic strengths and weaknesses. As he worked, a second program identified and presented

TRANSCENDATRAN war reports. The latest news was of a massive Bestial raid into Sol system a week before. The docks orbiting the Moon, the Mecurian power stations, and the mining centers on Juno had all been hard hit. As a result, there would be a delay of at least another month before Sol could send its fleet to Centaurus for the formation of the Grand Fleet of the Alliance. Numerous politicians, mostly Terran, were saying that no fleet should be sent until local defenses were strong enough to make a recurrence of the raids impossible.

In other news, the Sirian ambassador speaking as representative of the Outer System—effectively all human colonies outside Sol and Centaurus—had presented a strongly worded note to the Centauran Inner Council, protesting what he called the "self-centered overly defensive conduct of the war," the effect of which was to leave the Outer Systems essentially without protection. First Councilor Rascavia had responded by sympathizing with the Sirian ambassador's impatience but reminding everyone that military success against the Bestials depended on prudence and careful planning. Councilors Cowan, Epstein, and Kondrashin had issued a minority statement, which agreed with the Sirian ambassador's charges and stopped just short of charging the First Families with impeding the war effort to increase their profits.

"Master Chiang will see you now."

Benedict thumbed his microphone, thanking the secretary on the floor below for the announcement. He then left his room, took the elevator to the second floor, and threaded his way through the busy corridors to Chiang's main office suite. Motioning him in and closing the door, Chiang seemed in reasonably good humor. Benedict surmised that his early morning consultation with his allies and his disciplining of Couteau had gone well.

"Ms. Kim says you have a request."

"Before I left Ariel, Abbot Tsintolas gave me a prog-

ress report on the terraforming project to deliver to the
Father General of our order. I have learned that he is
visiting the Primate today, and he has been willing to set
aside time to see me."

"You could mail the report."

"I could. I would then have to forgo the opportunity
to sound out the Father General on any support he might
be inclined to give you."

Chiang grunted. "Why should the Order of Stewards
want to help me?"

"Many of your innovations, such as the *E. coli* that
devour heavy metals, have been very useful to us. If
Pierpont is successful in vanquishing Chiang Biosynthetics and establishing Industrial Microbiotics as a vir-
tual monopoly, those new inventions will slow to a
trickle.

"More importantly, the Stewards need worldly allies.
You heard Gould call for an investigation of Ariel. They
will discover nothing there concerning me, but they *will*
find a world ripe for the plucking. No matter how badly
they were burned on New Eden, Gould's friends will find
it almost impossible to resist the calls for 'homestead
territory.' At that time, the Stewards would very much
appreciate having a powerful friend on the Inner Council
who owes them a favor."

Chiang considered for a few moments. "Very well.
But be back here this evening. We will be leaving for
Neoptolemus then."

The driver from the aircar pool set down in the large
cathedral parking lot. Benedict thanked him, promised to
call when he was ready to return, and stepped out.

There were a few other aircars scattered about the lot.
The last station of the hovertrain line was on the left.
Benedict's glance followed the rail down the side of the
mountain to where Pierpont lay warm in the midmorning

sun. Beyond it, on the other side of bay, the government center seemed to float on the haze.

The Cathedral of St. John Henry Newman, hollowed out of the mountain's crest, stood directly before him. Huge doors of carved oak imported from Earth were hinged on the granite.

Benedict regretfully turned away from the cathedral, spotted a small sign, and took the indicated path to the chancery. He announced himself to the receptionist, who consulted her notes, nodded, and directed him back to "the apartments." He walked down the indicated corridor, coming into an area that was clearly living quarters. He knocked at a doorway and a voice bade him enter.

He stepped into a living room. Three men, who apparently had been deep in conversation, turned to regard him. One was dressed in the habit of the Stewards.

"Father General Muir? I am Brother Benedict from the Abbey of New Hierosolyma on Ariel. I bring you greetings from Abbot Tsintolas and a report of our work on that planet." Benedict bowed deeply, then handed the cassette to the Father General.

"Thank you." Muir seemed oddly hesitant. "Brother Benedict, allow me to introduce Archbishop Cardinal Kourdakov and his secretary, Father Barbet."

The archbishop was a tall, massively boned man with a boxer's jaw. His basso profundo voice seemed like a roar even when he was speaking softly. "Please be seated, Brother Benedict. We have much to discuss."

"I think not." Benedict did not take his eyes off Muir. "I have accomplished my mission for Abbot Tsintolas and so shall take my leave." He turned to the door.

"Brother Benedict," Muir said, "I bid you stay."

"It would not amuse me."

"Remember your vow of obedience!" Father Barbet's voice crackled with rage. Each hair on his well-trimmed beard seemed to stand out like a spear.

Benedict half turned in the doorway, cocking an eye

at the ceiling. "Do you really think I should?" he asked innocuously.

"Father Barbet," the archbishop said wearily. "For a Jesuit you are sometimes surprisingly unsubtle." He had taken a seat and was resting his head in his left hand, massaging his temples. Now he looked up at Benedict.

"I know what you want. You must know that I do not have the authority to give it to you."

Benedict's whole manner altered. "You are the Primate of the Centauran system," he said. "You are also a scholar whose works are highly respected outside the Church. You are the Pope's close friend and adviser, and are yourself the odds-on favorite to be the next pontiff. Your word carries immense weight."

Barbet seemed to be having difficulty controlling himself. "Would His Eminence please explain to me what favor this upstart monk is requesting?"

"Just yesterday, Brother Benedict manipulated a hostile Inner Council so effectively that it granted a legal endorsement of his human status. Now he seeks to do the same with the Church. As the Father General was just explaining to us, Brother Benedict's vows were accepted conditionally four years ago. If we now hold him to his vow of obedience, we elevate it above a conditional status."

"I have made a lifetime commitment to the Church," Benedict said. "It does not seem to me unfair that the Church should have to decide once and for all whether my vocation is valid, or if I am wasting my time, much like a dog who spends all his time practicing walking on his hind legs."

"The final judge of any vocation must be God," Barbet said judiciously.

"Well, yes," Benedict agreed with ill-concealed exasperation. "But it was always my understanding that the thing about holy orders and apostolic succession was that one was able to speak with authority about such aspects of the Deity's will. Or have we all succumbed to a fit of ecumenical enthusiasm while I was on Ariel, and become Unitarians?"

"Brother Benedict, pray calm yourself." The Father General was visibly distressed. "Archbishop Kourdakov spoke truly of the limits of his authority. When your request to enter the novitiate was forwarded to me, I needed permission from the Pope himself to grant even conditional admittance to our order."

"Furthermore," Kourdakov said, "you could hardly pick a worse time to press for a definitive ruling. There is a great deal of Defenders' sentiment in the Church, from parish level up through the College of Cardinals. The war has inflamed it all the more. A Church declaration favorable to most genetic variants and simulacra would risk almost certain schism. The Reunification would be shattered. In an instant, two centuries of ecumenical healing would be swept away in a firestorm. Can you tell me what would be worth that risk to the Body of Christ?"

"Our obligation to preach the truth of the Gospel without compromise," Benedict replied.

"Brother Benedict—" Barbet began hotly, but was stopped by Kourdakov's upraised hand.

"He has answered well," the archbishop admitted. "It is just that thought that keeps many of us awake nights.

"Now, enough of this fencing. You are not going to force from me what you came for. Any final decision on your status rests with Leo XV. In the meantime, discussion is to our mutual benefit. I ask you again to sit down, not because you have sworn obedience to your ecclesiastical superiors but because you wish to convince us that your vocation is indeed genuine and because we need your aid."

The words were placatory, though his attitude suggested a general accustomed to unquestioning obedience. Benedict sat.

"The reports leaking from the Inner Council yesterday were just sufficient to whet our appetite. Tell us the real reason you returned with Councilor Chiang."

"He threatened to destroy our every installation on the planet," Benedict said simply. "As earnest of his intentions, he vaporized one of our weather satellites."

"Why did you swear indenture?" Barbet demanded. "He could not have legally compelled that."

"I wanted to get him alone, away from his crew. That seemed a more likely event if he felt his hold on me secure."

"And now, how does he plan to use you?" the archbishop asked.

"The story for public consumption is that I can help in the war with the Bestials. That may eventually become true. My immediate task is to aid him in his struggle with the Inner Council. The First Families have always resented the threat to their dominance that Chiang represents. Eighteen months ago they shelved their own squabbles and began a systematic campaign to destroy Chiang Biosynthetics. Chiang assessed the situation and saw that he could stave off defeat but had no reasonable chance of victory. That was when he conceived the idea of altering the odds by tracking me down."

"Chiang's elimination would be quite disadvantageous to the Stewards," Muir put in. "The products his company produces are extremely useful to our work. He has also had a salutary effect on the prices charged by Industrial Microbiotics and its subsidiaries."

"I confess that I am less concerned with that than with the effect he might have on the war," Kourdakov said. "Chiang was at first strongly opposed to the war, then turned completely around and began favoring a more aggressive war effort. I had hoped we could influence him through his wife—ah! you did not know Chiang's wife is Catholic?"

"I did not know," Benedict said, chagrined both at his

ignorance and that his expression had betrayed his emotion, "that Chiang is married."

Kourdakov's laughter boomed across the room. "So much for the supernatural discernment of Multi-Neural Capacitants!

"His wife's maiden name was Roberta Gallagher. She is devout, intelligent, something of a mystic, and more than something of an upstart when it comes to her relations with the hierarchy. She leans toward pacifism but has apparently had no effect at all in influencing her husband in that direction.

"However, she is beside the point right now. You want the Church to declare your humanity. I want your aid in resolving this war. The two are more closely connected than you may believe. I would like to show you a report I received recently. The narrator is Father Terrence McIlvay, a Franciscan. He was specifically requested by the Clan Leaders, apparently because of the missionary work he did among the miners of Ross 128. His report was sent to his superiors, thence to the Pope, and from Leo to me."

Kourdakov touched a button on an arm of his chair. Hologramic ghosts shimmered quickly through the air as the Primate searched for a particular image. The playback slowed abruptly as he found it.

"—has been both my guide and interpreter for the duration of my stay among the Clans."

Benedict had never seen a Bestial at close range before. Nose and midregions of the face extended into a snout. There seemed to be too many inhumanly sharp teeth. The ears were large and pointed. Short reddish-brown fur covered the entire head.

Closer examination disclosed signs of human heritage, among them the large brain case and stereoscopic eyes. But many would never look that closely, and most who did would find little comfort in what they saw, for the human traces in some ways made the overall effect even more unsettling. A totally alien creature could have been accepted on its own merits. This, however, was too similar to one of humanity's oldest nightmares—the werewolf.

McIlvay was explaining that the visual portions of his report had been censored to prevent the disclosure of militarily sensitive information. There were apparently two factions among the Clans. The first held that they were an evolutionary jump ahead of mankind and so needed to make their own values and not be constrained by outmoded morals and sentiments. The other party emphasized their human ties and was searching for ways to make the rest of the race acknowledge these ties. It was this latter group that had sponsored McIlvay.

The hologram showed a room that had been chiseled out of living rock. Rows of benches spread out in a semicircle from a raised and ornamented table.

"This is the Chapel of St. Michael in Ravenhead, a planetoid circling Lalande 21185," McIlvay was saying. "At least it would be a chapel were it properly consecrated. There are dozens of these scattered throughout the domains of the Clans. Prayer and Bible services are held regularly. There are even informal baptisms. No communion services are allowed by the lay elders, although there is a growing body of opinion that the Eucharist may be celebrated by any body of believers.

"They only look like wolves. More and more I think of our Lord gazing out over the multitude, likening them to sheep without a shepherd. We are needed by these people. They labor under all the burdens of common humanity, and some unique to themselves. Young males pass through *testrarch* during puberty, a period during which they may become irrationally violent. Families have literally been destroyed by violence. And those who escape with only moderate physical harm are often crippled by guilt for the rest of their lives.

"On their behalf, I beg you to send missionaries to the

Clans. More, I beg that a bishop may be assigned to them and may ordain priests among them. There are many who have the desire to enter the priesthood and require only a year or two of study and formation. Without that, even the best of them must inevitably fall into error.

"I recognize that these are matters of great controversy, the more so because of the war, and that it may be years for their resolution. For this reason I am not returning as planned. Fully recognizing that I am going beyond my authority, I am nonetheless staying here to preach and administer the sacraments. The Clans are humans, I *know* they are! They can be denied the means of salvation no longer."

Kourdakov touched a button, and the images disappeared. "As a hypothetical, the case was recently posed to Cardinal Tortini of a priest who celebrated the Eucharist for Bestials. Cardinal Tortini declared that it would be the same as throwing the Body of Christ before swine. Such a priest should be defrocked and excommunicated. But if the recipients professed belief in the faith and contrition for their sins? A robot, the Cardinal replied, could be programmed to recite the Nicene Creed. It would not thereby be considered to have a soul. What was doubtless frivolous genetic programming should be accorded no greater dignity.

"Cardinal Tortini commands a large following."

Benedict exhaled slowly. "I am not asking the Church to make a general and definitive statement on all genetic variants. My own pedigree is, I believe, less complicated than that of the Bestials and presents none of the more difficult problems."

The Primate shook his head, smiling sadly. "Your viewpoint is reasonable, but it has no constituency. Tortini and others who follow the Defenders of Humanity line have a strict definition of humanity: any 'improvement' on the genetic base and you lose your membership card. The Defenders' opponents—call them idealists, liberals, whatever—want a behavioral rather than a genetic definition. Neither side is much interested in dealing solely with the last Multi-Neural Capacitant."

"One thing about which Father McIlvay was quite correct," Muir said, "is that the situation is complicated by the war. If the Church were to declare the Clans human, we would risk not only schism but charges of treason. And yes—" he held up a hand to forestall Benedict's comment "—we have a duty to speak the truth no matter what the consequences, but we also have a duty to be wise and effective in our actions. Martyrdom might win salvation for our souls but would be useless to our flock."

"That is one reason why the Church would like a negotiated end to the war,'" Father Barbet said. "When the killing stops, passions may cool and allow us to deal with this extremely complicated problem."

"No one negotiates unless they feel it to their advantage," Benedict stated flatly. "Right now neither side wants negotiations. The Allies are smarting from what they feel was an unprovoked sneak attack and want revenge. The Clans feel victory is necessary to prevent genocide."

"You may well be correct," the Primate agreed. "That is where we need your assistance. Councilor Chiang is currently backing the war party, but he is clearly no Defenders bigot. He might well come to hold the balance in the Inner Council, to be the difference between peace feelers and an unconditional surrender policy.

"You have done good work, Benedict. I have read Abbot Tsintolas's previous reports to the Father General. You should take satisfaction in your contribution to the transformation of Ariel from a wasteland into an Eden.

"Now you are called to a higher task. Unless something is done soon, millions of lives may be lost and entire planets turned to cinders. We will be relying on you to do everything you can to prevent this. Our blessing goes with you."

Kourdakov stood, extending his hand. Benedict knelt and kissed the ring. Then he stood and followed Barbet back to the entrance.

"You have a difficult situation," Barbet commented. "You are bound by your vows to the Church and by law to Councilor Chiang. You are aware of what our Lord says about those who attempt to serve two masters."

"I am."

They had come to the door to the outside. Barbet stared at Benedict, clearly dissatisfied with his answer. "But perhaps you have resolved the matter. Perhaps the Rénard in truth serves only one master: himself."

Benedict's smile was mocking. "You are insightful, Father Barbet. Until I have the pleasure of your company again." He bowed and strode through the doorway.

VI

THEY LEFT THE *GRYFFON'S PRIDE* THROUGH THE UMBILI-
cal tube that led straight into Chiang's home/factory/city-
state. Benedict moved with leaden legs. It was after
midnight, Chiron time, and he had been too mentally
restless to sleep during the three-hour flight to Neoptolemus.

A figure approached him as he stepped into a corridor. "Mr. Rénard? My name is Hélène. Master Chiang
has asked me to be your guide. Let me take your duffel
bag. Follow me to your quarters, please."

Benedict was too tired to protest as she took the bag
from his hand. A moving walkway led to an elevator;
they exited two floors up and stepped onto another
walkway. After little more than a minute, they stepped
off and threaded their way through a bewildering maze of
tunnels and corridors. The lighting was dim; there were
few people about. Then he remembered that Neoptolemus was run on Chiron time, since it was impossible to
synchronize to weeklong days and nights. At this hour,
everyone except the night crew would be in bed.

Hélène activated a thumb lock, and they entered a

private hallway. One large, ornately carved door was set into the left wall.

"These are your rooms," Hélène said, opening the door.

Benedict made no move to enter. "My thanks for your guidance." He held out his hand for his bag.

Hélène stood perfectly still. "I have been assigned to be your servant for the duration of your stay here. I will show you your rooms, answer any questions you may have, and generally keep myself available. Master Chiang wishes you to enjoy every courtesy."

Suddenly, he identified the sense of familiarity that had been nagging him for the past few minutes. Juliet. The hairstyling, the mold of face, even, as far as he could remember it, the perfume.

Damn you, Herter! he thought. You did earn your wages for a little while at least, didn't you?

Benedict forced a smile. "I would hate to so waste your talents. I need no servant."

Even the hurt expression was Juliet's. "Have I offended you? Master Chiang will be extremely displeased with me if I have."

"Master Chiang's displeasure will be with my intelligence, not with your performance. You may go now. One of the MPR units I saw on the walkways will be sufficient for my needs."

Hélène hesitated a moment, then handed over his bag and turned away. Benedict was careful not to look after her.

Entering, he was taken aback by the size of the rooms. Each could have been carved up into cells for at least a dozen monks. Benedict wondered for an instant how one could sleep in such a room without getting agoraphobia.

The bathroom was worse. After nearly a minute's examination, Benedict determined that what appeared to be a small indoor pool, complete with waterfall, was in fact a tub.

He walked through into the bedroom and put his duffel bag in a closet filled with suits and sportswear—all of which, he realized without examination, would fit him perfectly. The bed was uncomfortably soft. He had to maximize the air pressure to get a reasonable firmness.

The entire far wall was taken up by what Benedict had first thought was a huge mural. Now he realized that it was viewscreen. He lowered the apartment lights so that he could see more easily.

The picture was coming from the surface, twenty or thirty meters overhead. At first Benedict could see only the crescent of Achilles spanning the horizon, a rainbow bridge bisected by a white line that was, from this angle, as much of the gas giant's ring system as could be observed. As Benedict's eyes adjusted, he picked out the burning yellow of Centaurus A and then two other moons of Achilles that floated directly above the ring as if double dotting a celestial "i." Finally, there was the ground, covered with tall grasses bending before intermittent gusts. Beyond them, icebergs drifted slowly across a dark sea.

The door chimed. "Enter," Benedict called. He turned to greet his visitor.

A multipurpose robot glided into the room, hovering only centimeters above the floor. When Benedict had left civilization ten years before, the proud boast of the robotic companies had been that you could talk to one of their products for half an hour without realizing that it was artificial. Since then, statutes passed by the Defenders of Humanity had made such close mimicry of the human form illegal. The robot before him had the vague form of a tapering cylinder surmounted by what might have seemed a humanoid head had it not been so asymmetrically deformed. Recessed lenses regarded him. Heavy-duty mechanical grapples were hinged on two sides, while four evenly spaced segmented tentacles hung limply. Every visible surface was silvered as completely as the *Gryffon's Pride*. Anamorphic reflections of himself stared at him quizzically.

"I am CB-MPR 30," the robot said in a pleasant alto voice. "You may ask of me whatever you wish." It paused. When Benedict said nothing, it resumed. "Master Chiang desires your presence. Please follow me."

Benedict sighed and followed. The journey this time was short: around two corners and through large double doors into what were surely Chiang's personal apartments.

Chiang was seated at a long, highly polished wood table. He stared as Benedict entered.

"Did none of your new clothes fit?" he demanded.

Benedict shrugged. "I have no idea. My spare habit is all that I need."

Chiang grunted. "Bobbi, meet Paul Niccolo Rénard, last of the Multi-Neural Capacitants. For some reason, it pleases him to continue his masquerade as as member of the Order of Stewards. Beware of him: He is totally impervious to the charms of women. Rénard, my wife."

The small figure seated directly across from Chiang rose and extended her hand. Her hair was as dark as Chiang's, but the skin was lighter. The bone structure was fine, but any suggestion of delicacy was swept away by the lively blue eyes.

On impulse, Benedict took her hand and pressed it to his lips.

Chiang frowned. "My wife has been running the company in my absence and was about to bring me up to date. I though you would like to sit in."

Benedict took a seat on the same side as Bobbi.

"When I arrived in Centauran space," Chiang said, "the signal I picked up put our strength at eighty-seven percent optimum. Has that figure changed in the last two days?"

Bobbi shook her head. "No."

"That is surprising. Before I left, we judged that it might be down as low as sixty percent by the time I returned. Do you have any ideas?"

Bobbi grinned. "I *know*," she said. "At least, I'm pretty sure. The First Families have been war gaming this struggle on their computers just as we have. The one thing they couldn't anticipate was that you would suddenly drop out of sight. Running a simulation from their point of view, without any knowledge of your search for the Rénard, gave as most probable the answer that you were using me as a stalking horse, hoping to tempt them into an overhasty attack.

"Also, their computers have no personality profile on me. No one had previously thought me important enough to prepare the requisite data base. My actions were therefore unpredictable."

"Situational programs," Benedict murmured. "How did the Borgias and the Tudors get on, having to decide for themselves where their advantage lay and who could be trusted?"

"But there were still harassment actions," Chiang said.

"The general power of attorney you left with me was challenged a number of times," Bobbi agreed. "Legal was able to deal with that. Companies that refused to deal with me were threatened with expensive breach of contract actions. More serious is the fact that Industrial Microbiotics has launched a full-fledged price war against us. In some areas, of course, they have no comparable lines. I was able to convince some of our clients that while switching might be to their short-term advantage, the long-range result of driving Chiang Biosynthetics under would be to double their costs. Still, we have lost some business, and it does hurt. It hurts Industrial Microbiotics at least as much, but they have greater resources to absorb the losses.

"They have also been raiding our personnel. They can't offer a much better benefit package without causing trouble among their own workers, so what they are doing instead is spreading scare stories. So far we haven't had any crucial losses, but if we appear to be weakening, we can expect a stampede.

"There is also the problem of the Epsilon refugees. Supporting them has been a continual drain. If—"

"We are going to continue supporting them," Chiang interrupted. "I have given my word on that. What about our plan to work them into our operation?"

"It is progressing. They are making all the supply runs to L 726-8. Still, we can't fully integrate them until our current freighter contracts expire. And until then, the refugees are an expensive capital outlay at a time when our cash flow is thin."

"Arrange a meeting with them for tomorrow," Chiang said. "Also, ask Colonel Cassian if he can attend."

He turned to Benedict. "Nearly a year ago, the Allies decided that neither Epsilon Indi nor Epsilon Eridani were defensible. They therefore ordered their evacuation. That one action reduced some of the most intelligent and venturesome families in human space to paupers. Some joined the Solar or Centauran fleets in the hope of being able to fight to get their homes back. Others have been forced to rely on the dubious welfare of the state. I have been aiding as many as I can, getting them jobs either in my own company or elsewhere."

"Why?" Benedict asked.

Chiang looked uncomfortable. "I want their loyalty. I have a feeling they may be useful sometime. Their ships alone make up a small flotilla. There has to be some use for that. What do you think?"

"I think that your wife looks much too young to be the mother of those two beautiful children I see pictured behind you."

Surprisingly, Chiang grinned. "And yet she is, and has

many other talents as well. Ah, Rénard, I see that we are both too tired to do any serious work. Call on me early tomorrow morning."

Benedict took his leave and followed the robot back to his apartment. He fell into bed, his mind evaluating and balancing the First Families and the Unions, the Allies and the Clans, Chiang and Bobbi. But when he dreamed, all that vanished, and he was walking with Juliet along the windswept beaches of the Outer Banks, murmuring happy inconsequentialities. Yet within him a sadness grew, and he kept his head averted, for he did not wish to see that the flesh had melted from her skull, leaving only a death's-head with sockets so deep and dark that they could swallow the world.

VII

Mr. Sun stood rigidly at attention, his eyes staring straight ahead. He was of average height, but somehow the hard slabs of muscle sheathing his body made him look smaller from a distance. At first glance he could have been mistaken for a martial arts instructor. One who took a second glance might have noticed an unusual air of alertness and intelligence and deduced some slight degree of his dangerousness.

"So you understand both my disappointment and my anger," Chiang was saying to his security chief. "You checked out Herter for dangerous connections and gave him a clean bill. Nonetheless, he murdered two good employees and tried to murder me. The crew members of the *Gryffon's Pride* all have Prime security clearances, yet one of them programmed the on-board computer to awaken Herter. The same one planted an eavesdropping device on my clothing. Hiring Herter and searching for the Rénard were supposed to be completely secret, yet Rascavia knew about both."

"You may have my resignation if you wish," Sun said woodenly.

"I don't want your goddamn resignation!" Chiang exclaimed. "I want help. I want to know why my formerly tight organization is now leaking like a sieve."

"I have no explanation as yet," Sun said. "I have re-checked all our information on the individuals in question. Nothing has changed."

"That is clearly insufficient," Benedict said. "Let us be candid, Mr. Sun. Master Chiang has a multitude of enemies eager to destroy him. They are rich and influential enough that even you are not exempt from suspicion—"

"Not true," Chiang interrupted.

"Master, we gain nothing from hiding such obvious suspicions. Mr. Sun is intelligent enough to realize that so many sudden security breakdowns make him an inevitable suspect."

"No, this time you are wrong, Rénard." The prospect seemed to please Chiang. "There are some facts you should know. When it first occurred to me that you might not be dead, I gave Mr. Sun the job of finding you. He ascertained that your last recorded words to your secretary were that if anyone wanted to see you, they were to look for you on Lemnos. After a thorough search he was convinced not only that you were not there but that you had never even been to that Aegean island.

"He might have concluded at that point that your words had been intentionally misleading. Instead, he considered the possibility of an allusion and had a computer run made for literary references to and figurative meanings of Lemnos. This produced reams of material, as you might imagine, but he quickly decided the reference in Sophocles's *Philoctetes* was most likely to be fruitful. In that case, Lemnos might mean any faraway place of exile. He then went through three months of passenger lists for all interstellar liners. He didn't find your name, of course, but knowing your fondness for multilingual puns, the name Philip Head looked suspicious enough to run a fingerprint check on the credit voucher. That was the first part of the trail. He lost you again on Ugly Duckling in the 61 Cygni system. Nothing showed up on the passenger lists this time. Only when he extended the search to crew members did he spot a Philip Archer and remember that Philoctetes had been an archer. Archer had shipped out on the *Gypsy Dancer* to Ariel but was not listed on the crew sheet when the *Dancer* reached its next port of call.

"Now, I think we all agree that the reason Herter attempted to kill me was to prevent me from contacting you. Mr. Sun could have accomplished the same end simply by not reporting any of his leads.

"And if that is not convincing enough for you, consider one thing more. Mr. Sun is both lethal and intelligent. In the nature of things, I am vulnerable to my security chief in ways I am vulnerable to almost no one else. If Mr. Sun wished to dispose of me, he would do it himself and in such a way that everyone would believe it an accident. Isn't that so?"

"Quite right, sir," Sun replied.

"Then I trust that we can stop following this particular blind alley," Chiang said.

Benedict nodded, smiling slightly. "The case is well made. My apologies, Mr. Sun."

For just an instant, Sun became scrutable enough for his satisfaction to be observed. "I am pleased that you can trust me, for it will make easier what follows. I told Master Chiang that the information we have indicates no disloyal employees. That is true. The obvious course of action, then, is to obtain more information."

Van ter Haals scowled up at Benedict through the fringe of bushing, graying eyebrows. He sucked at an elaborately carved wooden pipe, puffing furiously.

"My friend, Mr. Doi, and I have been having an argument," he explained. "He thinks entrance into the Order of Stewards indicates a real change of heart. I say it's either a joke or part of a scheme."

They were in Chiang's great meeting hall, which adjoined his apartments. Nearly all of the refugee families from Epsilon Eridani and Epsilon Indi had sent representatives. In the months of their exile they had learned how to walk gracefully in the gravity of Neoptolemus, and their skin tone had adjusted to the point where it was indistinguishable from the natives'. Resentment and bitterness had grown, however, and almost by that alone could a refugee be picked out in a crowd.

"Your incredulity is understandable," Benedict said. "Nonetheless, my conversion was genuine, my profession of vows sincere."

Van ter Haals grunted. "Pity."

"Why?" Benedict asked.

"Well, meaning no disrespect to the clergy, even the Catholic clergy, it's the old Rénard we need to help us now, the one who ran the Sirian system from his vest pocket and nearly snatched New Eden from under the noses of everyone. Prayers and spiritual consolation are all very well, but there are hundreds of ministers who can provide that."

"I fear you are making the common mistake of equating serious Christianity with limp-wristedness," Benedict said. "It was not meekness and passivity that survived the persecutions of Nero and Diocletian and went on to conquer the ancient world. Think of monarchs like Constantine, St. Louis, and Richard Lion Heart. Think of Francis, daring the Saracens to trial by fire; Ignatius Loyola, a soldier to the end of his days who merely changed commanders. Think of the clerics who defied Hitler. Think of St. Joan, of Michael Archangel himself. There is more to all of these than pastels and pious sayings."

"They had fire," Van ter Haals conceded, belching forth a great gout of smoke. "But your present church is not so convincing. The Bestials attack us without provocation, and your Pope calls for negotiations. It's our homes they're negotiating."

"As you should want them to," Benedict said. "To take back your planets by force would take atomics. Fine, your fields will be for you sown with strontium 90. No, your complaint is not with the Church, nor even particularly with the Bestials. It is with the Allies who decided not to defend your homes even though the Bestials gave no indication of wanting to mount a full-scale attack on them."

"You think you can right that?" Van ter Haals asked.

"Such is Master Chiang's intention, and up until now his will has not been thwarted," Benedict said. "As for myself, my skills have been put to a higher use during the past ten years; they have not atrophied through neglect."

"Aye," Van ter Haals said, a shadow of a smile appearing on his face. "From what I hear of the way you handled the Inner Council, that's so."

Benedict cast a quick glance about. The reception appeared to be going well. Chiang had appeared imperturbably cool and arrogant, which irritated some but definitely inspired confidence in most. Benedict did his part, having first memorized the names and faces of all the refugees plus most of their biographical material. Thus he was able to greet his guests on a first-name basis and inquire after some trivial detail of their affairs in such a way that they were convinced that he knew everything about them. A lifted eyebrow, a shrug, a phrase quickly cut short became invested with import limited only by the imagination of the listener. Indeed, it was from the refugees that he heard that the rumor mills had learned of his visit to the Primate. Vast and intricate machinations were hinted; cabals were implied that spanned star systems and generations. *The Fox is on the move.*

It was very much like the old days, and Benedict was surprised to find he was enjoying himself immensely.

Bobbi was in one corner of the room, seated in the midst of several refugee wives, smiling occasionally, now and then making a comment, but mostly listening. It was done altogether artlessly and unconsciously. Bobbi herself was genuinely concerned about the women surrounding her. The result was that they opened up to her, gave voice to complaints or observations they might not have shared even with their husbands. With mingled respect and irritation, Chiang had admitted to Benedict that Bobbi would often come away from meetings like this with a truer picture of the situation than Chiang could obtain from sounding out the main actors.

"Rénard! Over here." Chiang's hand beckoned imperiously halfway across the room. Benedict excused himself from Van ter Haals.

A group of bearded, turbaned men, ceremonial kirpans strapped to their thighs, moved aside to let him pass. Chiang sat at one end of a modular divan, listening intently to a man in the dark dress blues of the Centauran Space Force.

"Rénard, this is Colonel Cassian. You will note his decorations for valorous action against the Bestials. More important to us is his strategic sense. He is the only officer I know of with any real idea of how to win this war."

Cassian rose to his feet, extending a well-manicured hand that was hard with muscle. His uniform was impeccable from the orange and yellow ascot to the permagloss boots. The face was surprisingly young and handsome. The eyes, however, were disturbingly out of place. Benedict sensed an overwhelming intensity just barely held in check, as if Cassian were studying an interior scene of such importance that Benedict faded into ghostly insubstantiality by comparison.

"I have heard much about you, Colonel," Benedict

said. "You inspire admiration and loyalty. And controversy."

Something seemed to open within Cassian's shuttered
expression: Benedict had captured a portion of the man's
attention.

"Among some I inspire envy. And fear," Cassian said
slowly. "Political appointees—sycophants playing at
war—fear exposure of their incompetence more than
they fear the enemy."

Benedict was quite still. "To whom are you referring?"

"He is talking about the General Staff," Chiang muttered, "but he is too good an officer to say so in public,
even at a friendly gathering like this. In the past, only a
too-truthful tongue has kept him from the star he deserves. Refrain from catalyzing his temper."

"Master Chiang says you have a plan for ending the
war," Benedict said.

A slight smile split Cassian's face. "I have a plan for
winning the war. Observe."

He touched a button on the side of the divan. A spher-
ical star field, more than a meter across, sprang into existence above the table. Conversation around them
stilled.

"The first necessity is proper perspective," Cassian
said. "Ask most politicians or generals to describe the
strategic situation and they will say that we are surrounded by Bestials."

"That is a fact," Benedict observed.

"A completely misleading fact," Cassian countered.
"A more correct characterization would be that the Bestials are a veneer on human-occupied space. The Allies
are more than twenty times as populous, more than two
hundred times wealthier. We have interior lines of communication; the Bestials do not. If they surround us,
they surround us like a balloon waiting to be burst."

"So far they have maintained the initiative."

"Because we let them maintain it!" Cassian said. "But now regard that star on the upper left edge." The star in question began to blink. "A red dwarf, far behind the lines, generally considered to have no strategic importance. For just that reason, the Bestials have set up what you could call a nursery there, a place where their children can be safe from the war. That is where I would take the fleet."

"You would destroy the future of a race, engendering implacable hatred, while doing little immediate harm," Benedict said softly. "Let me not distract you with questions of morality. Rather, let me ask if it is wise to so motivate an enemy while doing him so little military damage."

There was a moment of strained silence. Then laughter, rich and full, flooded the room. Benedict was motionless, a supplicant patiently awaiting enlightenment.

"You see, Chiang," Cassian said, cutting short his laughter, "even the Rénard, whose very name has become synonymous with precisely calculated duplicity, even he misses the point.

"Your concern for children surprises me, Brother Benedict. Is not one of your Scriptural prayers

'Blessed shall that trooper be
Who cummin on his naggie,
Grabs the wee bairns by the hair
And dings them on a craggie.'"

More laughter forestalled a reply. Cassian sobered himself. "I have no intention of making war on children. They are irrelevant to this war, except—" He raised his forefinger importantly. "Except that the Bestials, by setting aside a nursery world, have revealed that they place an inordinate value on their litters. We can take advantage of this weakness.

"I would send scouts first and let them be seen. Soon

after, I would commence skirmishing with their patrols. In deliberate steps I would escalate the conflict, yet never so quickly as to crush them. Only when they sent in transports for evacuation would I act decisively, destroying them so as not to lose my hostages. In a relatively short time, I will have forced them to engage the main part of their fleet. Then I will throw in the reserves and crush them."

"That is likely to be a costly proposition," Benedict suggested. "If the statistics I have studied are accurate, we will lose four ships for every three we put out of commission."

"The real figures are much closer to three for two," Cassian said. "That is irrelevant. We could lose two for one and still win. Some wars call for Alexander; others, like this one, for Grant. Always match your strength against the enemy's weakness. In this war, our overwhelming strength is our mass. Using it intelligently will let us crush our enemies."

He sat back, regarding Benedict intently as if waiting for a challenge. Instead, after a few moments, Benedict nodded. "It could work," he admitted.

Cassian smiled, accepting this due.

The message light was on when MacAndrews got back to her room. Luminescent letters sprayed across the screen as she touched the playback button.

CASH FLOW DIFFICULTIES PREVENT IMMEDIATE PAYMENT OF THE BONUS YOU DESERVE FOR YOUR WORK IN GETTING ME TO ARIEL AND BACK AGAIN. IN THE MEANTIME, TREAT YOURSELF AND A GUEST TO A FREE EVENING AT KUBLAI KHAN'S. CHIANG.

MacAndrews whistled. Given the prices at Kublai Khan's, this was probably worth more than the cash bonus she had expected. She considered briefly whom to invite. Kirsten would be going with Younger, that much was certain. Keith would be enjoyable—*if* he could tear himself away from his laboratory. But to her surprise, her call went through at once.

"Hi," she said. "How would you like to help me do some celebrating?"

"Celebrating?" Keith Russell replied. "How did you know? The official announcement isn't to be made until tomorrow."

Russell was all of twenty-nine and looked younger. It was hard to believe that this boy genius was not only the head of Chiang's experimental division but also personal physician to Chiang's family. In his own field he had few, if any, peers. Yet he regarded everything outside his field with a childlike wonder. When she was with him, MacAndrews felt older and more self-assured than usual and could explain for hours the ways of the world to his attentive ears.

Now, however, she was the one who needed an explanation. "Official announcement of what?"

"The Champagne Project, of course. We have succeeded, and three months ahead of schedule! Let's get together, and I'll tell you all about it."

They took the hovertrain, congregating in one of the minilounges on the observation deck. Russell hunched over, his voice conspiratorily low. From time to time, Younger boomed out a request that Russell talk more loudly, ignoring MacAndrews's warning glare.

"The problem is that champagne, all wines actually, are such exact mirrors of their environment. You start out with various types of Pinot grapes, grow in chalky soil, press, and blend. The manufacturing process is extensive, but it can only refine what is already there. Here we start off with a non-Mediterranean climate and soils that have percentages of elements different from any on old Earth. That's why it's been impossible, up until now, to do any better than our Chiron Bubbly brand."

Kirsten looked puzzled. "I have had real champagne once, and I must say, I like Chiron Bubbly better."

Russell looked a bit sheepish. "Well, so do I, actually. But the point is, it's not the real thing. Given its relative rarity and the huge freighter fees, real Terran champagne has become tremendously expensive in the Centauran system. But now we have produced a local synthetic that cannot be distinguished from the French original. We proved that today at a tasting test by stumping the most prestigious wine experts from Chiron and Neoptolemus as well as five flown in from Earth for the occasion. Tomorrow, an official announcement kicks off the advertising campaign. The snob appeal plus the lower prices we will be able to offer should make this one of our most profitable items."

Rapid deceleration made them all lean forward as the train slid into the station. They stepped out onto the enclosed platform. Outside, snow devils whirled fitfully in the predawn half-light. Looking to the sea, MacAndrews saw a wall of clouds on the horizon, dark against the lightening sky: the dawn storms that came with the planetwide low-pressure area that always faced Centaurus B.

A main walkway carried them down through a dark, spice-scented tunnel, which opened up abruptly into Kublai Khan's. Each time MacAndrews had come here, it had taken all her self-control to stifle a gasp. This time was no different. On the left, seven open levels stretched up to a high ceiling. The right was a seamless wall of glasteel pointed like the prow of a ship. The upper four levels of glasteel let in the wide gray and blue expanse of sky. The bottom two levels were underwater. Cryptic luminescent forms swam in the darkness. The ocean swell had play over the third level, where the incoming waves smashed themselves into froth. During the great storms that began and ended the weeklong days of Neoptolemus, waves would sometimes hurl themselves to the very top of the glasteel. If, at such times, attendance fell off a bit, the increased alcohol consumption of those who remained offset any loss in profits.

The hostess approached them, smiling. "What milieu would all of you care for?"

They had not discussed this yet. "If you don't mind," Russell said hesitantly, glancing uneasily at Younger, "I would suggest the gourmet milieu. Not only for the food, but the entire surroundings are much nicer. And the entertainment is good yet soft enough that you can talk if you want. I believe there is an especially good chamber group that will be doing Brahms's trios in the next few hours."

Younger shrugged. "Sure. Why not? I can get bombed in any dive, but with the boss paying, I might as well sample the finer things of life."

So they ascended to the seventh level and were seated in their leather chairs by one waiter while another put new logs on their fireplace. Then the waiters quietly retired, leaving their guests to the contemplation of the large, multipaged, gilt-lettered menus. Outside, snow began to fall heavily. The waves writhed higher.

"Captain MacAndrews! Delighted to see you. The entire Centauran system has been praising the first pilot to take extended conscious command of a ship in Space$_4$. Likewise they have been praising the navigator who got the *Gryffon's Pride* out to the edge of inhabited space under such trying circumstances. And more than a few surmise the crucial role Mr. Younger played in convincing the Rénard to return."

The speaker was short and overweight. Firelight gleamed off his skin. A dark, hairline mustache nearly lost itself in a broad expanse of face.

"So we're good," Younger said. "We already know that."

"Yet being good is, unfortunately, not enough."

"Good enough for what?" Kirsten asked.

The figure coughed delicately. "Forgive me for appearing crude. Good enough for continued employment."

MacAndrews decided that she definitely disliked this man. "Do we know you?" she asked.

"Excuse me. My card."

MacAndrews wrinkled her nose as she took the card from the perfumed hand. "Industrial Microbiotics. You work for Pierpont, Mr. Reese."

"As you should also. We can reward your talents most handsomely."

"We are happy where we are," MacAndrews said.

Reese looked sorrowful. "Your happiness will be short-lived. Master Chiang has offended too many powerful people. He will shortly pay the price of being impolitic. It would be a shame if he were to drag any more down with him than necessary."

MacAndrews felt her stomach knot. All the rumors she had heard in the past six months were suddenly cast into sharp relief. Even the fact that their bonus was payment in kind rather than cash confirmed what Reese was saying. Futilely she searched for words to throw at him.

"No," a voice next to her said. The tone was calm, like a parent patiently explaining something to a child. "No, it is not going to be like that at all."

MacAndrews looked at Russell in surprise. "You see," he was saying, then stopped as if searching for words simple enough for his hearer to understand. "You see, Mr. Pierpont and his associates have accumulated a great deal of power and a team of intelligent employees. But we—we are the best there is. And," he added, the kindness, almost pity, in his tone taking the edge off his words, "we are going to beat the living daylights out of you."

There was silence. Reese seemed to wilt under Russell's absolute certainty. The moment passed, and Reese forced a sickly smile to his lips.

"You may dream that it will be so. But in the meantime, keep my card. Your services are at their highest value now. When the collapse comes, there will be thousands like you, all clamoring for jobs."

He bowed slightly and disappeared into the shadows.

This time the silence lasted until the waiter returned. "We will start with drinks," MacAndrews said. "We all have a taste we would like to wash out of our mouths."

Bobbi walked softly through the corridors, which were dim now for the evening shift. She stopped at Benedict's door, announced herself to the microphone, and entered sideways, holding the tray carefully level before her as the door opened.

Benedict was at his work desk, flanked by a motionless CB-MPR 30. His eyes swung quickly back and forth across the readout screen while his fingers danced lightly across the keyboard. He glanced up as Bobbi approached.

"Mrs. Chiang, and with food! I seem to have lost all track of time. Please don't be offended if I keep working. One of the advantages of being a Multi-Neural Capacitant is that I can give full attention to more than one thing at a time."

Bobbi set the tray down at the side of the desk. "I thought you might like something since you are working late. And especially since you haven't had any dinner."

"I have been busy running variants on the situational programs," Benedict replied, a hint of apology in his voice.

"And?" Bobbi prompted as Benedict took a large bite from one of the sandwiches she had provided.

"Without exception, every program I run shows that my mere presence has made things much worse for Master Chiang. The time to crisis has shrunk abruptly from six months to one week or less." His tone was light, but Bobbi thought she could detect something dark and bitter beneath the words.

"That doesn't make sense," she protested.

"It makes perfect sense," he said. "Ten years ago I acquired a certain... reputation, much of which was deserved. Master Chiang's enemies fear that given sufficient time, I will once again be manipulating the levers of power, setting them at one another's throats while placing Chiang firmly and forever beyond their grasp. These fears, by the way, are correct. Therefore, a preemptive strike is called for. But since I have at my disposal much the same situation programs as they do, it follows that I will anticipate their move and try to strike first. The positive feedback continues, with the result that a premium is placed on very quick action."

Bobbi took a cup of tea for herself and sipped it thoughtfully. "If they move quickly enough, they may make a mistake."

"Perhaps." Benedict looked up from his terminal. "It is unlikely, however. They will make no move without having fully calculated its effects beforehand. No, in a game like this, where each side is examining its options the same way—" he patted the keyboard "—victory goes to the one with the significantly better data base, the one which, like the hedgehog, knows one big thing its opponents don't."

"Do we know anything like that?" Bobbi asked.

"Maybe. I'm not sure yet. In any event, it would be a breach of security for me to tell you. As you probably know, we have reason to believe there was a spy on the *Gryffon's Pride*. Mr. Sun is carrying out an operation this evening that we hope will net our quarry, but until he does, my advice has to be for Master Chiang's ears alone. Not that I have much to offer him. Our best chance appears uncertain and costly."

"Given our situation, I can't imagine John scrimping at expenses," Bobbi said.

Benedict met her eyes. "I was referring to lives."

For a moment, she was at a loss. Benedict touched

two buttons, grimaced at the figures that appeared on the screen, and tapped out another series.

"Such calculations seem odd for one in your vocation," Bobbi ventured.

"While I was on Ariel, we worked to spread life. We matched algae and bacteria to soil, plants to climate, animals to the plants, and all to each other, slowly building an intricate, interdependent structure, a living cathedral that fed on sunlight to bring an entire planet to fruition." His fingers were flying over the keyboard now. Data rippled across the screen and were replaced before Bobbi could gain more than an impression of irregular columns of figures and cryptic graphics. "After a while, I came to the conviction that Dom Diego Cervantes was correct, that this was the work for which God had created Adam, that it was the only work completely fit for a human being. For ten years I was, though I didn't appreciate it at the time, absolutely content. Your husband ended all that. I make these calculations not as a result of my vocation but at his behest."

"You are bitter," Bobbi said.

Benedict seemed to consider this. "No," he said at last. "Bitterness is a self-inflicted wound which I can well do without. At whom would I be bitter? Your husband is trying to keep his life's work from being destroyed. I have only sympathy with that. And I have to admit that the task in front of me, though less enjoyable than terraforming a planet, is more important."

They ate and drank in silence for a few minutes. "How did you come to be a Steward?" Bobbi asked. "Mac—Captain MacAndrews—tells me that you disavowed any kind of faith."

Benedict looked at her sharply. "She misquotes me. What I told her was that I came to Ariel for purely profane reasons. Which is quite true."

Figures continued to flicker across the screen. Benedict noted them, gently stroking the keyboard, moving the program toward its inscrutable conclusion.

"Cast your mind back thirteen years. Well, no, then —you were hardly at the age of consent and, I presume, totally uninterested in interplanetary politics. Just listen.

"Snowden produced eleven salable MNCs. Two had been 'tamed' surgically to be little more than human biocomputers for Snowden's Recombinants Limited. The personalities of three had shattered in schizophrenia— which is a professional hazard inherent in being a Multi-Neural Capacitant. For two, even catatonic withdrawal had not provided sufficient protection from all the voices that argued and pleaded with them. They had committed suicide.

"That left four of us: myself, Allele, Highspirit Rowley, and Caesare Valentino. Caesare invited all of us to a meeting. He was living in Venice at that time, in one of the huge, baroquely ornate old houses on a canal. After we were settled in our rooms, we were summoned to his great dining hall. There were only three of us: Rowley had not come. Caesare wisely kept no human servants; house cleaning and meals were taken care of by robots.

"We sat down, dazzled by the midafternoon sunlight that flooded in through the tall rectangular windows. Caesare announced that he had called us together as a war council. His presentation would take two parts: the first, on our own nature; the second, on the most important societal trends that could be forecast for the next five years.

"On ourselves: By selling MNCs to various patrons, Dr. Snowden had, wittingly or unwittingly, created inherently unstable situations. Since MNCs were much more intelligent and therefore potentially more powerful than their masters, they inevitably tended to operate in their own rather than their patrons' interests. We were all examples of this. Caesare had gained his freedom by blackmailing his patron. I had made my patron uneasy simply by being so many steps ahead of him. Knowing that he could not control what he could not understand, he had been quite willing to grant me my freedom, especially when I offered to purchase it for five times the price he had paid for me. Rowley had been purchased by the Sirians to formulate more effective smuggling controls; he had gone on to build the beginnings of a new model army of mercenaries. Allele had apparently gained her freedom by appealing to the conscience of her owner, a gentle but in her case effective means of persuasion. The important thing was that we had all obtained our freedom and now worked only on commissions of our own choosing.

"On society generally: Snowden had made Recombinants Limited one of the most powerful companies in inhabited space by supplying genetic variants for every purpose from prostitution to planetoid mining. The short-term profit had been great. The long-term cost would be extravagant. Many had been opposed to Snowden's experiments with human genetic material from the beginning. The success of his enterprise had aroused concern in his competitors as well as bitterness in the human workers he had displaced. Increasingly strict repression could be calculated for the next ten years unless it was catalyzed sooner.

"Caesare had located such a catalyst. Graeme Williams, a lay Baptist minister who worked as a miner in the Asteroid Belt, had begun preaching against 'beasts spawned by the devil to lead men to the depths of sin and degradation.' He rallied about him all who would be true Defenders of Humanity. To perceptions of threatened self-interest, Williams was giving a cloak of righteousness. Caesare showed us his calculations. Within three years, there would be a campaign to exterminate all human genetic variants. Including ourselves. In fact, it was already beginning. Rowley was not with us, Caesare informed us, because he had been poisoned less than a week before.

"We did not dispute his calculations; they were too convincing. Instead, we discussed ways to protect ourselves. I suggested that the Reverend Williams might meet an accidental death. Caesare smiled but shook his head: Williams's following was large enough now that death would only occasion his replacement with someone even more virulent. Caesare had contacted Snowden, broaching his fears and suggesting that some of the danger might be defused were Snowden to renounce all future experimentation with humans. Snowden had listened but seemed totally unconcerned. Perhaps he was even then beyond the boundaries of sanity.

"Allele had been growing ever more pale as we had been talking. I asked her for her suggested strategy. In a low voice, she said that she knew exactly how to quench the reaction. Caesare inclined his head ironically and asked for her solution. She only bit her lip and shook her head, muttering that she was not brave enough for her own solution."

Benedict took a long drink of tea and sat back, cradling the cup in his hands. "Even with hindsight, I still find it difficult to believe how pathetically blind we were. Supposedly three of the most ruthless beings in existence, certainly the three most intelligent, with the solution right before us, and we never so much as thought of it."

"Which was?" Bobbi asked.

Benedict snorted. "Kill Snowden, of course! Present ourselves to humanity as tortured grotesques driven to vengeance. With luck we would have ridden the wave of reaction Caesare predicted to a verdict of justifiable homicide. At worst, we would have been judged guilty of second-degree murder and been sentenced to seven years' ethical reeducation."

"Perhaps you never thought of it because Snowden was your father," Bobbi suggested.

"Our father," Benedict said slowly, as if studying the words. "Tell me, how close were you to your father?"

"I—well, not very," Bobbi said, confused by the change of subject. "He was a sky miner. He came to the Centauran systems from Sol and worked on and off for Flying Mountains. Most of his pay went to snorting syntho. He stayed with my mother—I really don't know why. Maybe because she took care of him. Maybe because she was cheaper than the whores. It didn't stop them from fighting, though. At least three times a week, when Dad was home, they would be yelling at each other and throwing things around the room."

She forced a small laugh. "I started going to church just to find a place where it was quiet."

"Did he ever culture cancer on your brothers," Benedict asked, "and cut them up to mount on microscope slides? Would it ever have occurred to him to give you gills, replace your limbs with tentacles, and throw you into a pool in order to note your adjustment to a marine environment?"

"No!" Bobbi said, disturbed.

"Then every night you should get down on your knees and thank God for such a father. Dr. Snowden was quite . . . otherwise. He knew no emotion, no morality, no loyalty, save to his overmastering curiosity. Curing hereditary hemophilia and inventing cheaper methods of producing nerve toxins were all one to him.

"He made more than one hundred attempts to create Multi-Neural Capacitants. Most were rejected as unsuitable before being brought to term. Many more were destroyed later for various unsuitable reactions. And, of course, the brain surgery itself was experimental. Many of my brothers and sisters succumbed to the learning curve.

"I must have been about ten years old, just beginning

to assert my independence, when Snowden took me through a laboratory bay I had never seen before. I turned a corner and recoiled, having nearly run into myself.

"The corpse was floating upright in a transparent case of preservative solution. The right half of the skull had been taken away. That portion of the brain had been delicately sliced into dozens of translucently thin leaves. Unseen currents moved them slowly. The left half of the face, which remained, was my own.

"Snowden, behind me, clapped his hand on my shoulder. 'Number 16B5. Such promise! Such a disappointment! I still sometimes study the neuronic structure in hopes of discovering what went wrong. You won't disappoint me, will you, my boy?' "

Benedict took a deep breath, as if trying to drag himself up from the past. "No, it was not filial piety that prevented us from contemplating his murder. It was a mindblock. Snowden had foreseen both our true potentials and the possibility of conflicting interests. I did not even guess its existence until a friend of mine, Brother Dimitri, removed it during my novitiate.

"So Caesare offered his solution. He proposed that the three of us seize power, not openly but behind the scenes, that we control and ultimately discredit the newly formed Defenders of Humanity.

"It was when he proposed setting up breeding factories that I had to object. We would have to be in control for two generations. Not only would we have to produce several thousand offspring but also supervise the brain surgery that would complete the transformation into Multi-Neural Capacitants. And we would have to do this in the face of growing opposition from groups like the Defenders of Humanity who considered us to be dangerous monsters.

"It was easy to demonstrate that the odds against such a plan were astronomical. Caesare was nettled.

What was my plan? he demanded. Low visibility, I replied. Instead of seizing power, we should make ourselves indispensable to power. Our price would be being kept well behind the throne—and pay sufficiently to establish and reach various boltholes if the need arose. Perhaps our main use would be against each other. Strategically, we were the intellectual equivalent of the atomic bomb. If we played our cards correctly, the humans would establish MNC breeding factories for us, for the same reasons the great powers of the twentieth century had established nuclear stockpiles.

"Caesare thought it too dangerous for us to allow ourselves to be used against each other. Allele concurred. Caesare said something else: 'No matter how far you go, no matter how well you hide, someday someone will come for you. He will pluck you from your hole, and there you will be, in whatever outlandish disguise still clings to you, totally at his mercy.'"

Benedict looked down at his Stewards' habit and smiled. "My brother was obviously a prophet."

"What happened then?" Bobbi prompted.

"The meeting ended inconclusively. Each of us had individual ideas on how to deal with the threat Caesare had pointed out to us. I kept in touch with him off and on over the next three years, sometimes helping him with minor problems. Allele seemed to withdraw into herself; we had only the most perfunctory notes from her. And all the while the Defenders of Humanity grew more virulent and influential."

He stopped, seemingly absorbed by his memories. His fingers continued to move, as if by themselves. Watching him, Bobbi was suddenly reminded of a pianist she had seen years before playing a nocturne, his right hand hitting one note repeatedly so that it sounded like a distant church bell tolling the hours before dawn.

"I was living at that time with a woman named Juliet. She was not an especially pretty woman, and certainly not what either one of us would call a good woman. Nevertheless, she was good to me. We were on vacation on Mars, landing at the spaceport at the base of Olympus Mons. As we walked across the concourse, a man lunged through the crowd, slashing down with a knife. Juliet died immediately."

"The murderer," Bobbi said. "He was a Defender of Humanity?"

Benedict nodded.

"How you must hate them."

"No. For a long time that bothered me. Surely I had every reason to hate them. But if a tidal wave destroyed your home, would you curse the individual water molecules? I could feel no more anger at them than at any other mindless natural calamity. And besides, they were correct."

"You can't mean that," Bobbi said, shocked.

Benedict forced a wry smile. "Oh, I don't mean they were right in identifying me with the Antichrist. Or that Juliet was 'the scarlet whore of Babylon' despite what the knife wielder shouted. No, they were correct in Caesare's way, in choosing not to allow themselves to be supplanted. A race that is too fainthearted to kill for its own survival is already moribund.

"Fear soon displaced and dominated sorrow. Juliet and I had been traveling under what I had had every reason to believe were impervious identities. If we had been located at Olympus Mons, there was no reason to believe that any of my boltholes were safe.

"Caesare would make his move within the next three months. By that time I wanted to be gone to ground. But where would the Defenders be least likely to look for me?

"That's when I thought of the Stewards. Several years before, my then-current patron had been Sky Miners, Inc. Like all Sol-centered enterprises, they were beginning to feel the crunch of Centauran competition. Like nearly every state or corporation, they believed they could get well by digesting New Eden. Remember, no one had seriously believed that the Stewards could terraform that desert planet orbiting Procyon. Proven wrong on that, no one intended to let them keep it.

"At the time I received my commission, the competing interests had pretty much canceled each other out. My plan was to have the Stewards give Sky Miners the planet. My patron would act as protector; the Order would become fabulously wealthy. So I proposed it to Muir, who had only recently been elected head of the order. I laid before him every possible temptation, but always dressed in moralistic finery. The money my patron would pay would be used by the Stewards to further extend their mission. By coming under the protection of Sky Miners, the Stewards would avert the possibility of war over New Eden. And so on.

"Muir listened intently to all my arguments and then, with ponderous deliberation, replied that while everything I said was true, there was no way that he could turn over a planet made fruitful and beautiful for the glory of God to a company that intended to turn it into a huge strip mine. Those are my terms; the Father General was much more polite.

"I left that meeting blind with rage, cursing Muir for being too much of a moron to recognize what I could do for him. Only later did it occur to me that he might be far on the other side of the human scale and that I had failed because I had nothing of interest to offer a saint.

"Giving no one advance warning, I dropped out of sight, hoping that my disappearance would be considered the result of a successful assassination attempt. I moved from world to world, creating a new identity in each one, and finally came to Ariel. Since the Order even then ran fairly sophisticated checks on long-term visitors, I went to the abbot and announced my true identity, claiming sanctuary.

"He was not at all pleased. He had watched my actions on behalf of Sky Miners from a distance and had drawn all the correct conclusions. Now he feared that I would attempt on Ariel what had failed on New Eden. My response was very close to the pure truth. By then, the Defenders of Humanity were near the height of their influence. The abbot could see that soon I might well have good reason to fear for my life.

"I said I would take sanctuary on whatever terms the Order found acceptable. Still suspecting me, Abbot Tsintolas said that the best disguise would be that of a novice. It was actually his way to subject me to scores of petty humiliations, putting me to work in the kitchen, serving tables, washing floors—in hope that angry pride would cause me to cast aside my disguise. The attempt was too obvious to work. Furthermore, though the abbot couldn't know it, he was gentler and much more careful of my dignity than Snowden ever had been."

Bobbi was frowning. Her tea was now lukewarm, but she hardly noticed it. "Your sister, Allele—I think I remember her now. I was hardly more than a teenager then. She had been videocording a paper—something to do with sociology—when a mob broke into her house. They were Defenders. They shouted terrible things at her; I guess they didn't realize the videocorder was still on. She pleaded with them, asked what wrong she had ever done them. She looked so vulnerable, so innocent. She almost seemed to sway them. Then the bludgeons came up, and I heard the snap of cracking bone and saw two thin streams of blood running from her nose. When I saw that on TRANSCENDATRAN, I decided that I wanted no more to do with the Defenders of Humanity."

Surmise flashed across her face like lightning. "Which was exactly what she intended! That was the plan she mentioned to Caesare Valentino, the one she was not brave enough for. And it worked, because from then on

the Defenders were looked on more and more as dangerous fanatics."

Benedict nodded. "You see it immediately. It took me
more than a year after the fact to admit that she had
planned her own death, that she had staged and recorded
it solely to discredit the Defenders. I was outraged! How
could she do anything so perverse? Caesare and I had
always understood that one played the game for one's
own benefit. For Allele to sacrifice herself was a violation of everything we stood for."

"So MacAndrews was right?" Bobbi asked. "Your
being a monk has never been anything more than a disguise?"

"That's hard—I mean—I . . ." Benedict trailed off in a
confusion so apparent that even though she felt ashamed
of it, Bobbi couldn't help being suspicious. For surely
the Rénard, even when utterly at a loss, would never let
anybody *see* that.

Benedict seemed to pull his thoughts under control.
"Several things conspired together. Allele's death. Dead,
she had much more presence to me than she had ever
had when alive. When I thought of her, I felt a mute,
insistent pressure.

"Then there was New Hierosolyma. I don't want to
overromanticize it. In many ways a monastery is not the
place for naturally good men: They can do very well in
the world. But for those who need an external structure
to order their lives, it is ideal. For the first time in my life
I was able to go to bed without wondering if someone
would try to kill me in my sleep, without trying to plan
for a dozen contingencies on the morrow. And the work
itself was so clearly good yet complex enough to retain
my interest. It took me four years to realize that I was
completely happy.

"Then there was the problem of 'good.'" His eyes
darted at her as if trying to provoke a reaction.

"There is no problem with good," Bobbi objected obediently.

"There was for me," Benedict said. "Growing up under Snowden's tutelage, I had been presented with a universe that was random and purposeless. Human motivation could be reduced to power and curiosity. Evil and pain presented no intellectual problem. They were the expectable state of affairs.

"But good? What was I to make of a man like Father General Muir, whose main motivation really did seem to be a disinterested goodwill? How could I account for those days when, against all odds and any rational expectation, everything would go right? Most disturbingly, how could I understand myself, and sweet troubling of my soul at a beautiful landscape or at some particularly haunting passage of music, or my wonder at the complicated interdependencies of the human body or society or the universe itself?

"I was not Prometheus, seizing grace from the heavens. It swooped from the sky and seized me in its talons. I submitted gladly, but to a mystery. I know Jesus for my Lord, but I have no idea why He insists we should love our enemies when their extermination would prevent so much evil. 'My ways are not your ways,' God says smugly. Well, that is for god*damn* sure."

Benedict seemed to lose interest in what he was saying as new figures marched across the screen. His lips thinned; his eyes had gone slate-gray. Without knowing why, Bobbi felt an almost overpowering sense of dread. Benedict's finger hovered reluctantly over the printout button then descended. There was a high-pitched whine as the paper began to fold itself out of the slot.

"But that is all old history now," Benedict said, his voice like a lightly scraping razor. "*Homo sapiens sapien*, victor over mastodon, Neanderthal, and carrier pigeon, triumphs yet again. The Multi-Neural Capacitants are seen to be an evolutionary failure. Snowden, our creator, has gone to his own bizarre end. Knowing that humanity considered me a stinking wound, I sought my own Lemnos. Now the great powers find that they need my bow enough to hold their noses. We are no threat, since all are dead save myself. And there shall be no more, for I am celibate, my pledge of harmlessness to the Defenders of Humanity."

Bobbi found herself on her feet, rage lancing through her like a firestorm. "Is that all your vows mean to you? You have taken what should have been the sign of your commitment to God and turned it upside down, made it the craven ransom for your hide so that you can continue to scheme and plot and never, never grow at all."

The words were true and spontaneous. Yet for an instant Bobbi seemed to be watching herself from a distance, trying to hurt Benedict on such a basic level that the pain would destroy his defenses and he would be forced to vomit forth the truth about himself.

His face shut like a door. Once again he was poised, courteous, ironic. "Well," he said, "I never claimed to be perfect, did I?"

VIII

CHIANG LAY BACK, STARING UP THROUGH FIFTEEN meters of water. Three rays were swimming in slow, confused circles above him, uncertain whether to orient on the sunlight overhead or the light beneath them.

There was still a pins-and-needles sensation in his fingers: the residue of cold sleep. Even the short flight back to Chiron had taken its toll. That and too little real sleep, too much time spent wondering over the solution the Rénard had given him, which, as he studied it, had shifted from incomprehensibility to become a viper, as liable to destroy him as to destroy his enemies.

The Rénard. In his mind, Chiang replayed Bobbi's account of her conversation with him. For a moment his thoughts were on his wife. Once again he marveled, almost fearfully, at the way people would disclose themselves to her. Her mere presence seemed to act like a catalyst, bringing forth from the most reticent the fears, the hopes, the shames they guarded deep within themselves.

Such had seemed to happen last night. Yet had it? Bobbi herself had doubts, half suspecting that it might be some elaborate show put on for her—and Chiang's—

105

benefit. But why go to the trouble to project such an ambiguous image?

"At some point, you will be faced with a decision," the Rénard had said. "Either you can trust me, or you cannot." The more Chiang thought about those words, the more they resembled a curse.

The noise was subliminal, but Chiang swung instantly off the bed to his feet. The door opened, and Rascavia entered. Close beard and mustache made his face an inverted A. Chiang could imagine him as the Devil's younger brother, not yet weary and bitter with the frustrations of seeking universal damnation.

Rascavia's eyes swept the room, quickly taking in the huge bed with its red silk coverings, the concave mirrored walls, the ceiling aquarium, the overly ornate vanity.

"Did you know, these places are more expensive without the whore?" Rascavia shook his head. "Undoubtedly due to some obscure economic factor with which, as First Councilor, I really ought to be conversant."

Chiang opened his mouth. Rascavia held up his hand. "'Especially,' you are going to say, 'since you know everything about prostitution.' You see, I am so determined that this meeting be a success that I am willing to take your insults upon myself even before you speak them."

"I am intrigued," Chiang admitted carefully. "Why do you think this meeting so important? And why is it *here*?"

Rascavia shrugged. "Even with all precautions, it is still impossible to be sure that no one knows your whereabouts. Best, then, to give them a false reason so that the spies may smirk and leer and never suspect that your motives are—relatively—virtuous."

He dropped the bantering tone. "As for why, I think you must have guessed. Your time is very short. Your neck is on the block. The blade is raised and requires no more than that—" he whisked his forefinger across his thumb "—to send it hurtling down."

"And this disturbs you," Chiang said.

"Yes, it does! Good God, Chiang, aside from myself, you are the only intelligent member of the Council. Who else could spit in the faces of the First Families and build up a multiplanetary corporation under their noses? Who else could have pulled off the coup of locating the Rénard? I still laugh whenever I think of the expressions I saw when his identity was confirmed in Council chambers.

"Whom will I be left with if you are thrown to the wolves? Murderous fanatics like Cowan. Sniveling bootlickers like Couteau. And smug, pompous bores like Pierpont and Gould who think the planets owe them a living because their great-grandfathers had the intelligence and initiative to settle this system. I can hardly bear thinking of it."

Chiang gazed at him earnestly. "You have no idea how touched I am to inspire such esteem. To think that you would risk a career begun with a marriage into the First Families and buttressed by being the balance of rival factions. That you would meet me to give warning in total defiance of the wishes of the First Families. That your affection is based entirely on my own sterling qualities, not at all influenced by the fact that even as I surprised everyone by producing the Rénard, so may the Rénard and I be preparing a surprise to be triggered as soon as my enemies move against me."

Rascavia laughed delightedly. "There, just as I said! We really are the two most intelligent men in the system. And you are right, of course. I have the permission of the First Families to sound you out. And they are just a bit worried about the Rénard. I myself consider it to be misplaced fear. Not that the Rénard is inconsiderable. However, even the resources of Multi-Neural Capacitants are finite. Were it not so, Caesare Valentino would be pulling all our strings."

"He is," Chiang said, improvising. "The Rénard told me this morning. When Valentino recognized the strength of sociopolitical currents ten years ago, he realized his only chance for safety was to arrange his own apparent death. That done, he disposed of Graeme Williams and took his identity. He then instigated this war with the Bestials to keep everyone distracted while he consolidated power."

"Don't play with me," Rascavia said. "I am here to do you an important favor, not to listen to fairy tales." Yet he fell silent, clearly turning the idea over in his mind. Chiang tried to look properly inscrutable. "Besides, you would never tell me such a thing if it were true."

"Unless my purpose was to make you discount such a belief by my suggesting it before you assembled enough clues by yourself to come to that conclusion," Chiang countered.

Rascavia passed a hand wearily in front of his eyes and shook his head. "You have been with the Rénard too much. You are beginning to sound like him."

"But you have a proposal," Chiang prompted.

"Yes, I do. The First Families recognize that even if you and the Rénard do not concoct an unpleasant retaliation, the effort of disposing of you would nonetheless entail certain . . . inconveniences. Being prudent businessmen, they wish to avoid these problems. Therefore, using me as intermediary, they suggest a reconciliation."

"On what terms?"

"Almost any terms you choose. You need not divorce your wife and marry into the First Families, although that would be ideal. You could even keep Bobbi as your mistress; such things are understood.

"Nor need you throw the Rénard to the Defenders. Though many would advise that, I personally would regret the loss of so unique a personality."

He paused, as if waiting for comment. Chiang remained silent, his face totally devoid of expression.

"Certain concessions would be needed, however," Rascavia continued. "You would have to transfer, immediately, fifty-one percent of your stock in Chiang Biosynthetics to Industrial Microbiotics. Likewise, fifty-one percent of your stock in your freight and mining companies would have to be transferred to Flying Mountains Mining. You will be paid handsomely, probably more than you could get on the open market just now. You will certainly never need to work again.

"If you choose to continue active, however, you will be executive vice-president in charge of research for Industrial Microbiotics. You will have a six-figure salary—plus generous stock options."

Rascavia looked at Chiang appraisingly. "Pierpont is not a young man. He has surrounded himself, for the most part, with yes-men and toadies. None of them will have the ability to run that company when he is gone. Play your cards right and, say, in ten years, you could be running everything."

Chiang got up and began to pace. Rascavia nodded, pleased that his offer was being seriously considered. There was flurry of motion in the ceiling as a ray, startled by something unseen, darted out of the light. Chiang stopped pacing and looked up.

"I didn't intend to form my own company. Not at first." He looked down at Rascavia. "I came here from Earth, during the Expulsions. I wanted a research job with Industrial Microbiotics. The interview went well to begin with. Then the interviewer let something slip, and I realized that Industrial Microbiotics, a company founded and run largely by those of northern European extraction, wanted a token Oriental to be placed in a high-visibility position so as to soothe the corporate conscience.

"I blew up. Slamming my résumé down on the table, I told the interviewer that I should be hired for one reason only: because I was without doubt the best qualified candidate she would ever see. She got nasty then, and I stormed out of the room, swearing to myself that I would push that patronizing bullshit down their throats. And for ten years I have been doing that."

"Until now," Rascavia said.

Chiang shook his head. "You said it yourself. The original settlers were smart and tough. Somewhere in the last three generations, though, the genetic material has played out. All that is left to the heirs is inherited wealth and a jealous regard of privileges. It is past time that they were put in their place."

"You are in no position to do that," Rascavia warned.

Chiang thought once again of the printout Benedict had showed him. He met Rascavia's eyes easily and held them. "You are wrong. Your earlier surmise was correct. The Rénard and I have indeed formed a plan. I had intended to spring it on all of you as a surprise, but your offer is not ungenerous, and my wife does, for some reason, have a weakness for mercy.

"Hear, then, my terms: We may continue on our various paths competing in the marketplace for whatever fortune we may obtain. If, however, the First Families move against me, I will retaliate and short-cut the competitive process. You saw how the Rénard could manipulate the Inner Council on the spur of the moment. We have now had weeks to plan, to make contacts, to set events in motion our way. Be warned."

Rascavia sighed deeply. "You disappoint me. Had you set pride aside, you could have been one of the great."

"I, too, am disappointed," Chiang said. "Had you any pride at all, you could have been a man."

Rascavia's eyes flashed. "That is your anger speaking. Because I am your friend, I will not hold it against you." He stood and strode across the room. At the doorway he turned. "Contact me if you change your mind. I will still intercede for you. But do so quickly. You have very little time left."

Benedict moved from the darkness into an island of multicolored light. The interior of St. John Henry Newman was illuminated not only by the tall stained-glass windows but also by skylights depicting the heavens as seen from a score of planets. From the great central rose skylight, God exploded in a fury of creativity, fashioning not only this but every universe.

It was the windows, however, that held Benedict's attention. Here Gregor Mendel was almost lost in the twining foliage of his pea plants. It was said that if one looked closely enough, one would see that certain of the leaves came together to form a monkey's face: the artist's way of acknowledging that Darwin's theory of evolution would have been insupportable without the monk's discovery of genetics.

He moved on to another window. In it, a rather obese Thomas Aquinas discoursed with Étienne Gilson and Jacques Maritain. In a third window, titled "The Writers," Saints Clive, Jacob, and Charles were dressed in tweeds as they sat around the fire in a study, reading manuscripts to one another.

One of the heavy oak doors to the rear of the church opened, momentarily flooding the interior with a nova burst of brilliance. A figure in silhouette moved forward uncertainly, letting the door shut behind him.

Benedict walked slowly from the side chapel in a way calculated to draw unobtrusive attention to himself. Out here in the nave the ceiling was much higher. He stepped under the central skylight. The sun was almost directly overhead so that he passed through bands of red to orange, yellow to green, blue to violet. In the center was a large shadow. The glass that cast it was totally black. Pictorially, it was God's mouth, representing, according to the viewer's perspective, the Logos, the Cloud of Un-knowing, the Original Singularity.

He passed from the shadow to the light. Around him, he could hear the clink of a rosary, the vacuum dusting of a workbot in one of the side chapels. Footsteps echoed behind him, approaching.

Benedict moved casually to the side to arrive, as if by accident, at a small, unlighted doorway. The room sensors noted his presence as he entered and slowly brought the lighting up to standard intensity. A moment later Epstein entered, blinking against the brightness.

The room was small and relatively barren. The only ornamentation was a small crucifix on one wall. A table and two chairs were the only furnishings. On the table lay a Bible and a few devotional works.

"The Reconciliation Room," Benedict said, waving his arm from the chair on which he had draped himself. "In an older ritual, called the Confessional. I am sure both of us have much to confess. A pity neither has the power of absolution."

"Your past indiscretions are not the point," Epstein said brusquely. "It is your future decisions that are now very important."

"Indeed. The reasons I called you here, Councilor—"

"—are likewise unimportant." Epstein spoke deliberately. Only the slight sheen across his upper lip disclosed that he was not as completely in command as he would have liked Benedict to think. "Doubtless you wish to haggle with me, to use your influence to get me to use my influence to do something favorable for Councilor Chiang. Conserve your breath for a more useful project."

"Why?"

"Because Chiang has joined the walking dead, although he doesn't realize it yet." There was excitement in Epstein's voice, as well as an obscure anger. "Within a week Chiang Biosynthetics will be in the hands of receivers. Your indenture will be worth no more than ten centimes per credit."

"That should please me greatly," Benedict said softly, "since it would bring my freedom that much closer. But if that is true, then why have you bothered to come at all?"

"Chiang is about to be removed from the game board, but you are still very much on it. There are those who wish you to share Chiang's fate, and worse. Cowan, for one, heads a faction of the Defenders of Humanity that looks for your death."

"Is that so?" Benedict looked at his fingernails, utterly unconcerned. "How novel. In my experience, only defenseless women have had reasons to fear the Defenders."

Epstein flushed. "Any movement, no matter how valid, attracts its share of thugs and fanatics. I am sorry about your sister and your mistress—"

"You are sorry. They are dead."

"—but you must realize that many people were pressed beyond their limit. Snowden was manufacturing biological machines to take their jobs away. Worse, by making these machines in the image of human beings, he took away their dignity, implying that they themselves were only arbitrary forms of protoplasm."

"Save it for the Spacers' Union elections. I'm sure that it gets the votes every time."

"Do you dispute a word that I say?"

Benedict pressed his lips together as if forcibly holding back a retort. Then his eyes slid away. "No, I don't. Snowden was an evil and dangerous man, too intelligent in the ways of biochemistry but too stupid to understand or care about the reaction he was provoking."

"You, too, are a victim," Epstein said. "He played with you, created you as a toy to please his whims, then cast you aside, leaving you nothing, not even your common identity as a human being. I don't know how you came to be with the Stewards on Ariel, but I can guess part of it. You were looking for the farthest corner of human space to hide in, with the people least likely to turn you out.

"That isn't possible anymore, now that you have been rediscovered. It may not be necessary. I can change things for you. I have great influence with the Defenders. I can show them that you have been hurt by Snowden as much or more than any of them. I can make, in terms they will understand, Councilor Ronan's argument, which convinced me of your humanity. Then, if you wish to continue as a Steward, fine. But if you wish, you will be able to go anywhere, your humanity undisputed."

"And the price for all this disinterested benevolence? Chiang's head, perhaps?"

Epstein shook his head violently. "Believe what I say! Chiang is already out of the picture. You are needed for more important things. In a matter of weeks, the Solar Space Forces will send a large contingent here to join with our forces and form an Allied fleet. For the first time we will be able to maintain a sustained offensive against the Bestials. But even so, the war will be difficult and costly. Your MNC talents would prove invaluable in formulating strategy."

"Why should I?" Benedict asked.

"As proof of your loyalty to humanity," Epstein said pointedly. "And because if the habit of a Steward means anything at all to you, you believe in justice. We were attacked and men were killed without any provocation by the Bestials. There can be no peace anywhere until they are defeated."

"Epstein, my dear boy," Benedict murmured. "To think that you have clawed your way up to leadership in the Spacers' Union, gained influence as one of the leaders of the Defenders of Humanity, and won a seat on the Centauran Inner Council, all the while remaining a naif.

"Forgive me if I grow serpentine. I shall force you to eat of the Tree of the Fruit of Knowledge and send you from this room bewailing your nakedness and your loss of innocence."

Epstein stared at the hand Benedict was slowly extending across the table as if expecting an apple to magically appear within it. "What are you prattling about? Speak plainly or not at all."

"How much do you know about the Bestials?"

"What everyone knows. I know that they were created by Snowden mainly to be workers on mining worlds, to be tougher than humans and more resilient while requiring less food and oxygen. For more than twenty years they seemed to work out very well, so that the number of human supervisors was gradually reduced. At the time, the mining companies considered this to be improved efficiency. Now we realize that the Bestials were consolidating their control over all the Periphery Stars, eliminating human interference so that they could prepare for war."

"Why should they want war?"

"How should I know? To gain their independence, I suppose."

"Which independence, you imply, was a necessary condition precedent to beginning martial preparations. Doesn't your reasoning strike you as circular?"

"How the hell should I know—"

"Quietly, please," Benedict said, holding a finger to his lips. "These rooms are only moderately soundproofed. You will frighten the dear old ladies in the pews."

"How should I know what motivates the Bestials?" Epstein asked in a more moderate voice. "I don't think they necessarily know. I understand they go through a period of irrationality..."

"*Testrarch*," Benedict supplied.

"When they are dangerous to themselves and everyone around them. Maybe that caused the attack."

"An odd and restrained irrationality that hits at the heart of the enemy's war-making capacity and *only* at military targets," Benedict commented. "Tell me, when did the mining companies become aware that the Bestials were founding colonies of their own and were siphoning off a good half of their productivity to support this effort?"

Epstein frowned. "Less than a year before the war began, I believe."

"And what did they do to get their erring children back in line?"

"I don't know. I wasn't a party to those decisions. Perhaps you should ask Gould."

"As it happens, I don't have to ask Gould. I have a decision document, obtained for Master Chiang by the ever-resourceful Mr. Sun. In it I read that the miners, including Gould, decided to stop shipment of hydroponic phosphorus and rare earths."

Epstein thought for a moment and nodded. "That makes good sense," he said, surprised approval in his voice. "Even the tightest food recycling system loses a fraction of a percent with each cycle. It's not important if the loss can be made up locally, but certain necessary trace elements in the rare earth series are unlikely to be found in the planets circling M-type stars. Phosphorus must usually be resupplied as well. Without those supplies, the Bestials would have to surrender."

"Or go to war to obtain them."

"That just shows how irrationally violent the Bestials are. They had plenty of negotiating leverage. The sensible response to their predicament would have been unionization and bargaining, not war."

"Really? Cast your mind back. What bargaining recognition could the Bestials expect at a time when the death penalty would be invoked against them merely for testifying in a court of law? At a time when genetic variants like Highspirit and Allele were killed by mobs of Defenders without even the pretense of law. So far distance had buffered the Bestials against the wrath of the Defenders. But now Williams's followers were calling for the extermination of all genetic variants, while the mining companies were tightening the screws, forbidding the supplies necessary for life. Of course, they could have submitted like trusting lambs."

Epstein was pacing now. His left eyelid flapped like a captive moth. "You exaggerate. Nobody seriously proposed genocide of all genetic variants. That was just rhetoric."

"Well, yes," Benedict said in a conciliatory tone. "I suppose it was. But how could the Bestials know that? When your enemy has both hands clenching your windpipe and is screaming that he intends to murder you—why, I would say, in such circumstances you can be forgiven for not perceiving that it is all 'just rhetoric.'"

Epstein had stopped pacing. The veins along his throat and head stood out like fracture lines in a granite boulder. He was staring at the floor and hardly seemed to hear when Benedict continued.

"You are correct, of course. The war is much more important than the fate of Chiang Biosynthetics. And you are also correct in thinking that you and I may have a pivotal role to play in ending the war. But before we can make reality we must understand it. I mean no insult when I say that today you have had as much reality as you can deal with. Think of what I have said over the next few days. Think, especially when you catch in a mirror the image of the one who started this war: it is you, *mon semblable, mon frère*."

The door slammed as Epstein fled the room. Benedict blinked, wondering how the Archbishop would like *this* report. Then he stood, finding to his surprise that he was trembling, and let himself out of the room.

Light spilled briefly out into the aisle before the sensors, noting his absence, extinguished it. True to his prediction, an old lady sat in a pew, an almost comically terrified expression on her face, with one round white eye staring back over her shoulder in the direction Epstein had gone. Then she glanced back at Benedict. Against the light, she could catch only the confused shadows of his habit.

"Ah, Father, it's a fierce one you have there."

"No, indeed, madam," Benedict murmured. "Rather, a deeply troubled soul. Pray for him, please. He suffers the disadvantage of being, basically, a good man."

IX

MEMORIES FLOATED IN DISORDERED CLUMPS, LIKE SPIN-
drift after a storm, being sucked back and then thrown
forward onto the sand, evaporating into incoherence.
She was shouting, they were chanting—something, over
and over. They were searching for someone, chasing him
down level after level into flaming darkness. Over everything a voice kept droning on, saying things she knew
were terribly important—if only she could comprehend
them.

Sensation itself was disjointed, as if bone and flesh
had been pried apart and scattered to the winds. There
was the heat of her cheek reflected off the rumpled
sheets. Tongue and roof of mouth were as dry and jagged
as the mountains of Mercury. From the teeth oozed
something that tasted indescribably foul.

The stomach emanated a bloated anxiety, an uneasiness that grew and intensified.

In her dream, she forced herself out of bed, just making it to the bathroom before her stomach crawled up her
throat and emptied itself in her mouth.

She dimly became aware that only escaping from the
bed had been a dream.

Ruthlessly she forced her will down her nervous system, conquering first the rebellious muscles, ordering them to contract together, to lever bones in ragged unison so that they could grasp the sheets and stuff them down the laundry chute. Then she scrabbled at the holophone.

There was a gap in memory. When self-awareness returned, she thought she must be dreaming again. Her sodden clothing had been somehow removed; the clean coolness of a nightgown now caressed her skin. A wet cloth was sponging her lips clean. MacAndrews allowed a small sigh of contentment to escape her.

"One thing I have to hand to you," Bobbi's voice said. "You sure do know how to enjoy yourself."

The words seared through MacAndrews's brain like laser cannon fire despite the fact that they had been softly spoken. MacAndrews tried to groan but only succeeded in producing a soft gurgle at the base of her throat.

"Here," Bobbi said. "Inhale while I squirt some No-Hang up a nostril." MacAndrews did as she was told. Almost at once a tingling warmth made its way up along both sides of her septum. The hammering in her head faded into the background.

Bobbi sat back on the bed, admiring her handiwork. "I suppose now would be the proper time for a lecture on the evils of drink," she said. "However, I fear that drinking may have been one of the least of your indiscretions."

"What do you mean by that?" MacAndrews asked, separating each word and articulating it carefully. "We only wanted to hear some chamber music."

"Well, that may have been so to begin with," Bobbi allowed as she placed MacAndrews's head gently in her lap and began massaging her temples. The action quickened the circulation of the NoHang, washing the pain out of the caverns of her skull. "However, sometime after the sixth bottle was consumed, you all decided to search out and punish some individual who had apparently offended you. So you staggered from table to table shouting, 'Greasy Reesey! Greasy Reesey!' "

MacAndrews groaned. The memories were beginning to come back with a painfulness no antihangover medication would be able to ameliorate.

"Not finding him on the seventh level, the lot of you carried the hunt down through Kublai Khan's level by level, stopping often to refresh yourselves with whatever was being sold for drinking, snorting, or smoking. On the second level, there was what has been termed an altercation. The stories I got were confusing. Either you spotted Greasy Reesey and closed on him with the intent of doing grave bodily harm or you mistook one of the waiters for Reesey. In any event, the Kublai Khan bouncers were all set to smash your skulls when Mr. Sun and some members of his guard force showed up and got you to leave peaceably."

The memories seemed almost ready to surface. Monstrous black waves shattered themselves against the transparent wall and climbed up the slanted surface, cutting off the sunlight like rushing thunderheads. Shadowed figures surrounded her, crouching, neurosticks extended like swords. One moved directly in front of her. Mr. Sun. MacAndrews shook her head. That made no sense. The element of memory fell apart, faded to ghostlike insubstantiality.

Unexpectedly, she laughed. "If only Mother could see me now. When I was growing up, it was always, 'Eileen, can't you behave like a lady for once in your life?' "

Bobbi continued the soothing massage. "I suspect you are being overly harsh on your mother."

MacAndrews closed her eyes, smiling. "No," she said. "That is your we're-all-moms-together tone of voice. This really happened. When I was five years old, I took down a chart that was hanging over my bed because it looked ugly. I wanted to replace it with a picture of flowers. Mother was furious! 'That is your genetic chart,' she yelled, at a ladylike level, of course. 'That defines you as a Terrestrial, the standard for what is human!'

"It's funny, actually. Most of my mother's friends look down on the Defenders of Humanity as being lower-class religious fanatics. But they absorbed the basic ideas of Defenders because they fit in so naturally with their own preconceptions. In fact, they are even narrower than the Defenders: They really believe that Earth, or Manhome, as they have taken to calling it, is the only planet of any importance, that the only 'real' humans are those born on Earth. And, of course, they have improved on their definition of 'real' by having Expulsion Laws rid them of all undesirables. They are, in fact, so self-centered— narcissistic would hardly be an exaggeration—that I will be surprised if they even send a fleet out from Sol."

Her glance fell on the wall chronometer. "Anyway, you can't be too harsh on me. It's only oh-seven-thirty hours. If I really did carry on as you say, I am doing extraordinarily well to even be coherent at this hour."

"Check the date," Bobbi told her. "You dropped an entire day."

MacAndrews sat up in alarm. "Christ, your husband will have my head! The *Pride* was on line to take him to Chiron yesterday."

"The crew of the *Sredni Vashtar* covered for you. Besides—I think John has more important things on his mind."

MacAndrews looked at her in sudden apprehension.

"Yesterday the Inner Council met and decided to withdraw the protection of the Fleet from L 726-8," Bobbi said evenly.

MacAndrews felt a roaring in her ears. "That makes no sense," she said weakly. She tried to remember what she knew of that system. It had only one planet of consequence: Pearl. "Pearl is a source of rare earths. The Bestials have been starving for those. Why should we suddenly give them away?"

"Different factions will give you different answers," Bobbi said, her voice betraying an edge of bitterness. "Militarists will say that it shortens our supply lines and makes our new perimeters more defensible. The peace faction will tell you that it removes one of the main causes of the war and so should make the Bestials more amenable to negotiations. The truth, however, is that Pearl has been forfeited for one purpose only: to destroy Chiang Biosynthetics."

It was, Bobbi thought later, similar to what it must be like to have received a fatal dose of radiation. On the one hand, you are already dead. Yet you may not feel any hurt at all. Instead, it seems almost as if time were suspended. And a great dread grows of how the body will begin to disintegrate when time resumes its march, how there will be weakness, nausea, bruises that don't heal and bleeding that doesn't stop.

Then again, it was like hearing a huge structure collapse from a great distance. Bobbi was not generally involved in the day-to-day operations of the company, but she kept hearing snatches of talk. Credit had been cut off. Acceleration provisions were being invoked in several important loans. And the rate of resignations had reached serious proportions.

There was nothing she could do. For Chiang it would be even more devastating, for he would see and understand so much more of the disaster than she could.

For his sake and as an exercise in humility, she began to prepare his favorite meal. Despite materials that electrostatically repelled dust and computerized food preparation facilities, Bobbi was at best an indifferent homemaker. So it was also something of a penance as she prepared the carrots, string beans, and onions, took down the great cleaver—which frightened her more than she liked to admit—and cut the flank steak against the grain into thin slices.

When Bobbi next noticed the clock, it was early evening. Curiously, although she had been working all afternoon, she felt nearly as refreshed as she would have had she spent the time meditating in a float-tank. Now, all that was left to do was to choose a drink to go with dinner. Normally John favored a slightly bitter local beer. Tonight, though, there should be something special. She took down the bottle of Olde Earth Champagne that Dr. Russell had presented to her the day before. John would be pleased by the reminder of one project that had turned out perfectly.

Bobbi had just finished setting the table when she heard voices approaching.

"...understand how crucial this is," Chiang was saying. "I was just getting started ten years ago. Pierpont was trying to freeze me out. Most of the big suppliers were forbidden to deal with me. The smaller outfits who were willing to sell to me did so at exorbitant rates. That was when one of my scout ships chanced across Pearl. It was purest accident. Pearl has a highly eccentric orbit and probably originated in another star system altogether. Nobody could expect that such a system would harbor a planet so rich in phosphorus, in rare earths, in everything I needed. I filed my claim immediately, mortgaged everything I owned to obtain title and to begin development. Within three months, I was able to undercut substantially all of my competition."

"A Pearl of great price, indeed," Benedict murmured.

"On which Chiang Biosynthetics has been totally dependent. I thought I had the votes to prevent this. But Couteau voted with the First Families, figuring I would be too busy struggling to survive to repay him as he deserves. The hell of it is, he's right: I don't have time for vengeance."

"At least," Benedict said judiciously, "we now know the identity of our spy."

Chiang's laughter was sharp. "And the psychological profile Sun has taken shows that our spy really is one of my most loyal employees. What an absolutely pathetic waste of time that was!"

They sat down at the table, hardly noticing Bobbi's presence. Benedict spooned rice onto his plate, and then the spiced beef. "It could be worse. This is what we predicted they would do. And, as I have said, you need not lose Pearl."

Chiang glared at him. "You offer me carnage."

"You prefer capitulation?"

"I prefer an edge—no, hear me out. You have an idea, a good idea, something no one else has even considered. If we were solely interested in fighting Bestials, you would be the hero of human-occupied space. But we have taken your—insight—and programmed it into the simulation computers, and the odds against us are even then not as good as fifty-fifty. The refugees are proud and brave and angry, but they are not fools. No, put your mind to work on something else, something I might be able to use."

Benedict assented silently. Bobbi poured the champagne for him, explaining as much as she knew about Dr. Russell's project and why it was so important for Chiang Biosynthetics. Benedict sipped and made appreciative noises.

"Let the Jesuits and Dominicans glory in displays of rhetorical and intellectual skill," he said. "The truth is that no religious order can be said to have arrived until it has had a wine or liqueur named after it. Take Dom Diego's old order. They brewed a potent cordial that was once the envy of Europe—so much, in fact, that the revolutionary French government not only seized the abbey but tried to continue producing the liqueur itself.

As you might expect with bureaucrats in charge, quality went quickly to hell. Then—"

He sputtered and seemed to choke. Bobbi got up in alarm. Then she realized that he was *laughing*. To her utter consternation, he proceeded to rise, refill his glass, and do a kind of dance with it. And, in between gasps of laughter, he was singing:

> *"There be none so jolly*
> *As our friend* E. coli
> *Today."*

Bobbi looked down at her own glass of champagne and hastily sampled it. It was cool and slightly tart, surely no more than twenty proof. He had taken only two glasses.

Yet, she thought, he had been on the rather spare diet of the Stewards for ten years. His tolerance for alcohol had surely decreased. Perhaps—

As if catching her thought, Benedict turned to her, mad glee dancing in his eyes. "You must not think me drunk, madam. Why, it's hardly nine o'clock in the morning!"

"If your time sense is that warped, you are drunk indeed," Chiang said sourly.

Benedict controlled himself with a visible effort. "I have found our edge," he said earnestly. "The odds have just shifted drastically in our favor. But we have no time to lose. You must put me in touch with the Primate at once. I may be able to arrange a stalling action through him. And we need to get Russell immediately. He is the key to everything!"

Chiang rose, his face hesitantly beginning to mirror some of Benedict's enthusiasm. "Very well, then. Let's go."

"What about my dinner?" Bobbi demanded.

Chiang stopped at the door. "Send down coffee and sandwiches," he said. "*Lots* of coffee."

X

THE OUTER AIRLOCK DOOR OF THE *SHERE KHAN* SLID
open, allowing the residual air to puff out. Benedict felt
it tug at him, trying to pull him out into the bottomless
interstellar blackness. His breathing sounded unnaturally
loud in the confines of his pressure suit.

As his eyes adjusted, he made out the black shape of
the other ship floating without apparent motion against a
scattering of stars. Still, he did not spot the grapple until
a second before it hit and magnetically clamped onto the
hull of the *Shere Khan*.

"I'm going now," he said.

"Sir, we can stay on station until you return. I think
Master Chiang would prefer that." Captain Faoud's
voice sounded anxious in Benedict's earphones.

"Belay that, Captain. No need to tie your crew up out
here indefinitely. My hosts will get in touch when negotiations have been concluded."

Benedict pushed himself off and grabbed the line. He
had expected that he would have to pull himself hand
over hand to the other ship. Apparently, though, they
could see him, for as soon as his hand touched the line, it
began to reel itself in. Benedict, his weight off center,

started to swing around it. For one terrifying instant, vertigo had hold of him. The *Shere Khan* circled below/behind/above him. The line seemed intent on throwing him off spinning into the void.

He closed his eyes and held on, forcing his breathing into the meditation pattern he had learned as a novice. He had returned to calm by the time hands reached out and pulled him into the airlock.

Benedict removed his helmet as soon as he was inside the craft and regarded his companions. Intelligent brown eyes surrounded by auburn fur looked back at him. The lips pulled back in what might have been intended for a smile, revealing disturbingly sharp teeth. There was a heavy, wet, slightly acrid smell in the air.

"Paul Niccolo Rénard."

"Yes," Benedict said. "You can check that with a retinal scan or skin sample."

"There is no need. Come with us." Unceremoniously, the two Bestials grabbed his arms and thrust his weightless form through a hatchway.

He seemed to be in an alcove lined with overly large file drawers. Briefly, he thought of a morgue. Then he saw the dials by each handle.

"Get in," one of the Bestials directed, gesturing to an open cold-sleep capsule. "We will be traveling in Space₄."

Benedict complied, letting them cinch the straps around him and administer the preliminary injections. Only when the anesthetic mask was placed on his face and the smell of Bestial became overpoweringly strong did he experience a moment of claustrophobic panic. That passed almost—

—immediately. Something else was wrong, though. He felt a pressure over every centimeter of his skin, as if a body were lying atop him. With an effort, he opened his eyes. He could see nothing to account for the sensation. Benedict tried to sit up. Nothing happened.

Darkly furred hands grasped him beneath his armpits and pulled him upright. Brilliant, soundless fireworks exploded across his field of vision. For an instant he nearly fainted. Two Bestials helped him swing his legs around and stand. He walked like a two-year-old, staggering uncertainly, bracing himself heavily on his companions.

"You will have to be very careful going down the hatchway," one of them warned him. "I'll go down first, to support you."

The ladder seemed as high as a cliff. Rung by rung he descended the entire length of the ship. He wanted to stop and rest but feared that if he did, he would not have sufficient strength to make it to the bottom.

At the base, he leaned against the wall, gasping. His limbs were shaking with fatigue; sweat burned in his eyes. He was helped into an overly large black thermosuit with a tinted face mask. Then the airlock was opened, and they stepped outside.

A red sun, appearing slightly larger than Sol from Earth, glared without warmth from a milk-white sky. All about them was the white of snow so that it was almost impossible to say where the horizon was. Benedict's eyes sought hungrily for some object with which to establish perspective. The concrete landing field on which they were standing stretched into the distance until it seemed to blend in with the snow. Several domed buildings, which might have been as large as five stories, were connected by closed-in walkways.

Off to one side he spotted fumaroles of rising steam. That explained the location of this base: geothermal energy. Despite its frigid appearance, this was probably the hot spot of the planet. Not only would this provide the Bestials with badly needed energy, it would also serve to mask their own energy leakages from orbital detection by an Allied scoutship.

Mountains of snow seemed to tower on every side of the field. Many were nearly covered in patches of what appeared to be low-lying greenish-black shrubs. Benedict was reminded of the grass that held the dunes together on Provincetown Island and wondered if the shrubbery performed a similar function: preventing the field from being buried in drifting snow.

A gust of wind sent snow whirling across the field. The wind died as suddenly as it had started, and the snow dropped abruptly to the ground.

Other thermosuited figures approached. They were guiding a powerchair with rubberized wheels. Irregular brownish stains decorated the cushions.

"Sit here," one of them commanded. "You will need its aid in this gravity field."

Benedict gratefully surrendered himself to the embrace of the powerchair. They made their way to an airlock door in one of the enclosed walkways, where Benedict's face mask was covered with a dark cloth.

The entry was into an area of sharp, metallic echoes. They turned left toward, according to Benedict's memory, one of the large domes. The blindfold presumably was to keep him from noticing any military secrets. Or if Benedict's evaluation was correct, to keep secret the much more potentially damaging information that there was nothing here worthy of secrecy.

No one, he realized, had been identified by name yet. Perhaps, like primitive savages, they feared that to give their names would give him a magical hold on their souls. And perhaps it might, at that. Like most genetic variants, they had not been individually named by their creators. When, later, they took names, they would be names that meant something to them. It had certainly been that way for Benedict, who had been through the process twice.

The quality of the echoes changed. The floor over which he traveled had become smoother. Benedict guessed that they had left the walkway and entered the dome. A hand touched his chest, shutting off his thermosuit.

Several meters further on they stopped, turned him sharply, and then backed him a short distance. Benedict felt rather than heard the door close in front of him. A fraction of the awful weight seemed to lift from his shoulders. Automatically, Benedict started counting. At twenty, full weight and more pressed him firmly against the contours of the powerchair. The doors hummed open.

There were fewer echoes here; all sounds were muted. Benedict had to strain to hear the tread of his guard.

They stopped after traveling what Benedict estimated to be approximately fifty meters.

"The minister will see you shortly," a voice announced behind his left shoulder.

Benedict sighed and settled himself down for a long wait. The pattern had become unmistakably clear. It was, in fact, one of the classic diplomatic gambits. To enhance negotiating leverage, one went to any length to discomfit one's opponent.

The next item on the agenda, if he gauged his hosts correctly, was to be an interminable wait, during which he would be expected to gnash his teeth in helpless, impatient rage. Well, Abbot Tsintolas had admonished him more than once for spending too little time in meditation and contemplation. He would certainly never have a better opportunity.

Automatically, his breathing slowed and deepened. He summoned up images before his mind: Chiang, Pierpont, Rascavia, Epstein, the Primate, the Bestials . . . *Dear Lord and Father, show me what is good and*

*needful about these Your children. Make clear Your will
concerning myself and them.*

For the first time since leaving Ariel, he allowed his
mind to float freely among ideas and memories, not trying to weigh and calculate, not trying to force people into
predetermined niches dictated by self-interest. The figures advanced and retreated with his breathing. After a
time, they arranged themselves on a chess board. God
loomed over them, an amiable, nondescript grand master.

Then it was as if Benedict's point of view had suddenly shifted. The board was not a chess board but a
matrix of some kind. And God was not so much playing
against an adversary as against the pieces themselves,
trying to set them in a particular set of relationships that
would—Benedict's vision, or imagination, failed at this
point. There was only the hint of something unimagin-
ably grand and exciting. But the pieces obstinately insisted on going their own way, wreaking havoc on the
delicate balance of energies within the matrix.

Benedict scrutinized the matrix intently, certain that if
he studied it just a few moments longer, the intended
pattern would come clear to him.

"Idiots!" The voice was deep and hoarse nearly to the
point of incomprehensibility. "Is this the way you treat
an honored guest? Strip that thermosuit off him before
he is overcome by his own body heat. You must remember that human beings are *delicate*."

Hood and face mask were removed from Benedict's
head. He was lifted to his feet as the rest of the thermosuit was stripped off, then gently deposited back into the
powerchair. His sweat turned suddenly cold. He repressed a shiver.

"Leave us," the voice commanded. Benedict focused
his attention on the speaker: a large Bestial, fur jet-black
except where fringed with silver. He was dressed in
loose-fitting silks of black and white, pulled tight at

ankles and wrists, cinched at the waist by a wide leather belt.

There were three dark pits on each side of the muzzle: infrared sense organs. Night vision was the least important of their uses. By registering minute changes of surface temperature, a Bestial could tell a split second before that an adversary would spring. He might even be able to tell when Benedict was lying.

The room was oak paneled. The built-in shelves were crammed with reading and holotapes. A hutch with beveled-glass doors occupied one corner. The desk top between them appeared to be of a native marble; its polished surface was broken only by the computer console.

"Welcome," the Bestial said. "I am Gubbio Lupus, Foreign Minister of the Confederated Clans. And you are Paul Niccolo Rénard, or—" he looked down at the piece of paper on his desk "—I see I should say Brother Benedict of the Order of Stewards. Thinking of you as a monk will take some getting used to."

"Since leaving Ariel, almost everyone I have met has seen fit to doubt the sincerity of my vocation," Benedict said. "I confess that by now I find it wearisome."

"You mistake me," Lupus replied. "I do not find it at all unlikely that a man such as yourself would undergo a conversion. I am only surprised at your lowly station. I would have expected you to be, say, bishop of Hippo by now. Perhaps even a member of the Curia."

Benedict smiled wordlessly at the flattery, convinced that it was only setting him up for the ax.

"Here, let me show you some hospitality." Lupus took two cut-crystal liqueur glasses from the hutch and filled them with a colorless liquid. "This is a local product of which we are quite proud. CH_3CH_2OH, ethyl alcohol, or, as it is known to the vulgar, vodka."

Benedict sipped gingerly. It burned the inside of his mouth and felt as if it were searing away the mucous lining of his throat. Yet almost magically the discomfort was transformed to a feeling of warmth and contentment.

"It is really quite an honor to meet you," Lupus continued after gulping down his own drink. "You have achieved near-mythical status among my people. All of our cubs are taught strategy through a role-playing game, the game of Fox and Lion. We try to teach them that although bravery and strength are essential, they can too easily be turned against themselves without subtlety. You were the model for the Grandfather Fox of the game.

"Now, it is one of the rules of the game that Grandfather Fox, unlike the Lions, does not usually assert himself personally. He prefers to work behind the scenes, to remain completely unnoticed, if possible. Only in the most unusual, and important, circumstances does he voluntarily place himself on the board.

"Comes now the true Grandfather Fox, back, as it were, from the grave, craving an audience with me! You have my . . . interest."

"My mission is simply stated," Benedict said. "I am sure that your dossier on me reveals that I have been put at the disposal of John Lei Chiang. Your intelligence may have informed you that the Centauran Inner Council has voted to withdraw the protection of its Space Force from L 726-8, around which circles the planet Pearl. Pearl is the keystone of Master Chiang's empire. It is about that planet that I have come to negotiate."

Gubbio Lupus studied his glass as if fascinated with the way the crystal prismed the light. "Your problem," he said in a low rumble, "is that you have nothing to negotiate. You will lose Pearl. We shall gain it. In fact, my nephew Brand shall be Pack Leader of the Pearl occupation force. Such are the fortunes of war."

"Pearl, by itself, has a limited value," Benedict responded. "It is valuable to you only because of its rare earths. Master Chiang is required by the Inner Council to blow up his processing plants as he evacuates to prevent them from falling into your hands. For the proper consideration, this demolition could be almost completely ineffective."

Lupus raised eyes full of danger. "The Centauran Councils would call what you are suggesting treason."

"This is Master Chiang's difficulty, is it not? The fact is that the refining works, the loading docks, and the workers' quarters all have a market price that can be readily ascertained. For you, the worth is somewhat higher since you are under embargo and could not easily obtain the material and skills you would need to make Pearl quickly productive.

"At the same time, Master Chiang greatly needs ready cash to stave off the dissolution of Chiang Biosynthetics. You have that cash. We have everything to gain by negotiation."

They got down to haggling. Benedict found himself tiring quickly. He forced himself to relax, focusing all of his energy into his mind, his eyes, his voice.

He started by demonstrating, with aid of the financial tapes he had brought with him, the market worth of the Pearl facilities.

Lupus snorted in reply, claiming that there was not that much currency in all the Confederated Clans. Benedict countered that kilos d'argent terrestrieme were not the only acceptable medium of exchange. Anything readily convertible would do: heavy metals such as platinum or uranium, gems from beyond the periphery such as Cartherite, which flashed through all the colors of the rainbow in changing light and had soared in price since the war and cut off supply.

Even then, Lupus complained that the Clans simply could not meet the price. That might, Benedict reflected, be true. If so, it was irrelevant. There was a specific amount he needed, and given the uncertainties, he dared not settle for less than twice that amount. So, slowly, he let himself be forced down. From time to time Lupus would tap briefly on his computer keyboard as if marshaling his resources. Or perhaps, Benedict thought, he was getting needed concurrences.

The final agreement was KDT thirty million: one half to be sent back with Benedict, the rest to be paid after the Clans took possession of Pearl and assured themselves that it was substantially intact.

Lupus leaned back in his chair. "I may have played the game too much as a cub. I wish I could be assured that you have prepared no...surprises...for my people."

"Minister Lupus," Benedict said, forcing his aching muscles to hold him upright. "Let us understand each other. This is no arm's-length transaction between businessmen looking for mutual profit. It is a forced sale between parties at war with each other.

"I swear to you, in the presence of God and as I hope for salvation, that you shall have the Pearl facilities just as I have promised. Nevertheless, once you have them, it is up to you to keep them. You know that they are worth three times what you are paying for them, and to Master Chiang they are worth far more than that. Right now it is all he can do to fight off bankruptcy. But I prophesy you this: One day he will come back for Pearl. Pray on that day that strength and quickness are with you."

For a second he feared he had gone too far. Lupus's claws slid out reflexively as his nostrils flared. But then he seemed to relax and nodded.

"I understand Master Chiang's attitude; it would be mine as well. And I appreciate your honesty.

"We have negotiated your offer. Now hear our offer. Join us, Benedict. You are nearly as much an outcast as we are. If the Defenders of Humanity are triumphant in this conflict, they will be more repressive than ever. In peacetime you will be worse than useless: you will be dangerous. They will deal with you as they dealt with you brother, Valentino, and your sister, Allele.

"Our offer extends to Master Chiang as well. We recognize that the First Families are making Chiron a haven for privileged mediocrity. The Clans certainly know better than to attempt the destruction of the best biogenetic mind alive. He would have with us the honor due him."

It seemed suddenly so eminently reasonable and desirable that it was all Benedict could do to keep himself from accepting. "I will convey your offer to Master Chiang," was all he said.

There was an oddly embarrassing silence. Benedict's mind turned to the constellation of insight his host's name had given him.

"There are some other things we have in common," he began hesitantly. "For example, I would guess you have met Father McIlvay."

"A friend of yours? You know him?" Lupus seemed to consider the implications. Benedict watched him cautiously, perturbed at the reaction he had provoked. "That may make things easier. Follow me."

Lupus led him out into the corridor, taking such lengthy strides that the powerchair was hard put to keep up, even at top speed. The marble and oak finishings ended abruptly, confirming Benedict's guess that he had been in an area created with the sole purpose of impressing foreign visitors. A tunnel of bare rock stretched out before him, lit at intervals by microwave squares attached to the ceiling. From time to time they passed shadowed cross tunnels. There were also rooms that had been carved out of the rock. Some gleamed with unfamiliar equipment, but most were shrouded in darkness.

The air currents gusted alternately hot and cold. There was an almost subsonic rumbling that seemed unmechanical in a way Benedict could not define. He wondered how close they were to the geysers he had seen on the surface.

A whiff of hydrogen sulfide, surrounded by other, less identifiable smells, caused him to gasp. There were now extrusions in the rock: some an angry reddish orange, others the deepest cobalt-blue.

Two guards in livery of silver and black leather stood to either side of a doorway. They held long falchionlike swords vertically before them in a motionless salute. Neither seemed to notice as Lupus and Benedict passed between them.

The room beyond was dim, lit only by candles. On one wall was a being made of stars. As his eyes adjusted, Benedict stared with increasing wonder. The mosaic was still incomplete, but enough had been done that the artist's intent could be discerned. The star field engulfed nearly half the hemispherical room. The being's eyes were novas. The guard of his sword was an elliptical galaxy; the blade was a cosmic jet.

Moving forward, Benedict could now make out the silhouettes of a raised altar with a crucifix suspended above it. At the foot of the altar was another shape, low and narrow. Benedict moved his powerchair to its side and looked in.

McIlvay lay there, eyes closed, hands folded across his chest with a rosary wrapped around them. Even the most loving application of the mortician's art could not fully disguise the ravages to which face and neck had been subjected. Benedict frowned, trying to discern other shapes more deeply shadowed, clustered around the body. Then he winced, recognizing the heads for what they were.

"Why?" he asked Lupus.

"He preached love, forgiveness, peace." Lupus's voice was soft, a throaty half growl. "Perhaps more offensively, he preached the Incarnation and the great honor that brought to Humankind. Some among the Clans claimed that he wished to make us weak, to chain us to merely human morality when we have evolved beyond good and evil. Yet he was becoming increasingly influential, so they stopped his tongue in the ways most familiar to them.

"The leaders escaped into space when reaction turned against them. Our cruisers followed and closed. Their deaths were unjustly merciful.

"As for their henchmen, those who actually shed the Just One's blood . . ." Lupus picked up a head and fondled it almost lovingly. "If they did not have a true foretaste of hell before they died, and so ample reason to repent their sins, it was not for want of effort on our part."

He replaced the head. "We thought it only fitting that he should have companionship on his journey. Perhaps he will win himself extra merit by interceding on their behalf. Or if the earlier Church Fathers were correct, chief among his heavenly blessings will be a continual vision of the torments of his enemies." From his tone, this was no doubt what Lupus's choice would be.

"Tell his superiors that he died as they would have wished him to. Here, in this chapel. Preaching the Word he had been given, asking mercy for his attackers as his own blood bubbled in his throat." Lupus looked over at Benedict. "They had no honor, they who would attack a man who could hardly stand in this planet's gravity."

Benedict licked his lips and swallowed. "I will do as you ask," he said. "I will also try—I cannot promise: you must understand that my own status is subject to debate—I will try to see that the purpose for which he gave his life is accomplished."

Lupus stood, head bowed, haloed by candlelight. A distant rumbling vibrated the stone around them. His eyes, when he raised them, were unreadable.

"That will take powers even greater than those of Grandfather Fox."

XI

THE TABLE BELCHED OUT A CARD AT MACANDREWS. The ambassador views with alarm your recent activities. Lose 20 points.

Crap! MacAndrews scowled across the game board. The enemy, in the persons of her new engineer, de Toledano, and the new gunner, Dalton, would be ready to make their attack in the next cycle of play. She would need all her points for a finesse, yet her putative allies were more concerned with the niceties of diplomatic etiquette than with winning the conflict. She moved her remaining tokens to strengthen her perimeter and sat back as the turn passed to Kirsten.

It was not her idea of how to break in new crew members. Ideally, they should have a long shakedown cruise. That would give them time to get to know each other, to discern each other's weaknesses and work on strengthening them; time to learn how to compensate for those weaknesses which could not be fully strengthened. Enough time so that in an emergency their reactions would automatically take them through the first four moves of solving a problem before their brains could fully register that they had a problem.

But they were grounded. And confined to flight quarters. MacAndrews had put them through the simulators for ten hours a day at first. She threw at them every situation in the book and several of her own invention. They surfaced into Space$_1$ in the midst of a Bestial battle fleet, and Younger and Dalton had to prioritize targets and either take them out or at least raise enough havoc to keep their own ship from being blasted in the three minutes it would take for de Toledano to get them back into Space$_2$. They surfaced at random somewhere within twenty light-years of Alpha Centauri with all their navigation equipment dead: Kirsten had to rough out their approximate position and plot their course back to Neoptolemus solely on eyeball navigation. Their quantum drive became unbalanced and jumped into an uncertainty loop; de Toledano had to stabilize it to keep them from being blown out of the Multiverse, and then had to recalibrate the drive in deep space with only on-ship resources. And on and on.

Younger was heard to mutter that she was pushing them too hard. "What would you rather be doing?" she demanded. "Watching the goddamn paint peel?"

Part of this was her own frustration. In a rare moment of relaxation that she had allowed herself, she had tried to put a call through to Russell. Mr. Sun's face had materialized instead.

"Dr. Russell is working on Priority Prime matters for the company. He will be told you called and will return your call as soon as he is free." *And don't call him again until he does*.

Yet when the printouts showed that the effectiveness scores had plateaued and were even beginning to decline, she had to face that fact that Younger was right, that they were all approaching burnout.

She cut back simulator time to two hours a day. Another two hours were specifically set aside for individual rest and relaxation. For the rest of the time there were autobiography sessions, tall story contests, cooking contests, dirty limerick contests.

One part of her mind told her that it was useless working so to mold these individuals into a smoothly functioning crew. The business dailies all agreed the Chiang Biosynthetics was like a dinosaur that had been killed but was too stupid to know it was dead.

Yet nobody around her was acting that way. Instead, there was a sense of repressed excitement, a feeling—an image suddenly surfaced from that lost night at the Kublai Kahn—of putting everything on one last throw. Even that stone-faced Sun somehow exuded smugness. Sun was the most hard-nosed, realistic person MacAndrews knew. If he remained confident, then somehow they must still be in business.

Kirsten jumped up with a shriek as the alarm sounded. MacAndrews grinned, glad to see that someone was more on edge than she was.

"That's us," she said unnecessarily. She slapped the switch, killing the game board as she ran out the doorway.

The dome above the *Gryffon's Pride* had already opened, letting in snowflakes that melted before they hit the hangar floor. A hangar crew was loading a long cylinder into the cargo hold.

"Captain MacAndrews. These are for you." The chief of the loading crew handed MacAndrews a flight cassette and an envelope with her name on it. She tore it open.

Hi Mac!
    All our chips (yours and mine, too) are riding on this little beauty, so take good care of it. Try to stay sober this time!

                                        Keith

Conceited bastard, MacAndrews thought, smiling despite herself. Then she hurried beneath the ship, jumped, and caught the moving ladder, which quickly carried her high into the *Pride*'s interior. She swung off at the bridge and strapped herself into her chair.

The telltales were a cheery green. Another winked on as the cargo hatch was dogged shut. "All secure," the loading chief reported over the intercom. MacAndrews acknowledged.

"Gunners?"

"All okay."

"We're loaded for bear, Captain."

"Engines?"

"Everything's in balance."

"Navigation?"

"All instruments are go. If I had any idea where we were going."

"I think I can give you that right now." MacAndrews inserted the flight cassette. Chiang's face appeared on the screen.

"The coordinates of your destination are being fed directly into your navigation computers," Chiang said. "You will be told your destination and the instructions for the rest of your mission when you surface in Space$_1$."

It would seem, MacAndrews thought, that I am about to get my wish for this crew.

She hit the warning alarm to clear the hangar. Seconds later, the *Gryffon's Pride* leapt toward the cold and bitter stars.

The docking bays of Bolthole were humming with quiet activity. Newly installed banks of cutting and welding lasers gleamed brightly, awaiting eagerly the ships they would make lethal.

Benedict nodded, satisfied that everything was in order. Of course, it would have been helpful had there been more bays. As it was, valuable time would be lost as each ship took its turn. That was, though, the least of their problems.

Turning away from the bay, Benedict jumped, caught a guideline, and proceeded to propel himself along its length. The leisurely swimming motions gently stretched muscles that had been cramped ever since he had been on that unnamed iceball of a planet of the Clans. One was not technically weightless on Bolthole. But since the mass of this snowball in Proxima Centauri's Oort cloud was only about that of Deimos, that technicality was very easy to forget.

He heard Sun's voice coming from an open doorway as he sped by. "I suppose most of you consider yourself security guards," Sun was saying. There was a shuffling and apparently a fair number of raised hands. "That's what I thought. Congratulations on your promotions. You are now Marines."

It worried Benedict that so much of their strength was concentrated here. Should Pierpont or Gould mount a frontal assault on Chiang Biosynthetics in the next few days, Bobbi would not have the resources to fight them off. With luck, though, it would be some time before anyone noticed their absence. Bobbi was using both Chiang's and Benedict's credit cards, sending in a steady stream of transactions for the benefit of the intelligence agents who would be trying to trace their movements. At the same time, she would be causing considerable consternation among their enemies by paying off debts with cash that Chiang Biosynthetics was not supposed to have on hand.

Those ploys should divert attention just long enough.

He coasted into the main meeting room. Most of the Epsilon refugee leaders were already there. Benedict took his place just to the right of the lectern. He strapped the retaining net about his hips to keep himself from floating away in the air currents and waited for Chiang to begin.

Chiang swam in, nodding to several of the more influential refugees, attached the lectern tethers, and began without preamble.

"Twenty-eight days ago the Centauran Inner Council met and decided to withdraw Fleet protection from the L 726-8 system." Two M-type stars appeared on the wall screen behind Chiang. "As most of you are aware, Chiang Biosynthetics has an exploitation license for the planet Pearl in that system. It has proved an invaluable resource for phosphates and rare earths." A yellow dot appeared on the screen and began tracing a highly eccentric ellipse focused on the center of mass of the two stars.

"Withdrawal was effected five days ago. Almost immediately, the Bestials moved in with a garrison force. Three battlestars were placed in orbit about Pearl." The planet expanded on the screen. Three blue blips appeared defining a triangle the sides of which would be tangent to the planet's surface. A legend to the bottom left of the screen gave the carrying strength of a battlestar: five dreadnoughts, fifteen cruisers, thirty fighters. And beyond that, the battlestars had armament specific to themselves: fusion lasers and state-of-the-art smart missiles.

"There are also three freighters presently loading, traveling in a six-cruiser convoy. Obviously, the number of convoy craft will vary from week to week.

"Possession of Pearl has been essential to the financial viability of Chiang Biosynthetics. Without it as a source of raw materials, I would be forced to curtail the majority of my operations. Not the least of these operations is the support I give you.

"However, I do not intend to accept corporate dissolution so easily. I intend to retake Pearl—"Chiang paused for emphasis"—by force of arms. I ask and need your aid in this endeavor."

Van ter Haals was the first to break the stunned silence

that followed. "How the hell do you propose to accomplish this?" he asked plaintively. "Just look at the firepower you have put up on that screen. The Great Allied Fleet itself, if it ever comes into existence, would have a hard time dislodging that force. Forget about the convoys. Forget about carrying strengths. Deal just with the armament of the battlestars, the fusion lasers that can vaporize us light-seconds before we could get in a shot, the smart missiles that close at 1500 gees and can follow a target anywhere in $Space_1$. How do we fight that?"

Chiang nodded coolly, like a professor receiving an expected question from one of the class's brighter students. "This is the weapon you will use against the battlestars," he said, tugging free the shroud from the large object floating to his left. Someone in the audience gasped. "I see that some of you recognize this. This one is quite harmless. The fusing element has been removed from its head.

"This is a 75 megaton device of the type commonly used in splitting asteroids or in nudging them into more convenient orbits. At its base, you see the megatesla assembly used to magnetically shape the explosion.

"These devices will be deployed in the following manner: Of the three battlestars, two will be attacked by two vessels each." On the screen, dotted parallel lines began to approach two battlestars. "My vessels will make their runs in $Space_2$ according to a computerized flight plan. When they are within ten kilometers of their target, they will surface in $Space_1$, launch one missile each, and dart back immediately into $Space_2$. They will be in $Space_1$ less than one second." The battlestars flared and faded as the dotted lines continued away from them. "Most likely the missiles will be hit by laser fire within two seconds. That itself will detonate them. At ten kilometers, the combined heat and electromagnetic pulse from the blast will easily render the battlestars inoperative."

"Councilor Chiang, a question." The speaker was Mr. Doi. "What surfacing error are you allowing?"

"Fifty percent. Plus or minus five kilometers."

"That is unrealistic," Doi said flatly. "Pearl is more than ten light-years from here. Space$_4$ stresses over a journey of that length will cause an accumulation of random deviations from norm in all parts of the ship, but especially in the navigational equipment and in the quantum drive itself. After ten light-years, a surfacing error of a hundred kilometers is considered excellent; errors of a thousand kilometers are not uncommon. You cannot possibly meet the necessary tolerances."

Chiang glanced over at Benedict. "My colleague will answer that."

Benedict stood, smiled briefly at Doi, and let his gaze sweep the audience. They were extremely intent: a good sign.

"Some of you may have heard of Joseph Nsbugu," he began. As he spoke, the screen flashed Nsbugu's section in *Compton's Scientists and Engineers*, fifth edition. "Before he joined the Order of Stewards, he had carved out a career of great distinction with Quantum Mechanics, Ltd. He still contributes to the technical journals. Presently, he oversees the Steward shipyards on Ariel.

"Ariel may be described as a long way from anywhere. All ships touching down exhibit a good deal of the Space$_4$ distortion to which Mr. Doi has alluded.

"Father Nsbugu has kept careful overhaul records over the past six years. As Mr. Doi states, any ship exhibits increasing distortions the longer in Space$_4$. Since these distortions are randomized, there is no way any one ship may compensate for them while in flight.

"However, Father Nsbugu has noted that the distortions of several ships tend to average out. Averaging the errors of five ships will bring you within twenty percent of norm. Ten ships will reduce the error to ten percent; forty will bring it down nearly to two percent.

"This is our plan. We will make the jump from here to L 726-8 surfacing one hundred eighty degrees away from Pearl so that the bulk of the two stars will shield our Cerenkov wakes from the Clans' detectors. We will then average the readouts of our quantum drives and navigational devices and so bring them back very close to the norm. At the proper time we will make our attack on Pearl, traveling twenty light-minutes in Space$_2$. Damping fields should prevent any further deviations in the drives. We will easily be within the necessary tolerances."

Doi was looking at the screen, still not completely convinced. "Why are you not attacking the third battlestar?"

"We need to leave a command structure that can order a withdrawal. Remember, our objective is *not* to destroy enemy battlecraft. It is to retake Pearl at the least cost to ourselves and to the facilities on the planet. There will be over two hundred Clan workers in the mining base. If we have to take it room by room and corridor by corridor, they could make it prohibitively costly for us. And if we destroy their command structure and their transportation, they will feel that they have no choice but to fight to the death."

Which was true, even if it was not the real reason for that particular decision.

Wai Cheung was signaling for attention. "If we do not destroy that battlestar, we will have to contend with it and with fifty other battlecraft of varying weight. If all of us join in this attack, we shall have scarcely forty-five—"

"Forty-seven," Chiang corrected.

"—battlecraft. Furthermore, we will be going up against professional fighters with much more combat experience than ourselves. These do not seem to me favorable odds."

"Not only that, but you will be taking on fighters who have quicker reactions and greater tolerance to high-gee stress," Benedict agreed. "However, when we attack, they will barely be able to fly their vessels. They will be slow to react and be unable to anticipate our moves; they will find it very difficult to coordinate with each other."

"How is that going to happen?" someone asked.

"That is a secret for now," Benedict said, blandly staring down the questioner.

"It *is* still a risky proposition."

"So it is," Chiang snapped, irritation edging his voice. "That, after all, is war. 'We do not ask that others spend their treasure and risk their lives to protect our freedoms. Give us the arms and let us do the fighting. Then we will defend ourselves and you as well.' Who can forget that ringing statement, or the brave men who signed their names to it, or the shame they caused in the Centauran General Council? Was it all empty bombast? I am giving you the weaponry and the opportunity to use it."

"While you no doubt will command everything safely behind lines," Van ter Haals said testily.

To everyone's surprise, Chiang smiled. "Not at all. The Rénard will be responsible for coordinating the attack. I will lead the ground assault on Pearl itself."

Benedict turned, opening his mouth to object. Chiang's eyes glared warning at him. Slowly, Benedict compressed his lips and bowed his head.

"What if we choose not to participate?" someone asked from the back.

"You will be my guests here until the operation is concluded," Chiang replied.

"Prisoners, you mean," Van ter Haals said.

"I mean guests. Whether or not you choose to participate is up to you. You will be granted every comfort and liberty I can provide. But as you value the lives of your comrades, you will recognize that this requires the highest degree of security to succeed. I simply cannot allow any possibility of compromising this plan.

"Now, if you are quite done with your questions—"

"Not quite," Doi said. "I am intrigued by the question of treasure. Outfitting our craft for the type of attack you outline should prove quite expensive. I would estimate that it would cost at least KDT ten million. Do not take offense, but it is common knowledge that your current financial position cannot support such an outlay."

"A benefactor who prefers to remain anonymous has donated KDT thirty million to our cause." Chiang waited for the astonished murmuring to die down. "Now, if we may proceed with our preparations . . ."

XII

LATER, THERE WAS TOO MUCH TIME TO THINK, TO REmember, to second-guess.

The Epsilon refugees had given their unanimous, if somewhat grudging, support to the attack plan. Only forty hours had been needed to refit their ships with rocket launchers and more highly powered lasers. The jump from Bolthole to L 726-8 had been accomplished without incident, and once there they had worked frantically to restabilize the quantum drives and bring the navigational equipment back to norm.

But when that was accomplished, there was nothing to do but stare at the stars and at the darkness between the stars. To Benedict's fancy, the twin suns became the angry red eyes of a malevolent adversary.

With MacAndrews's help, he programmed attack simulations and broadcasted them to the other ships at extremely low power to prevent interception. He expected complaints. What surprised him was their nature.

"The first few runs, you had the Bestials weaving all over the sky like syntho sniffers. They were turkey shoots. Then, the last run, they meet us with decent defense formations and begin maneuvering smartly—and you have us turn tail and run without firing a shot!" Van ter Haals sounded more than usually irritated, probably because of the long zero-gee enforced abstinence from his pipe.

"Pray that they are indeed weaving all over the sky when we come in," Benedict replied. "If they are not, we are unlikely to escape alive."

That was more of a possibility than he liked to admit. Russell had been given so damn little time to work. And the Clans were both smart and suspicious. They certainly would have examined every centimeter of the ground station to make it secure. The only hedge against discovery was the estimate that the Clans did not possess sufficiently sophisticated analytical equipment and would not know exactly what they were looking for. Right now, that hedge appeared pitifully uncertain.

Alarms went off, nearly deafening him with their shrillness.

"Cerenkov wake off to port," Kirsten reported.

"This is the *Shere Khan*." On the intercom, Captain Faoud's voice betrayed just the slightest trace of excitement. "The Bestials have had two docking accidents and one landing mishap in the past forty minutes. I can't make out the radio chatter, but they sound very concerned. One ship just made the jump to quantum space, heading outbound. My guess is he's going for help."

Benedict flicked his communicator to Chiang's command frequency. "That's our cue."

"All craft, shift to attack vectors immediately," Chiang ordered.

Benedict felt himself pressed into his chair with increasing firmness as the *Gryffon's Pride* came around and commenced acceleration. Configurations shifted: Chiang, in the *Sredni Vashtar*, had sunk to the bottom of Benedict's screen and was pulling away. The entire battlegroup was fragmenting into four distinct parts. To come out of Space$_2$ with the proper speed and direction, it was necessary to go into Space$_2$ that way. There would be no chance for corrections.

Seconds raced backward on his readout. Zeroes marched in slow and stately procession, left to right, until only one column was left.

Jump.

A red haze blotted out all vision. For seconds, pain tolled through his head, obliterating awareness of everything but itself.

He forced his breathing to be calm and steady. Gradually, his sight cleared and the pain receded. This extra sensitivity to quantum jumps, which even the damper fields could not adequately reduce, was the curse of being an MNC.

The *Gryffon's Pride* coasted through emptiness, engines shut down, only passive sensors operative. Slowly it rose above the bulk of Pearl, which had shielded its Cerenkov wake. Twin red suns illuminated the planet beneath them, making it appear as if it were splashed with blood. The three battlestars orbited in silent, stately procession. They seemed dangerously close, but unless one of their observers happened to focus sensors in just the right spot, the *Gryffon* would be effectively invisible.

Benedict found that he was holding his breath as a second countdown wound its way. It should be just about . . . *now*! For an agonizing second, nothing happened. Then twin lobes of eye-searing brightness blossomed about two of the battlestars and engulfed them.

The battle had begun.

Chiang's attack wing tore through Pearl's scanty ammonia and methane atmosphere, the wake of their passage trailing far behind them. Their speed greater than the planet's escape velocity, the ships had to apply downward thrust to follow the planet's curve and keep from being hurled into space.

"Pearl station on the horizon," Navigation informed him. "Five ships are already on their way to orbit."

"Let's make sure no others get off," Chiang said. He spoke into the communicator: "Launch AT6 fragmentation missiles."

The missiles streaked away from the ships and down, homing in on the underground hangar complex to blast whatever ships remained while they were still on the ground.

The five Bestial ships continued their ascent, apparently unaware of the attackers closing in behind them.

"Lasers on the lead ship," Chiang commanded. "Fire!"

Fingers of light from Chiang's attack wing reached out and touched the Bestial ship. Abruptly, it exploded. Shrapnel caught the two ships behind it. They seemed to stagger. Their flight paths became curving ballistic arcs.

The remaining two ships split left and right, bringing themselves around to meet their enemy.

Fighters had erupted from the Command battlestar. They circled ahead and behind its orbit, seeking the cause of the destruction of the two other battlestars. Their flight paths were curiously exact, as if the pilots, not trusting themselves to take manual control, had put their craft entirely on autopilot.

They discovered the refugees' ships circling near the corpses of the battlestars. The Bestials opened fire. The refugees returned fire and retreated in evident confusion. The Bestials called for reinforcements. Heavier ships, cruisers and dreadnoughts, launched themselves into orbits going over the north and south poles of the planet. They converged on the other side of Pearl, forming a three-dimensional pincer where their fighters had already backed both refugee wings against each other. Seeing Bestial reinforcements arriving above and below them, the refugees seemed to freeze in panic.

Benedict called down the rest of his forces. They jumped through Space$_2$, surfaced, fired, and jumped again. In less than three seconds, twenty Bestial ships became charred, drifting hulks.

"Sir," Kirsten warned, "the Command battlestar is leaving orbit, swinging over to where our ships are fighting."

Benedict touched his communicator. "Mr. Doi. Drop a fusion device thirty kilometers dead ahead of the Command battlestar. We don't want to do any serious damage, but we do want to brush them back."

"Sir."

He saw the bomb explode on the screen. The Command battlestar ceased its powered flight and swung back into its original orbit.

Reports from the surface were fragmentary. Chiang seemed to be having some trouble establishing control of the main base. That attack had been a point of dispute. Benedict had wanted to concentrate solely on the battle in orbit. Victory there would give them the ground installation without a shot. Chiang had objected that that would give the Bestials too much time to sabotage the base once they realized they were losing. He had decided on a two-pronged attack to take and hold the fusion plant and the main processing buildings, to be led by himself and Sun.

From the way the battle seemed to be going, it was unlikely they would achieve less destruction than intentional demolition would have. That, however, was not Benedict's problem.

There was a constantly shifting ratio in the upper-left corner of Benedict's screen that had for the past several minutes been approaching unity. Suddenly, with the destruction of a straggling Bestial cruiser, it reversed itself and disappeared. In its place appeared a blinking green square.

"Disengage." The command went out to all his ships.

Almost immediately, each made a Space₂ jump to an individually predetermined position a light-second from the *Gryffon's Pride*.

Benedict shifted to the Clans' general hailing frequencies. "This is Benedict on the *Gryffon's Pride* calling Pack Leader Brand. Acknowledge."

There was a pause, then Brand's face appeared on the screen. The fur around the eyes and mouth was wet, matted down. The whites were dangerously bloodshot. "What is your message?" he asked, voice rough and broken.

"I am sure you have much the same tactical programs I do," Benedict said. "You must realize by now that there is no possible way for you to win this engagement. I call on you to surrender and avoid needless bloodshed."

"Perhaps we cannot win," Brand responded, "but we can make you pay dearly for victory until you choke on the word."

That was more true than Benedict cared to admit. The Bestial ships that still survived were showing signs of shaking off their artificially imposed drunkenness. The remainder of this battle, if it must be fought, would prove much more costly than it had been so far.

"I grant that," Benedict said. "But think: Your uncle must have told you that I was once Paul Niccolo Rénard. There is great dishonor in learning nothing from the encounter. If you do not force me to obliterate you, your people will study this battle, and perhaps the next time I go against them, they will be prepared."

Brand was motionless for a long second. "Very well, then. What are your terms?"

"An immediate cease-fire. Call your men up from Pearl. And then depart."

"There may be survivors on the other two battlestars. I must put aboard search parties to find any."

Benedict considered. "Granted. Pull all craft not involved in evacuating Pearl or in landing search parties into a holding pattern within two kilometers of your battlestar. All communications will be sent in clear on this frequency. The unexplained departure or disappearance of any craft will be construed a violation of the cease-fire. Is this understood?"

Brand exhaled raggedly. "It is understood." He cut contact.

The search parties visited the first battlestar only briefly. Its surface was too hot for entry crews to work on it. Instrument readings implied that the central core was at least 250° Centigrade. Nothing could be alive in there.

The second battlestar was considerably cooler. Transparent domes went up as artificial airlocks were established and entry crews cut their way in with heavy-duty lasers. They relayed a running commentary as they made their way inward, ring by ring.

Those in the outer rings had been killed immediately by the heat pulse. Blackened, charred bodies—those who had not been spot welded to whatever they had been touching—floated in the superheated air.

Bestials further in had died of depressurization. Traceries of clotted blood trailed out of their mouths like spiderwebs.

Finally, in the core, they began discovering survivors. Even these were suffering from second- and third-degree burns, dehydration, and anoxemia.

MacAndrews had been growing progressively more ashen-faced as she listened. Her hand reached for the speaker controls. "I don't think we need to listen to all the gory details," she said.

"Oh, but we do," Benedict contradicted. "When first we met, Captain, you told me you had taken service with Master Chiang because you wanted more action. Well, here it is. Study it. Savor it. This is the stuff of glory, of reputations and promotions. If we are honest craftsmen, we should not flinch from the results of our handiwork."

Radio chatter indicated that the battlestar's medical staff was being overwhelmed. Several of the doctors were unconscious. Half of the rest were so unsteady as to be useless.

Benedict put himself back in communication with Brand. "Administer an emetic to your doctors; in fact, do so to any personnel you need operative. After it takes effect, they may have water but no food." That way, Russell's recombinant *E. coli* bacteria—which had spread through the air ducts of Pearl, been absorbed by the Bestials working there, and then transmitted one to another until all Bestials on the battlestars had been infected—would have nothing that they could ferment into alcohol.

The last ships came up from Pearl, completing the evacuation. The search parties pulled back from the wrecked battlestar with the last of the survivors. A general call went out to the ships of the Clans, asking for antiradiation medicine: The meager supply on the command battlestar was exhausted.

Benedict called up data from the computer memory banks. He activated his communicator. "We have 2500 units of antirad, which we will make available shortly."

"The hell we will," Wai Cheung objected. Benedict had been broadcasting on wide beam; all of his own ships had heard him. "I came here to kill Bestials, not to play doctor to them."

Benedict sent his reply back on a tight beam, which would be heard only in Wai Cheung's ship. "You came here as part of a paramilitary force with a military mission. That mission has been accomplished. Any further deaths we cause, by acts of commission or omission, will be murder. Furthermore, the refusal to carry out any order will be considered an act of mutiny and will be dealt with accordingly. Do I make myself understood?"

It was a bluff. Benedict was not about to fire on one of his own ships for voicing an attitude that was widespread among the refugees. It was just too dangerous, given the force of Bestials still present. Still, it was gratifying to hear the quiet clicks from the Gunners' positions as Younger and Dalton unquestioningly and without direct orders locked their weapons on their erstwhile ally's ship in readiness to blow it to bits.

"Understood," Cheung said thickly.

Benedict shifted back to wide-angle beam. "All ships will come alongside Mr. Doi's craft in battle order sequence to convey to him their antirad supplies."

It was done. Doi delivered the medicines to the battlestar, then moved his ship back. In less than half an hour, the Bestial ship broadcast quantum drive warnings and disappeared.

Benedict posted picket ships. He was suddenly so weary that he could hardly move. "Well, then," he said, broadcasting to the rest of the ships, "let us go down and take our prize."

XIII

CHIANG'S ARMADA CAME OUT OF QUANTUM SPACE IN the prescribed entry corridor, ten light-seconds from Chiron, and was immediately challenged by Centauran warships.

"Chiang Biosynthetics freighters carrying processed mining goods from Pearl."

"Pearl is under Bestial control," the Centauran commander objected.

"Not anymore," Chiang said laconically.

Word went ahead of him. By the time his ships were coming alongside the first of the orbital factories to which he was contracted to deliver rare earths, his receiver was jammed with calls both from businessmen and civil officials. He ignored them all, putting through a call of his own in the company code to his comptroller in Gryffon House. He gave instructions concerning the rates that were to be negotiated in all new contracts.

"Begging your pardon, sir," the comptroller said, "but since you've been gone, the price for phosphates has gone through the sky, what with Pearl being believed lost. We can easily charge fifty percent above the price you've stated and still undercut the competition substantially."

"That is well reasoned," Chiang agreed. "However, at that price, the incentive for those firms presently under contract with Flying Mountaineers to breach those contracts and come to us would not be quite so compelling."

"Uh. Well, that is more your area than mine. It was just a suggestion."

"Perfectly all right," Chiang replied.

In the last few weeks before the assault on Pearl, Chiang Biosynthetics had entered into a series of requirements contracts with various firms. Normally, many of the companies would have checked on the tonnage Chiang Biosynthetics was already committed to deliver to other buyers. Having analyzed that information, they would have refused to enter into contract, realizing that without Pearl it would be impossible for Chiang to honor all these commitments.

But times were not normal. To the First Families, it had appeared that Chiang was scrabbling desperately for capital. They encouraged their subsidiaries to accept the contracts. Soon, they reasoned, Chiang's reserve would begin to run out. Company after company would put in its demand orders, which could not be met. Chiang would be sued for breach and so would be forced neatly into corporate dissolution.

Now, however, Chiang had his main source of supply back. And if he could lure away a few more companies, Flying Mountaineers would suddenly find itself with next to no market for its goods.

He made another call, and soon frigates swarmed up to meet his fleet. Phosphates and rare earths destined for his own factories and storehouses on Neoptolemus were transferred into these just-hired ships. It would, of course, have been more economical for Chiang to have sent the goods in his own ships. But Chiang had another use in mind for them.

* * *

On the second day, TRANSCENDATRAN got hold of the tapes of the battle of Pearl. Defenders of Humanity exulted in seeing their enemies devastated before their eyes. Yet other viewers found themselves oddly moved by the rescue efforts that followed.

"Those Bestials are mean sonsabitches," a bartender said to a reporter, "but I've got to admit they're brave sonsabitches, too. And they really do take care of their own."

Attitudes throughout the Centauran system were undergoing a subtle readjustment. Epstein, watching the interview, remembered how once before the broadcast death of a simulacrum had had unforeseen results for the Defenders. He rubbed his beard and nodded, seeing in all this a hand other than Chiang's.

On the third day, Chiang appeared before the General Council. There was a standing ovation. Reporters with gyro-stabilized holocams perched on their shoulders like friendly crows relayed the speeches live as Councilor after Councilor got up to praise Chiang's daring or to pontificate on the importance of this victory to the war effort. Through it all, Chiang looked attentively bored.

There were no reporters at the afternoon meeting of the Inner Council. It was much more interesting.

Gould arranged a private meeting with Chiang just before the start of the afternoon meeting. "What the hell do you think you're doing?" Gould demanded. "Even with Pearl you can't possibly fill all the contracts you are making."

This was perfectly true, but it was also just a guess, and Chiang saw no reason to tell Gould that he was correct. "I am expanding my operations on Pearl. In the past, I was content to process only enough for my own needs and to provide some cash on the side. Since the commencement of hostilities"—they both understood that he was not referring to the Bestials—"I have come to realize that accelerated exploitation of these raw materials can eliminate my rivals."

"It will take more than that to drive us under," Gould said between clenched teeth.

"That may be. If so, your continued survival will be quite painful. However," Chiang added as Gould turned to leave, "that pain can be mitigated."

Gould turned back warily. "How so?"

"I have worked up an estimate of the profits you will lose over the next year given the drastically curtailed market for your goods. I imagine you have already done the same. I am not an avaricious man. For a mere third of that sum, I will rescind most of the new contracts."

"That is blackmail," Gould exploded. "My company will never pay it."

"As you wish." Chiang said agreeably, and left Gould where he stood.

He entered the Inner Council chambers in good humor. Nearly all the chairs were filled. Only Couteau was conspicuous by his absence. Pierpont began before Chiang reached his seat.

"Your ships are in violation of military law, Chiang. They have positioned themselves in orbit around Chiron without proper clearance and have refused orders to land. Unless they comply immediately, they risk being fired on by Centauran dreadnoughts."

Several council members were on their feet at once.

"That is hardly the way to greet the man who has given us our greatest victory against the Bestials," Kondrashin objected.

". . . really think that dreadnoughts will be more effective than battlestars were?" Chiang was asking. He shrugged. "Let them try. The results should prove amusing."

There was a sudden stillness. Chiang was so much the center of attention that Benedict slipped in almost completely unobserved. The lighting emphasized the four parallel scars on Chiang's left cheek, gained as he had fought his way into the fusion plant on Pearl. In that momentary silence there was something that was more than respect but not yet fear, something that attached itself to the new title by which some were already beginning to refer to Chiang: Warlord.

"Yes, we have been hoping Councilor Chiang would share with us the secret of his reconquest of Pearl." Rascavia's insinuating tone made it clear that he had very little hope that Chiang would share any secrets at all but that he would have to work very hard to justify his reticence.

"Indeed I shall," Chiang responded, surprising everyone. He slipped a cassette into a slot in his desk. Microholograms and graphs appeared in the air above them. Chiang described Russell's combination of mutated yeast genes with *E. coli* bacteria. The recombinant bacteria had been packaged into what looked like air freshener pads and then attached to the inside walls of the ventilation tunnels, timed for release after the evacuation of Chiang's workers.

"That sounds very much like biological warfare to me," Gould interjected. "I am sure that Councilor Chiang is aware that the penalities for such illegal action are severe."

Chiang turned a mildly surprised gaze on him. "I am certainly aware that the involuntary subjection of humans to biological agents is illegal. However, their use on animals is generally considered good husbandry or wildlife management, depending on the situation. Our relationships with the Bestials, both before and since the outbreak of war, have been predicated on the belief that they are no more than unusually intelligent nonhuman animals. Perhaps Councilor Gould would care to dispute this with Councilor Cowan. Our entire approach to these hostilities may need revision."

Gould flushed and sat down.

"Until now," Chiang continued, "quantum drives have been used in support of warfare in much the same way cavalry was before the invention of the stirrup: as a way of moving the troops quickly to the scene of the battle, where the fighting would then proceed along conventional lines. Now we can surface anywhere we wish within the enemy's defensive perimeter, fire a salvo, and be gone before fire is returned."

He explained Nsbugu's theory of in-space quantum drive correction and showed how it had been applied to his ships. Above them, the attack unfolded again.

Ronan sat forward, concentrating intently on the scene. "Are we watching this in real time?" Chiang nodded.

The battle surged toward a climax. In a sudden flurry of action, three Bestial ships came under attack and detonated almost simultaneously. Chiang's ships winked out of range, and Benedict's voice called on Brand to surrender.

"They were fighting better toward the end, weren't they?" Epstein asked. "They were beginning to compensate for their own inebriation."

"Run that last part of the battle again," Ronan demanded. "Slow it down this time."

Chiang complied. In slow motion, the ships displayed a ritual gracefulness, as if part of some interplanetary ballet. The three Bestial ships spotted a lone refugee craft and made a pass at it, vectoring so as to form a triangle enclosing it. Suddenly, other refugee craft appeared around them like atoms crystallizing out of a supersaturated solution. Laser fire burned itself across the intervening blackness, and for an instant before the explosions, the crystalline lattice was complete and balanced.

"What sort of tactical computer program were you using?" Ronan asked.

"No computer program was necessary," Chiang said, nodding at Benedict.

"In fact," Benedict explained, "use of a computer would have disadvantages. I couldn't write a program that would *control* the battle because I was not sure under what circumstances I would want the ships to disengage, to feint, to initiate new attacks. Too much depended on unknowns, on how effectively we had justified our quantum drives, on how disabled the Bestials were by the mutated *E. coli*. On the other hand, if a computer were used in merely an advisory capacity, the interfacing time between computer and human commander would slow our reaction time to an unacceptable degree. It was much simpler and quicker for me to evaluate the battle as it occurred and send out the necessary orders."

"You were able to do this by yourself?" Madame Sorabji asked.

"Multi-Neural Capacitants were created to deal with n variable problems in economics and sociobiology. The evaluation of a space battle on two quantum levels is technically much simpler."

"How many ships would you be able to control in such a situation?" Ronan asked.

"That would be limited only by the resolving power of the screen I was using."

"You would be able to control, say, the entire Centauran fleet?"

"This line of questioning is getting out of hand," Cowan expostulated. "Whether this creature has the technical competence to command any fleet is irrelevant to anything!"

"Not if we were to put him in temporary command of our forces," Ronan observed.

There was an instant uproar. Cowan could be seen shaking his fist, purple veins standing out along his wrist and jaw. Every Councilor was trying to make himself heard over the others. Rascavia gaveled for order for more than a minute and eventually was able to regain control of the meeting.

"Is this a serious proposal?" he asked Ronan. "The Rénard, remember, is not even a Centauran citizen. We only barely defined him to be human here a few weeks ago—granting him that much power would be extremely unpopular with our Defenders of Humanity constituents. And I don't even like to think how I would explain to our General Staff putting an outsider above them."

"I am quite serious," Ronan replied. He looked over at Cowan, Kondrashin, and Epstein. "The Defenders of Humanity should be placated by the fact that the Rénard has already inflicted more damage on the Bestials than they have suffered during all the rest of the war. As for the General Staff—First Councilor, in my experience, there are two varieties of military men: those primarily interested in winning battles and those primarily interested in their own prestige. The former will be grateful for an opportunity to learn how to defeat Bestials. If the latter are too greatly offended, their presence will not be greatly missed."

Councilor Sankla was frowning. "Mister—uh, Brother Benedict, you stated that you were not able to construct a controlling program for the battle of Pearl because you were too uncertain of the effects of the mutated *E. coli* and the justification of the quantum drives. You know all those things now. Couldn't you now write such a program?"

"I could now write a program to handle the Battle of Pearl," Benedict agreed cautiously.

Sankla caught the tone. "But what?"

Benedict hesitated, letting it appear that the truth was being dragged out of him. "There will never be another battle like Pearl. The Pack Leaders of the Clans are extremely intelligent individuals. Now that they have seen that quantum space jumps can be integrated into battles, it is only a matter of time before they realize how it is done. I would guess that it would be a short time. When next we join battle, both sides will be maneuvering on two energy levels."

"My God!" Fiertag exclaimed, imagining the result. "Nobody will stay put long enough to be shot at."

Benedict shook his head. "It might seem so, but in fact they will, in order to get their own shots off. The problem is how to do that most advantageously. I haven't been able to come up with a definite solution. Most programs I have worked on turn into infinite loops."

"So you would not be able to aid us in any case," Cowan said. "Let us move on to other matters."

"I agree," Chiang said quickly. "The Rénard is indentured to me, and I do not intend to risk him on any further military ventures."

"I am sure you do not," Ronan shot back. "You intend to use him in commercial matters. Some of us," he said, glancing significantly at Pierpont and Gould, "have already suffered from that use.

"Understand me, Chiang. You have been fighting for your corporate life, and I do not begrudge you your victories. But it is good health you deserve, not hegemony. The Rénard has proved too powerful a tool to be left in one man's hands. You told us when you first returned with the Rénard that he was to be used for the common benefit. It is time to make good that pledge."

"How could we trust Rénard with the sort of power you propose to give him?" Kondrashin asked practically.

Ronan shrugged. "He won't really have that much power. Our troops will be instructed that his authority is binding only in battle against Bestials. Defenders' sympathy is strong in the ranks. Any attempt to seize, say, the capital would meet with instant mutiny.

"Furthermore, you should study the Rénard's history more closely. He has done many legally questionable things, but he has never betrayed a client—not even Chiang, who obtained his services in a much more procedurally dubious manner than we propose to employ."

Chiang glared angrily at Ronan but with difficulty held his peace.

"Has it occurred to any of you to ask my opinion of the suggestion?" Benedict asked harshly. "Has it occurred to you that pleasing as all of this may be to Paul Niccolo Rénard, I am nonetheless now Brother Benedict, and as Brother Benedict I would prefer to use my time in a way more constructive than teaching hot-blooded fools more efficient ways of killing themselves?" And please, please don't throw me in that briar patch.

"It displeases you? Good," Ronan said coolly. "The more quickly you give us victory, the more quickly you can go back to culturing slime molds or whatever it is Stewards do."

There was no need for Rascavia's vote this time. Only Chiang and Cowan voted against. Chiang's indenture was to be "held in abeyance" pending the end of hostilities. Benedict was inducted into Centauran Space Forces with the temporary rank of Sky Marshal.

"You fools!" Cowan breathed. His face was ashen, and his voice was trembling. "Do you realize what you have done? This is what Valentino schemed and plotted for, what he would have achieved by force of arms but for a patriot's laser. And now you have handed it over to his brother! *Don't you understand*?"

XIV

THE COUNCIL GRANTED BENEDICT THREE DAYS TO TIE up his affairs with Chiang. There was little, in fact, to tie up. Benedict had time for the sweeter things in life, such as rest, recollection—and revenge.

Couteau's face in the holoscreen was unpleasantly lifelike. Perspiration glistened on forehead and scalp. A perpetual tremor in the underlip made itself felt through folds of fat to the far side of either cheek. Benedict watched in fascination. How easy to forget that this was a human face at all, to imagine instead that it was an entire planet of the verge of eruption.

"W-what do y-you want with me?" Couteau demanded. "I h-have very little time."

"Less than you imagine," Benedict said agreeably. "The Warlord is quite upset with you for reasons you are well aware of. Twice you have failed to honor your obligations. The first time, the lack of your vote nearly cost me the legal recognition of my humanity. Your second defection made possible the cession of Pearl."

"Little enough damage either of you took from those votes," Couteau said with a defiant bitterness.

"That is true," Benedict said. "In other circumstances

170

Master Chiang might be willing to forgo his recompense. But you must understand his position. As a member of the Inner Council, he receives deference and favor from many. If word of your unpunished treachery became common, petty insurrections would sprout up everywhere. No, even though it may be wearisome in the extreme, it is sometimes necessary, in the interests of domestic harmony, to post heads on pikes."

"There is nothing he can do to me," Couteau said, anger suddenly flaring. "I have new friends now, friends who can protect me—"

"Friends like Gould?" Benedict asked. "He'll not be able to underwrite your bad debts once Chiang forecloses. Gould is feeling the pinch himself right now. And why should he? Your limited usefulness is already spent. Surely not from a feeling of loyalty. Gould recognizes that even as you betrayed one patron, so you would betray him the instant it appeared profitable."

"You glory in this, don't you?" Couteau asked. "The destruction of little people like me. Despite that cross hanging around your neck, you have no pity, no mercy at all."

Benedict's eyes became suddenly bleak. "Don't prattle on things beyond your understanding. Even now, if you had any true penitence, I might intercede for you. But all you have is fear for your own wretched hide. To regret doing a wrong simply *because* it was wrong—well, I can see from your face that the idea fills you with complete incomprehension.

"No, Couteau, your disloyalty is exceeded only by your shortsightedness. There is little in you for salvation and scarcely enough for damnation.

"Here are Chiang's terms: Resign immediately from the Inner Council and as president of the Landholders' Association. Divest yourself of all Landholders' stock within one standard day. If you meet these terms, Chiang's support of the Landholders will remain in place and the details of your mismanagement will not be publicized."

"One standard day!" Couteau seemed to be struggling for breath. "Unloading that much stock that quickly will depress the price to below half its worth. I'll be ruined!"

Benedict shrugged. "Such is life. And even at half price, your stock will net you a hefty sum. Perhaps enough to emigrate to Earth and set yourself up in a town house."

Couteau took a deep breath. "I won't do it. *You* can't force me now that Chiang is being gelded of you."

Benedict sighed. "Your case would be removed from my control in any event. I had just hoped I could use this last chance to resolve things peacefully. Mr. Sun will take over from here."

"S-sun?" The tremor reappeared with renewed force.

"Yes. Are you familiar with him? I must say, I don't altogether approve of his methods."

"I'll g-g-get back t-to you later." The image disappeared.

Benedict leaned back and turned to Chiang. "He'll be gone within three hours."

Two hours and forty-five minutes later, the new head of the Landholders' Association, Jacob Newstadt, called Chiang to pledge complete cooperation. Couteau's name was not mentioned.

At the end of the final day, Chiang and Benedict walked down one of the long corridors leading to Chiang's docking bays. Between them rolled a multipurpose robot, one of its metal tentacles wrapped firmly around the duffel bag, which now, even as when he had first landed on Neoptolemus, contained all Benedict's worldly goods. As they walked, their reflections rippled across the robot's silvered surface, now separating, now merging.

Chiang was in voluble good humor. "Things finally

seem to be ordering themselves properly," he said. "I received this morning from Councilor Gould the first installment on KDT 60 million—which he is paying me to not enter into contracts that I do not have the resources to complete. Much of this first installment I have made over to Councilor Ronan for his marvelous performance the other day."

"Any news from Pearl?"

"The shipments are arriving on time." Chiang shrugged. "The Bestials might retake it at any time, given the small holding force we have. But by the time they realize how they were defeated, they will also realize that they have much more important targets."

"Then you are content."

"As much as is possible." Chiang's expression was midway between a grin and a grimace. "At least now my enterprises will stand or fall on their own merit, which is all anyone can ask."

They walked a few meters in silence.

"Then perhaps there are certain formalities—" Benedict began.

A tentacle wrapped itself firmly around his chest. Abruptly, Benedict found himself staring up at the ceiling. A stuttering hum came from the MPR unit. From a lens located near the head, quick bursts of laser light lanced beyond his field of vision.

Something tinkled against the metallic skin of the robot and fell to the floor. A cylindrical metal pellet nearly two centimeters long fell near Benedict's eyes and rolled in diminishing arcs, blue sparks erupting sporadically from two parallel prongs.

"Rénard." Sun's voice came through the robot's speakers. "Stay down. My men will secure your area shortly."

"You had better hurry," Benedict said. "Chiang has been hit."

The metal tentacle released him. He looked quickly

up and down the corridor. Two unidentifiable forms lay motionless at the far end of the corridor.

Benedict crawled across to Chiang. The pellet had burned a circle just below the sternum, and Chiang's eyes were rolled up into his head. Benedict felt vainly for a pulse.

Running footsteps approached. Sun's security personnel raced to the end of the corridor and stationed themselves, guns drawn, surveying the cross-link. Behind them, Russell, leading a team of three medics, dragged a tubular life-support chamber.

They picked Chiang up and tucked him gently into the coffinlike structure. Electrodes were fastened to wrists and neck. The front of his shirt was deftly cut away, and two metal disks were placed on his chest. Russell flicked a switch, and the chamber lid closed itself, leaving only Chiang's face visible through a glass port. His lips were blue-tinged. Remembering the modified life-support chambers in Snowden's laboratories, Benedict felt a chill of irrational dread.

"Can you bring him back?" he asked.

Russell glared at the chamber readout and punched a series of buttons. "Perhaps," he snapped. "If I am not distracted by needless questions."

Benedict accepted the rebuke quietly. At Russell's signal, the aides rolled the life-support chamber quickly down the corridor and out of sight.

There was an unnatural quiet. Benedict had to shake off a feeling of unreality, an illusion that everything that had happened in the past few minutes had been no more than an unusually vivid dream.

He walked to the end of the corridor, the robot gliding after him. Sun and one of his men were examining the two bodies. Sun's hands sifted through their longish hair.

"Three, four weeks ago, that hair would have been quite closely cropped," Benedict observed.

Sun grunted, nodding microscopically.

Benedict looked back down the corridor, gauging the distance to where they had been when they had been fired upon.

"The first shot was low," Benedict said. "A few centimeters higher and every nerve in Chiang's heart would have been fried, making resuscitation impossible. They overcorrected on the second shot: The electrodart meant for me bounced off the robot nearly half a meter over my head."

He met Sun's eyes. "These men were not familiar with projectile weapons. Most likely, their training was with standard-issue lasers."

"I follow your thought," Sun said. "It is not proof, however. And the identity records of these men have almost surely been erased from the Comp central data banks."

"True. But I think we both know who may be able to identify them for us."

Benedict nodded. "I will send for her immediately."

Cassian received the call in his headquarters.

"Mrs. Chiang, what—"

"Colonel, I need your help immediately." Bobbi took a deep breath to steady herself. Her eyes were shadowed and smudged. "My husband has just been assassinated. John died less than five minutes ago."

Cassian's pulse began to pound. "Do you have any idea who the killers are?"

Bobbi shook her head. "Not the actual triggermen. They've been killed themselves to cover up the evidence. But I know who was behind them: the Rénard and Mr. Sun, my security chief.

"Colonel, John always spoke very highly of you. I *need* you now. The Rénard is trying to take over all of Chiang Biosynthetics. I am barricaded in the computer room. If you come quickly, I can keep a corridor clear and give you entry here. You may be able to do something with the computer codes. Take only a small aircar and a few men. That way you should be able to get in unnoticed. If you approach in force, Sun will fight until there is nothing left."

"Give me ten minutes," Cassian said.

A domestic robot guided them from the little-used surface entrance to the computer room. Cassian posted as guards the four soldiers who had accompanied him.

"Sir," Cartello ventured, "there may be trouble in there. Shouldn't at least one of us stay with you?"

"I'll be able to handle Mrs. Chiang without any aid," Cassian said blandly. And without any witnesses. Cartello was silent, but his smug smile was eloquent enough.

Cassian entered the computer room. Bobbi was seated at the end of a long table, her head bowed, her hands clasped before her. Only the lights directly above her were on. She was so obviously wrapped up in her own grief that Cassian found it difficult to speak.

"Mrs. Chiang, even though I know you must be wondering how—"

She sat up quickly. Her hands held an electrodart gun, pointed directly at his chest.

"Wondering how it is that an ally has turned traitor and murderer," Chiang's voice supplied. The lights came up. Chiang was seated on Cassian's extreme right, encased up to his neck in a med chair. Some doctor with a familiar face —Russell, Cassian remembered belatedly— stood just behind Chiang, paying close attention to the dials of the med chair. Holocams set on tripods regarded him incuriously from two corners of the room. Just beyond their range, Sun and two of his guards stood with laser rifles pointed at him. Thermosights made the swivel-mounted muzzle tips follow his every move. So long as the rifles were pointed in his general direction, there was no way a shot could miss.

"Councilor Chiang, I thought you were dead—"

"I'm sure you did," Chiang said. His voice altered. "This tribunal is convened under the Emergency War Powers Act. A charge of treason is lodged against Col. José Cassian. Specifically, he is charged with twice attempting the assassination of Inner Council member John Lei Chiang and with the murders of J. James and A. Faisal, both of the *Gryffon's Pride*. How do you plead?"

Cassian opened his mouth to call Cartello. There was the sound of quick movement from behind the door. A cry was cut off almost before it could be heard. It was followed by several muffled thuds.

"As the accused has remained silent, a formal plea of not guilty is entered in his behalf." Chiang glanced from the holocams to Cassian. "Your men have only been stunned. Their sentences will depend on their responses while under truth enhancers.

"The first witness is Captain Eileen MacAndrews of the *Gryffon's Pride*." As if on cue, MacAndrews entered the room. Chiang continued. "Be warned that your testimony is under oath.

"Captain, you entered my employment approximately eighteen months ago. Your records show that you had just resigned your commission in the Centauran Space Force."

"In fact, I did not resign my commission. Colonel Cassian ordered me to pretend to resign and to obtain employment with Chiang Biosynthetics."

"Why?"

"You had told him that you were beginning a search for Paul Niccolo Rénard. Colonel Cassian had grave misgivings about this venture. He felt that the Rénard would be too dangerous to be useful if he were located. I was to obtain a position of trust so that I would be able to protect you if the Rénard were found."

"Tell us about your instructions concerning Dr. Herter," Chiang said.

"Dr. Herter was a passenger on the *Gryffon's Pride* during our flight to Ariel. He was an expert on all Multi-Neural Capacitants, including the Rénard. Colonel Cassian contacted him several weeks before we left Neoptolemus, but I don't know the nature or the extent of their conversations. I do know that Colonel Cassian ordered me to set the computer so that Dr. Herter would be awakened in his cold-sleep cubicle while we were still in Space$_4$, about a light-year from Ariel. He didn't say why, except that Dr. Herter would have to make preparations before we encountered the Rénard."

"Did you have any idea that these preparations included murdering two of your crew members and attempting my own murder?"

MacAndrews repressed a shudder. "No, certainly not."

"In fact," Cassian interjected, "is it not true that I never at any time ordered you to take action detrimental to Councilor Chiang's interest? Nor gave you any reason to believe that Dr. Herter was to act in any way save for the Councilor's benefit?"

"That is true," MacAndrews said, her voice unsteady.

"Since you did not denounce me immediately," Cassian continued, "I presume you had some explanation for Dr. Herter's actions that did not involve my malfeasance."

"I thought I did," MacAndrews acknowledged. "It seemed to me that the stress of being conscious while in Space$_4$ might have driven Dr. Herter temporarily insane. God knows, it was hard enough on those of us who had quantum space experience. Dr. Herter, to my knowledge, had none."

"A reasonable guess," Cassian said approvingly. "Certainly much more reasonable than supposing I would run immense risk by attempting, for no discernible reason, to have Councilor Chiang killed."

"Let us continue," Chiang said. "Several hours ago I was the target of a second assassination attempt. Four individuals were brought down by my security forces." Three-dimensional images appeared in the space between Chiang and Cassian. "They bore no identification. Querying the computer networks on Neoptolemus and Chiron produced no result."

He turned back to MacAndrews. "Can you identify them?"

"Yes. Lieutenant Shirley Kurtz. Lieutenant Juan Ortega. Captain James Holloman. Major Francois Leroi-Gourhan. All of these have been members of Colonel Cassian's personal staff."

"She is lying," Cassian said.

"Her testimony was taken first under truth enhancers. Will you allow yourself to be questioned under similar conditions?" Cassian was silent. "I thought not. In any event, even though their primary records have been erased, we have found several secondary references that confirm that these individuals have been under your command within the past year.

"Do you have any further evidence you wish to present?"

Cassian compressed his lips and shook his head once, violently.

"In that case, little remains except to pass sentence. However, before I do, I would like the answer to one last question. You have stated that the case against you is weakened by the fact that you have 'no discernible reason' to seek my death. That is true, though given the weight of the rest of the evidence, it counts for less than you would prefer. Still, I would like to know why you have sought my death. For more than two years I have done everything in my power to advance your cause. I have obtained choice commands for you; I had your views on tactics and strategy published and given the attention they deserved. Yet somehow it was evidently not enough. Why not, Colonel? Did my competitors promise greater rewards?"

Cassian had been staring at his feet. Now he looked up with eyes that burned like acid. "You know very well why! You never intended to give me my due. You wanted someone more clever, more powerful. That's why you wanted the Rénard and why I determined you should not have him. Herter was really appalled at your plan to track down the Rénard and put him once again at the centers of power. It was easy to talk him into taking whatever steps were necessary to prevent you from making contact with the Rénard.

"When you came back with him anyway, it was clear that my fears had been justified. When I was introduced to the Rénard at the reception for the refugee families, he at once began to belittle my strategy for defeating the Bestials. And when you returned in triumph from Pearl, the Rénard was made Sky Marshal, but not even crumbs were thrown in my direction. I wanted you to know that I am not that easily discarded."

Chiang was silent for long seconds, his face unreadable.

"I suppose that I have been somewhat slow," he said at last, almost apologetically. "The past few weeks have been quite busy. My first priority was to keep my corporation from being devoured. And then, when I was able to take time for other things, I held the news back from normal channels because I wanted to tell you personally."

He held out a folded sheet of paper. Cassian's hand trembled as he opened it.

"Your promotion to general," Chiang said. "It was my intention to use the Rénard to complement your talents, not to replace you. For all my many deficiencies, I have always put great store by the pagan virtue of loyalty. Each of us misjudged the other in that regard, I guess.

"Well, do you have anything final to say?"

When he raised his eyes from the promotion order, Cassian's face was full of such bleak despair that Chiang involuntarily glanced away.

"The sentence is death," Chiang said. "Mr. Sun, take him outside and dispose of him."

XV

ONE INSTANT, BENEDICT AND THE OTHERS WERE LOOK-ing on a representation of barren star field. In the next instant, seven scoutships appeared simultaneously in the void. Six moved outward, each at right angles to the rest. The seventh was motionless for more than a minute, then abruptly it vanished.

The remaining six continued to coast, defining an ever-larger sphere. This lasted just long enough for the generals and Councilors seated around Benedict to start shifting uneasily in their seats. Then, near the center where the scouts had first appeared, fighters surfaced into Space₁. Dozens, scores, of fighters appeared to follow the scouts, with more behind them until the screen had to alter scale to fit in the hundreds of craft that were coasting through space, filling the star field like a giant flower unfolding.

And behind them came scores of cruisers and dreadnoughts, each sweeping out to the perimeter as it took its predestined position in the battle order. Finally, with slow and solemn majesty, the battlestars appeared. Twenty-five of them.

"Christ," Councilor Kondrashin whispered. "Our entire Space Force has only fifteen!"

"And you can be sure that they kept more back around Sol to defend their precious Manhome," Rascavia said. "Building them all is what has delayed the formation of this fleet."

The battlestars drifted to the control points for their divisions.

"I don't understand how Ishige gets that dispersion pattern," General Mèffert murmured.

Benedict raised an eyebrow.

"When you surface from quantum space, you maintain the same vectors, speed, and direction that you had originally in Space$_1$," Mèffert explained. "If all these ships seem to be coming from a common center, Ishige must have split his fleet, placing half of it on opposite sides of Chiron and calculating his ships' jumps so that they would surface just past each other. That calls for incredible precision, and to no purpose that I can see."

Benedict quickly checked the coordinates at the base of the screen. "It's an illusion," he said. "Those ships aren't just expanding from a common center; the whole sphere is coming in our direction. You don't see it because the screen adjusts the perspective at the same rate to keep everyone in view. When they surface in Space$_1$, all they have is their vector in our direction. After they come through, they add the vectors that form the sphere."

General Turner-Smith, one seat over from Mèffert, was frowning. "What puzzles me is the sequence of the craft. I mean, I understand why he sent the scouts first, even though we had assured him that that quadrant of space would be safe. But if he was being that cautious, why not send the really big guns, the battlestars, through after the scouts. Better to have the heavy stuff on line immediately if you are expecting trouble."

"It is indeed suggestive," Benedict said.

The sphere was no sooner complete than it began spinning itself out as the craft of the Solar Commonwealth Fleet moved from battle formation into a series of orbits about Chiron.

"Time to go topside," Rascavia announced. "Our guests will soon be here."

They took elevators to the surface, to the plain on the far side of the river Alice from Pierpont, where the reviewing stand had been erected. Generals and members of the Inner Council took their appointed seats. The wind whipped fiercely off the Inner Sea, snapping the flags with sounds like rifle shots. A military band playing for the assembled dignitaries could be heard only fitfully.

Three dreadnoughts, silvered hulls gleaming like secondary suns, descended quickly out of the west. The huge, egg-shaped vessels blotted out the sun, casting the field in shadow.

It was only a token force for ceremonial purposes. Somehow, that fact made it even more impressive. First came the colonial regiments from Mars, the Moon, and the Jovian dependencies—each with different uniforms proclaiming an independence from Terra that was more apparent than real. Then the Terran Marines passed in review. Bagpipes, trumpets, and drums echoed thunderously off the reviewing stand.

The colors passed and bowed to each other: the blue and green of Terra, the yellow and orange of Centaurus. Behind them came what was, for Benedict, the only interesting feature of the afternoon. Toshiro Ishige, Sky Marshal of the Solar Expeditionary Force and generally considered to be the reason why the Moon, Mars, and the Jovian dependencies were not fully independent. Scion of samurai, master strategist, he was reputed to be most content when playing the koto.

He looked anything but content now. Squinting against the sun, stiffly erect, he seemed to exude dys-

peptic disapproval. Perhaps, Benedict thought, he is as
bored by this as I am.

He was able to study the Sky Marshal more closely at
the state dinner. The seating had been arranged so that
Benedict would sit to Rascavia's right and Chiang to his
left. Ishige was to sit across from Rascavia, flanked by
his staff and commanders.

Rascavia introduced them as soon as the opening
speeches were finished. "Sky Marshal, this is Paul
Niccolo Rénard, a Multi-Neural Capacitant. Despite his
Stewards' habit, he recently helped Councilor Chiang
win a most singular victory over the Bestials. I am sure
you heard of it. For that reason, though it is admittedly
quite irregular, he has been given the rank of acting Sky
Marshal for the Centauran forces."

"I have not only heard of the Battle of Pearl," Ishige
said, "I have spent the last week studying it. I am grati-
fied to meet you. I knew your brother before his un-
timely death. Had he read your sister's work more
closely, he would have understood that the greatest
power is usually exercised invisibly."

"Valentino was always impetuous," Benedict said
agreeably.

"Whereas you are very, very patient."

Rascavia frowned, nettled that he was not in control
of the conversation. "The Rénard has made the point,
and I quite agree with him, that we will need intensive joint training in the new method of warfare he has
devised. In fact, to ensure a successful campaign—"
Rascavia hesitated a half second, well aware of the sensitive ground upon which he trod "—we must discuss
unification of the commands."

The slightest of smiles quirked Ishige's lips. "First
Councilor, I fear you overestimate the extent of my authority. The days of *honor*," he said, his emphasis on the
word oddly jarring, "the days when one hero could put
himself and his army at the disposal of another hero sim-

ply because he recognized the other's superior virtue—those days have long since passed. The force that presently orbits this planet has been assembled for one reason and one reason only: because the Terrestrial Commonwealth feels threatened by the repeated incursions of the Bestials and believes that the most effective way to deal with them is with the aid of the Centauran Confederation.

"That does not mean that our interests are necessarily identical. I have been charged and restricted in my authority by certain postulates that the Commonwealth considers vital. One of these is my responsibility as commander of my fleet. I am not allowed to delegate or abdicate that responsibility, even if I would."

"But, surely, joint exercises cannot be in contradiction to your orders," Benedict suggested. "I note that we are already in agreement in some areas. For example, you sent your battlestars last through the jump here because you recognized their vulnerability, about which I am still trying to convince my own generals."

Ishige shook his head slightly. "I will be most pleased to cooperate in joint exercises. I am sure that I can learn much from Rénard. There is surely much he should learn from me.

"And in any event, I feel I should at least begin by being agreeable to hosts who are fêting me with the finest of French champagnes," Ishige said, unsmilingly taking a sip.

"But that is not French champagne," Chiang said.

"No?"

"No. And the story behind that may give you additional insight on the Battle of Pearl."

XVI

ISHIGE WAS SURPRISINGLY COOPERATIVE. BENEDICT'S own generals were the problem. Five were so insulted at having an outsider appointed over them that they tendered their resignations. To their complete astonishment, these were accepted.

Other problems began even before Benedict was able to commence training exercises. Even his choice of a command post sparked controversy.

"You will, of course, control from Battlestar One," General Mèffert said, as if nothing else were conceivable.

Benedict's answering glance crackled with repressed irritation. "If the Battle of Pearl taught you nothing else, it should have taught you that battlestars are nothing but very slow-moving, vulnerable, and expensive targets."

"Well, then, sir, why not a dreadnought rather than a cruiser?" Turner-Smith suggested. "That would give you maneuverability plus firepower."

"That is true," Benedict agreed. "But it will also give me a visibility I would do without. There will be hundreds of cruisers: It should be virtually impossible for the Clans to determine which one I am in. Furthermore, the *Gryffon's Pride* suits me. I understand the limitations of both the ship and its crew, and I am quite comfortable."

"This will be a much larger force than you had at Pearl," Mèffert protested. "A cruiser's comm screen won't be able to display them all."

"Point well taken. Order a large screen installed immediately."

Benedict sat in the command chair, nearly engulfed by the wraparound screen. He had ordered half the fleet to the sunward side of Chiron, hoping to shield the manuevers from the Bestial scouts who were surely monitoring everything from the fringes of the system.

First, to get them used to the new style of fighting, Benedict had scheduled a variation of the Battle of Pearl. Five Terrestrial battlestars were designated Team Mantichore. Twenty Centauran cruisers and dreadnoughts became Team Dragon. They floated now in the emptiness, observing radio silence, waiting for the narrow-beamed message from the *Gryffon's Pride*.

"Attack," Benedict ordered. The Dragons disappeared. For an instant they flashed into being clustered around the battlestars. Dummy missiles were launched and were countered by high-power infrared lasers. The Dragons vanished again.

The computer scoring was complete before they resurfaced in Space$_1$. Four Mantichore battlestars were completely destroyed. The one remaining was so severely damaged as to be out of action for all practical purposes. None of the Dragons had been harmed.

Benedict grinned. Let that lesson sink in among his troops and they would be much more interested in what would follow.

"Sky Marshal Rénard. This is Ishige. Please run that exercise again. I have made some adjustments."

"Indeed? Very well." Benedict thought a second and

directed the Dragons to attack from a quadrant ninety degrees away from the first vector. Again the computer read out the toll of demolished battlestars. This time, though, all attackers were also listed as casualties.

"I have bypassed the recognition programs," Ishige said. "Unless there is a manual override, any object within fifty kilometers will be automatically vaporized. The recognition bypass speeds the response just enough to hit attackers before they jump back into Space$_2$."

"Very good," Benedict said. "Still, a battlestar for a cruiser would generally be considered an excellent trade-off. And I will work on having my attackers drop their missiles more quickly."

The hours passed as Benedict developed and taught a vocabulary of attack. How do you fight a battle when both you and your adversary can appear suddenly, fire, and disappear? To most of the officers and men under Benedict, the idea suggested complete chaos. Bit by bit he showed them that this was not necessarily so.

An attacker might surface in Space$_1$. However short the time until he vanished again, his motion in the interval defined a vector. When he resurfaced in Space$_1$, it had to be on the line of that vector, moving in the same direction and at the same velocity he had held during the attack. Of course, the line was infinitely long, and if it was an isolated hit-and-run attack, the chances of deducing where the attacker would surface were infinitesimal. But if the attacker was part of a fleet, he would want to resurface in relatively short order to make another run. He would need to be close enough to receive orders from his commander and to see the battle he had left behind in something close to real time. That distance would be subject to somewhat arbitrary definition, but to Benedict a light-second seemed reasonable. Just under the distance between the Earth and the Moon.

If, as again seemed reasonable, the Bestials had chosen a like limit, then an Allied vessel could determine the

Bestial's vector the first time it surfaced and jump to intercept it.

A Bestial could do the same. So they developed countermeasures and counter-countermeasures. To peed response, Benedict set up a program so that basic commands could be sent by touching just one of the keys on his keyboards. When he had had the larger screen installed, he had also directed the installation of a second keyboard. This left-hand keyboard could, at a touch of the proper combination of keys, put Benedict in instant contact with any vessel or group of vessels in the fleet. The right-hand keyboard was reserved for the vocabulary of commands.

Ishige was the past master of conventional space warfare. He was quickly learning the advantages of maneuvering through the quantum spaces. Benedict made Ishige his constant adversary, now on offense, now on defense, as they fought combat scenarios varying from single-vessel up to division combat. With each mock engagement, he gained more insight into Ishige's sense of strategy.

He was also gaining insight into his subordinate commanders. At the end of each engagement, he made short comments on lessons learned. Ishige soon began to do likewise. From their responses, and even more from their subsequent actions, Benedict learned to distinguish the more promising officers from the deadwood.

They drilled that first day until Benedict noted with surprise that his voice was hoarse and his hands were beginning to shake. Glancing at the chronometer, he saw that they had been working for twelve hours. From then on, he kept the training sessions to ten hours a day. Each day he learned more about the capacities and limitations of this creature that was the Allied fleet. It was as if he were growing into it, encompassing it, so that the scouts were his eyes, and fighters, cruisers and dreadnoughts his fingers, which could work delicately or close into a first of steel. With the fleet as his body, he strode across the Centauran system, an infant giant learning to walk.

There were two interludes. The first was a summons from Rascavia after the second day of training. Benedict had been lodged in a visitor's suite in the government center, above the chambers of the Inner Council. He stepped from his door to the enclosed aerial walkway that connected the government center with the First Councilor's Residence. Outside, it was already dark. Pierpont sparkled beneath him like a dewed spiderweb catching moonlight. Far out to sea, windblown waves glowed with a more subdued and mysterious phosphorescence. The guards recognized him and wordlessly allowed him to enter.

Rascavia was in his study. Small Persian rugs lay scattered like darkly colorful islands on the parquet flooring. Rascavia had been seated in an alcove by a small table. Bookcases filled with music and reading tapes and a few actual, bound books towered into the ceiling shadows.

"Sky Marshal, thank you for responding so expeditiously to my summons. I realize you must be tired after such a long day. Please accept a cordial. It was once brewed by one of your own orders. Your namesake, in fact."

Benedict obediently took the small glass offered to him and sipped politely. The cognac base burned his lips and tongue before the taste of the herbs insinuated itself up the back of his nose. He continued to watch Rascavia closely.

"Please be seated," Rascavia said. "There are some matters we must discuss."

Benedict lowered himself into the leather chair across from Rascavia. He had been in zero gravity all day, but as the exercises had progressed, his back and shoulder muscles had unconsciously tensed themselves. Chiron's gravity, pressing him against the leather, effectively subjected him to a passive massage. Like it or not, Benedict found himself relaxing.

Rascavia studied papers on the desk in front of him. "I hear extraordinary things about you. You seem to be turning the Allied fleet into an instrument of unimaginable potency." He looked up for Benedict's response.

"We are making progress," Benedict said cautiously. "We are fortunate that the Commonwealth sent Ishige. I have learned volumes from him."

Rascavia seemed to study that for hidden meanings. "I am sure you have," he said at last. "I, personally, have nothing but praise for the way you have taken command. Nonetheless, reports have been made against you. These reports could damage your position unless we can take effective action against them."

Benedict let his head lie back against the chair. He regarded Rascavia between hooded eyelids, the slightest of smiles on his lips. Not for Rascavia was Chiang's blunt way of calling a subordinate to account. Especially not when that subordinate possessed great, not entirely measured, power. No, Rascavia would put his criticisms into the mouths of others, explaining them to Benedict in the guise of an ally and confidant and couching his commands in the form of countermeasures against a common enemy. It was hypocritical but, at that, Benedict's own preferred method of operation. He stretched catlike, waiting for Rascavia to come to the point.

"I was unaware I had given anyone cause for displeasure."

"It is said that you have exceeded your authority with regard to the Centauran fleet. Your temporary rank of Sky Marshal is fully effective only during actual engagement with the Bestials. Rather as if you were a *dux bellorum*. I fully comprehend the awkwardness of that arrangement, but I can give you no more permanent a position without causing complete disaffection among the military and a perhaps irreparable rift with the Defenders of Humanity.

"Despite this, you have taken command of every squadron and have been training them so mercilessly that the crews return wringing with sweat and on the verge of collapse. The General Staff, which formally is supposed to be in command of our fleet, has been reduced to the state of messenger boys occasionally granted a tutorial by you or Ishige. There are questions in Council, and I am very hard put to answer them."

Benedict's gaze had strayed to the diamond-paned alcove window and, beyond it, to the gash of darkness where the city ended and the harbor began. Perhaps the greatest burden of a Multi-Neural Capacitant was his own prescience, his ability to foresee the plans, actions, often the very words of those around him. Having comprehended everything in an instant, he would find the succeeding weeks as torturous as having to listen to an interminable symphony played at half speed.

It had not been so on Ariel. Accelerating that planet through fifty million years of compressed evolution was the most difficult task Benedict had ever faced. Then had come Chiang, completely unlooked for, in straits so difficult that but for the miracle of mutated *E. coli* provided by Russell at just the right time, even Benedict might not have been able to save him. At the same time, the difficulty of trying to please two masters, authoritatively held to the impossible, had been enough of a balancing act to require his full resources.

But now, having to intrigue with and against Rascavia and placate every jealous impulse in the General Council and the Centauran high command filled him with ennui and distaste. It was all both too petty and too predictable. The temptation was to let things slide, to allow the odds to accumulate against oneself so that the struggle would become interesting again.

Perhaps that was why Valentino had made his doomed

attempt on the Terrestrial Commonwealth. Not because he believed he could succeed, not even because he felt it necessary to protect himself from the Defenders of Humanity—only because that action alone offered long enough odds to be worthy of his attention.

It was a terribly dangerous fascination. The work he was engaged in was too important for him to risk it—or himself while he was necessary to it—in order to satisfy his craving for excitement. Only half of his obligations had been paid. The lesser half.

Rascavia was looking at him sharply, disturbed at the time it was taking him to answer. "Is Chiang one of those raising questions?" Benedict asked.

"No." The ruefulness of Rascavia's tone showed that he understood the reproof. Chiang was now the second most powerful member of the Inner Council. Had it suited him, he might well have been able to displace Rascavia as First Councilor. By implication, if he was not questioning Benedict's behavior, nobody of importance was.

"That does not dispose of the matter," Rascavia said, trying to maintain his offensive. "There are some, Cowan chief among them, who believe that you and Chiang connived to have you made Centauran Sky Marshal. They see your extension of authority within the fleet to be the first step of a coup."

"Do you see it the same way?" Benedict's voice was soft, nearly inaudible.

Rascavia shook his head. "If you were preparing to seize power, there are . . . certain steps . . . you would have taken." Rascavia's reluctance to name those steps showed his fear of disclosing too much to Benedict.

His voice took on a harder edge, as if something beneath urbanity and good fellowship were showing itself for the first time. "If I did believe you were plotting a coup, I would have had you killed already. I am smart enough to know that I am not smart enough to control you any other way."

Benedict nodded approvingly. "That being so, the sole remaining motive for my actions must be that I am attempting to carry out my commission."

"The Council has specified the methods and the authority necessary to do that."

"The Council cannot judge!" Benedict's voice was as sharp and as merciless as a surgeon's scalpel. "If the Council knew enough to direct me properly, it would be able to do without my services altogether. You are like men who go in great pain to a doctor and beg him to accept your case, but as soon as he begins to prescribe, you object: 'No, I have no time for exercise.' 'Don't give me such disagreeable medicines.' 'Those are my favorite foods; I *won't* give them up.' You jealously hug to yourselves the very causes of your distress.

"Chiang and I had this same discussion when first we met. The patron chooses the end, the goal. He employs me to reach it. I choose the method. Right now, I judge that a thoroughly and *quickly* trained fleet is paramount. If my efforts to achieve that are blocked, I will submit my resignation."

Rascavia's eyebrow shot up. "You did not obtain your position by responding to an advertisement. You were— how can I put this delicately—inducted. You are not legally competent to resign."

"How can you prevent me?" Benedict countered. "Will you have Marines hold lasers to my head while I direct the battle from the *Gryffon's Pride*? Or will you have me imprisoned? My ecclesiastical superiors have been criticizing me for spending too little time in prayerful meditation. I will be grateful for the spare time."

"I do not wish to do either," Rascavia said, restraining himself with some difficulty. "I wish in fact to smooth your path by eliminating extravagances on which your enemies might seize. Look at this, for instance." He slid a paper across the desk to Benedict. "Do you have any idea how much animosity we will provoke if we take over the three orbiting observatories of the Astronomical Union, as you demand?"

"It will only be temporary, and it is necessary," Benedict replied. "We need instruments that sensitive to detect Cerenkov wakes at a distance of five light-hours. I don't want scouts from the Clans reporting back every battle tactic Ishige and I work out."

Rascavia was not listening. "And then you completely bypass the Council in ordering the Terrestrial fleet to leave the orbit of Chiron and take up station near one of our Trojan points—"

"I did not order that," Benedict interrupted. "I suggested it to Ishige. He agreed that it was a prudent move."

"It suggests fear. You of all people must understand how the hyenas gather when they smell fear in a victim. How can you possibly take such extravagant safety precautions despite having joint command of the largest fleet ever assembled?"

"I am not that concerned with inspiring confidence. I am concerned with keeping 'the largest fleet ever assembled' from being cut down to size." Benedict paused, making sure he had Rascavia's full attention. "The fleet, in its present form, will never leave the Centauran system. The Clans are going to attack. With all of my precautions *and* by the grace of God, I may be able to save the Allied fleet from annihilation."

Rascavia looked at him aghast. "You can't be serious! They would have to be crazy to attack a fleet this size."

"They would have to be crazy not to. Once the two fleets are trained and integrated, they will be unstoppable. The Allied fleet will go from stronghold to stronghold of the Clans, reducing each in turn, until none is left. And then they will be under the vengeful and victorious military rules of governments that grant them a legal status comparable to that of cobras."

"They cannot muster the numbers for a successful attack," Rascavia insisted.

"Perhaps you are correct," Benedict said. "That will not stop them from trying. Indeed, I expect them to be numerically inferior. Their vessels may or may not be as good as our own. But man for man, their pilots and gunners completely outclass ours: They are quick, more precise in their reactions; they can operate effectively under much higher g-forces. As nearly as I can calculate it, the advantages of each side cancel out."

Benedict sighed, glancing again into the darkness beyond the window. "Ishige reached the same general conclusions on his own. That was the main reason for the spectacular way he entered our system. He considered that to be the time of maximum vulnerability. He fully expected the appearance of his fleet to trigger an all-out attack."

"And he was wrong," Rascavia said.

"They did not attack," Benedict conceded. "But you must understand that it is much more difficult for them to assemble their forces. Sol and Alpha Centauri are only four light-years apart. The systems controlled by the Clans are as much as twenty light-years apart. And to bring their vessels together from the extreme points, they have to either traverse our space or go around, tripling the distance."

Rascavia was pacing now. "If you are right, when will they attack?"

"I don't know." The stars in the sky outside were dim and ambiguous. "However, the fleet moves out in ten days. Clan intelligence must know that. So it will be before then. Sometime."

The second interlude occurred three days later.

Benedict walked slowly down the hallway to his

apartments. At every sixth or seventh step, he would stop and breathe deeply. With effort, he could force his eyes to focus. With more effort, he could hold the rolling nausea that threatened in spasms to overwhelm him.

His door was open. Father Barbet somewhat guiltily put down his glass of sherry. "The door was keyed to my thumbprint," he explained, "and your recording *did* invite me to make myself at home—" He stopped, regarding Benedict narrowly. "Are you well, Brother Benedict?"

Benedict allowed himself to be assisted to a chair. He let his head loll back and closed his eyes. "I am—as well as can be expected. No, don't call the doctor. A couple of tranquilizers from the bed stand will do. And a glass of that sherry wouldn't be amiss."

Barbet found the tranquilizers and handed them to Benedict with the sherry. Benedict crushed the capsules over the glass and began to sip slowly.

"As part of today's exercises," Benedict explained, "we played through a scenario in which my command ship was under attack. The idea was both to give my crew some training in evasive tactics—they've had very little to do the past few days—and to see how well the rest of the fleet would do without my constant oversight and correction.

"My crew did very well. The fleet did acceptably. I thought I was going to die."

Benedict paused for a sip. His stomach knotted up, pulling him forward. He forced slow deep breaths through clenched teeth. The muscles slowly relaxed.

Barbet was watching him with concern. "The brain of a Multi-Neural Capacitant is a finely tuned instrument," Benedict continued. "The very chemistry of the synapses is modified to allow one to think as much as a hundred times more quickly than an unmodified human.

"Unfortunately, there are times when it is too finely tuned. If conscious in $Space_2$, it responds to every

microsecond-long surge and weakening of the damper
fields. For most people, this results in a slight, almost
indefinable discomfort. For me, it is acutely painful. And
after several jumps, I found that I was becoming confused."

He looked up at Barbet with a bitter smile. "I have
fashioned the most potent, most dangerous machine in
the universe. And I am its weakest piece."

Barbet had the look of someone debating what he was
going to say. "I don't like arguing with a sick man—"

"That will be a blessed relief," Benedict murmured.

"—but from what you say, I may not have to. The
Primate is concerned about your elevation to the rank of
Sky Marshal. It is unseemly for a religious to be in command of so much destructive power. Your task is to bring
peace, not to destroy one of the combatants."

"Sometimes the one is necessary for the other," Benedict said seriously. Something in his eyes made Barbet
glance away. "Tell me, Father, are you a pacifist?"

"No, of course not," Barbet replied.

"Then why do you think it unseemly for a religious to
be a commander? Is it the hypocrisy of the steak-eater
whose stomach turns at the sight of a slaughterhouse? A
war either is just or is not. If it is just, why should the
Church be anything less than zealous in its prosecution?
Our God is, as Moses said, a god of war."

Barbet bit back his immediate retort. Benedict was
not simply baiting him. In some obscure way, his answer
was important.

"The particular job—calling—of the Church and
those in it," Barbet began slowly, "is to wait on God's
word and be obedient to it. God is sometimes, well, obscure. So we have to listen very attentively. In time of
war, it is very difficult to listen honestly: The blare of
passions drowns out the voice of conscience.

"A general, now, is not concerned with the niceties of
moral theology. His aim, his proper aim, is victory. Al-

though he is bound as a human being to refrain from atrocities, he is simply not in a position where he can stand back from events and dispassionately weigh the pros and cons of each side.

"The Church has to at least try to do that. That's why many orders such as the Stewards still maintain vows of celibacy and poverty: They are aids to disinterestedness. A disinterestedness that is intolerably strained when we become one of the main combatants.

"You say a war is either just or it is not." Barbet felt himself getting excited, as if he had opened a dusty box, long taken for granted, and found inside intricately wrought jewels. "I challenge that. A war isn't a static thing. It is dynamic. It may begin justifiably and decay through brutality into senseless slaughter. The only way in which the Church can hope to maintain perspective is to stand somewhat apart.

"Besides," Barbet concluded, looking sharply at Benedict, "I understood from your reports that you had been largely successful in making Councilor Epstein doubt the justice of this war. Therefore, you are hardly in the position to assume that as justification of your own role."

Benedict looked up blearily as a sudden lethargy nearly overwhelmed him. He had no taste for arguing with Barbet. Yet because those behind Barbet were at a nexus of events, he forced himself to continue.

"In truth, we have the not uncommon situation where both sides sincerely feel that they are in the right and they are both wrong. And not only are they matched in self-righteous zeal but also in fighting strength. The Allies have the edge, but they would win only after both sides were bled nearly to death, leaving generations of bitterness as their legacy. That can be avoided if this war is ended with one swift, decisive blow. And that is why it is necessary for me to retain the rank of Sky Marshal—"

Barbet opened his mouth as if to object.

"—necessary but not sufficient," Benedict went on.

"For victory to be more than a breathing space between hostilities, we need something more. A basis of understanding. News of which I have been hoping you would bring me."

Barbet looked distinctly unhappy. "There has been movement, but it has been slow. Cardinal Tortini vehemently opposes any change in the Church's official definition of human life. He has substantial support and not a little logic on his side. Three centuries ago, people were killing inconvenient children because they were not defined as human until the umbilical cord was severed. The Church fought long and hard to change that definition to the moment of conception, when human egg unites with human sperm. Tortini argues that if we abandon that definition, that inconsistency will endanger the precarious progress we have made."

Exasperation took the edge off Benedict's exhaustion. "There is always risk," he said. "The point is to recognize the deeper consistency. Humans owe a duty to each other—not just to protect their lives but primarily to recognize each *as* human. Sometimes, though, the line dividing human from nonhuman is not all that clear. So you measure the space of the ambiguity and plant your definition at its extremity, because if your definition is overly inclusive, you've done nothing worse than waste money and make yourself look foolish. But if you've been overly restrictive, then you have licensed murder and horror.

"Three centuries ago the only question was at what point humanity began. Conception was the most logical and morally safest point. But that answer presumed a normal sperm and egg. Now that presumption has been rebutted, and the question has become, How much can you tamper with genetic material and still have a human being result?"

Benedict passed his hand across his eyes. "I don't

know the answer to that. I do know that it is a question that must be answered. Soon."

"I can understand why you take this so personally, but—"

"You're goddamn right I take it personally!" Benedict said. "But that is not the reason the Church has to decide. I saw your face when I told you that it was necessary for me to be Sky Marshal. You thought I was boasting or using alleged necessity to cloak my own ambition.

"Believe this: What I said was literally true. But even if I were to decimate the fleet of the Clans tonight, the job would only be half finished. Because without some link of recognition between both parties, there can never be any relationship other than fear, exploitation, and warfare.

"I am Grandfather Fox. I am just about as clever and farseeing as my legends credit me with being. I can win this war, but even I cannot establish peace."

The eyes that looked up at Barbet burned like acid. "We both know who may be able to. If he has the courage to take the risk."

After Barbet left, Benedict walked out to the terrace and stretched himself out on the recliner. His stomach was still too upset for food. Instead, he took his glass with him and continued to sip slowly. An evening breeze was gusting off the sea, chopping the water into rolling, spume-topped hills. He felt he could watch it forever, and the shifting patterns of light across the water would move so quickly that only for an instant might they seem to disclose—a human figure, a vessel, perhaps only the hint of something completely unnameable.

He considered the meeting just finished. Perhaps more important than the Primate's urging that he resign as Sky Marshal was the fact that he had not ordered him to do so. He wondered if he would. He wondered if he would obey such an order.

The sky darkened. After a while the glass slipped from his hand. The air became colder, and he huddled more closely into himself. Just before dawn the wind stilled. It was now so cold that he floated halfway to consciousness, vaguely aware that he should get up and go inside to his bed.

His eyes opened. Three stars shone against a dark blue sky. Below them, a line of brightness was beginning to define the horizon. The brightest of those stars, he remembered, was Sol.

As he watched, the three stars were joined by a fourth companion. And then another.

Undefined alarm gave him the power to get up from the recliner and stumble through his apartment. Even now, he was not yet awake enough to know what had frightened him so.

He was halfway to the dropshaft when the sirens went off.

XVII

BENEDICT THREW HIMSELF INTO THE COMMCHAIR AND
snapped stomach and chest belts in place. At his nod,
MacAndrews began the final check.

"De Toledano."

"Both drive systems go."

"Kirsten."

"Nav and communications all green."

"Younger."

"Ready."

"Dalton."

"All affirmative."

"Kirsten, sound a priority one clearance. We're going
up at five gees, and I don't want any fool blundering into
us."

The hangar hatch above them opened. The *Gryffon's
Pride* lifted quickly into the brightening dawn sky. Increasing acceleration pressed Benedict ever more heavily into the water-filled acceleration couch. His breathing
became slow and labored. Cheeks and lips pulled themselves back from his face in a grimace, vainly seeking
separation from his skull.

"Three heavy cruisers at seven o'clock." Kirsten reported. "They're moving away, maybe for an attack run on Pierpont.

"Dreadnought bearing down dead ahead!"

The dreadnought fired before she finished speaking. As the beam from its laser cannon touched the skin of the *Gryffon's Pride*, three things happened simultaneously. Coolant in the hull raced through the area under attack, trying to dissipate the laser's heat. The vessel twisted 180 degrees, again trying to keep the heat from building up to a melt-through but at the same time presenting a smaller target to the attacker.

And then it threw itself into an instant ten-gee acceleration, at right angles to the attacker's vector. Through slitted lids, Benedict watched the dreadnought plunge by them and continue on down.

"Must have just been swatting at any Allied vessel in its way," MacAndrews muttered. "Thank God it wasn't serious about going after us!"

They were high enough now that the atmosphere of Chiron had become visible as a brilliant blue-white band girdling the planet. To the west, where it was still night, spots of light blossomed and grew like luminous flowers unfolding in the darkness. On the surface, firestorms would be making a false dawn. Benedict wrenched his attention away from the battle below and started taking input from the forward sensors.

The sky was falling.

Thousands of shards of every size and with varying velocities coated the sky above them. They were descending quickly. Calculating number and position was made harder by the snowy haze that tended to white out everything.

"It *is* snow," Benedict breathed. "They've blown up the comets."

He remembered approaching Chiron for the first time with Chiang and being amazed at the comet nuclei that had been pulled from parabolic orbits around Centaurus

A and thrown into orbit around Chiron, where they waited like floating icebergs to be carved up and sent below to increase the water budget of the semiarid planet. The Clans had speeded up that process considerably. Most of the shards would burn up in the atmosphere, doing no damage to the surface. But up here they effectively cut off any view of the battle above.

And with velocities approaching six kilometers a second, they would have explosive impact.

"The main component of velocity is still the orbital speed they had before they were blown apart," MacAndrews announced. "I'm going to match direction and velocity as much as I can as we go through. Gunners, set your lasers on minimum power and cycling time. I don't want anything larger than three centimeters getting within fifty meters of us."

They entered the cloud of debris. Then forward lasers stuttered rapidly, like apologetic machine guns. There were quick, unpredictable jerks sideways as MacAndrews dodged something too big to vaporize at such low power. Several times Benedict was thrown forward sharply against his restraining belts as the *Gryffon's Pride* plowed into an evanescent atmosphere created by its lasers.

Then, suddenly, they were above most of it. Ruptured comets spread out beneath them like fog. Scattered chunks of ice above the main mass caught the sunlight and threw it back in dazzling coruscations.

A new sun erupted on the western edge of the planet. Benedict shut his eyes against the glare even as the screen automatically dimmed to compensate, leaving only a rolling ball of incandescence visible.

"That was one of our battlestars," Kirsten said in a shaken voice. "I've been trying to raise some of the others, but all I get on my screen is wreckage and very, *very* hot gas. Maybe on the other side of the planet—"

"I doubt it," Benedict said crisply. "The Clans have

just proved my point about the vulnerability of battlestars. Let me see what is left of the fleet."

Bestial ships flitted in and out of range on attack runs. A few squadrons of Centauran ships were following the attackers and engaging them, as they had been trained. Too many, though, were milling around helplessly. There were no Terrestrial vessels in evidence.

"Time to retreat and reform. Put me on the general command channel," Benedict said to Kirsten.

The blare of static was nearly deafening. Kirsten turned down the volume and began spinning through the channels.

"They've got screamers in several of their ships," Kirsten reported. "They're drowning out all the communication channels with static. There's no way a general call will get through."

"How can they be communicating with their own ships?" Benedict demanded.

Kirsten frowned as she tried to extract meaning from the aural chaos. "There seems to be . . . gaps . . . in the static at predetermined intervals. I find the same thing on all the channels. My guess is that if you know the sequence of channel changes, you can get all signal and no static. But we don't know the sequence."

"These bastards learn too well," Benedict muttered. "All right, then. Give me tight beams to the dreadnoughts seriatim, with an order to relay instantly."

Kirsten nodded. Benedict tapped a key with each index finger. There was an instant countermand. Turner-Smith's face appeared on screen.

"Sir, the Bestials are making bombing runs on Chiron. We can't retreat now. We must stop them."

"The attack on Chiron is a diversion," Benedict snapped back. "As soon as we move away from the planet, they will come after us. There are only two realities: their fleet and ours. This war will be won or lost in the next few hours depending on what happens to these fleets. Our necessary first move is to retreat. Confirm."

His fingers hovered over the keyboard. In an instant, commands could be transmitted that would trigger an attack of Centauran vessels against a craft that only later they would realize had belonged to one of their own generals. At Pearl, he had been bluffing when he had threatened to attack one of his own ships for disobedience. To be sure, it would be a shame to kill a man for excessive love of his planet—especially since he had demonstrated the intelligence to move his command post from the too-vulnerable battlestars. Mèffert and the others had not been so wise. Yet appalled as Benedict felt at his own ruthlessness, he had no doubt that he would eliminate Turner-Smith in the most expeditious manner available if the General continued to balk at his command.

Something of this must have communicated itself to Turner-Smith. "Confirmed," he said.

Benedict touched the command keys again.

Jump!

Through a red haze, Benedict saw the blips of the Centauran fleet tumbling into existence around him. He stroked the keys again, pulling the vessels around him into a dynamic matrix, bringing each ship except those on the outermost perimeters into position where it could be protected by six other ships. The overall shape of the fleet was a sphere, but a sphere whose component parts surged and pulsed like schools of interstellar fish, smoothly changing patterns from moment to moment so that no attacker could be quite certain what their disposition would be during the next second.

Chiron was off to port, several times smaller than it had been before jump. On Benedict's screen, the Bestial ships seemed to be buzzing around the planet like bees disturbed from their hive. By now they must have spotted the Centauran Fleet.

And there was still no sign of Ishige!

The perimeters were most vulnerable, Benedict decided. He moved more ships to the outer layers, strengthening the interlocking defenses. At his direction, MacAndrews attached the *Gryffon's Pride* to one of the "schools" of ships erratically making their way from the center to the outer edges of the fleet.

Bestial ships suddenly blotted out the screens, terrifyingly close. Lasers on the *Gryffon's Pride* automatically fired on the incoming missiles, but there was no such defense against the Bestial lasers that were pouring energy into the ship's hull.

Benedict lunged at his override panel. From the corner of his eye, he could see MacAndrews stabbing at her controls, so he could not be sure which of them activated the quantum drive as he yelled:

"Jump!"

A second later, light caught up with them and they could see the ships that had attacked them burst into searing brilliance under the attack of the surrounding Centauran vessels.

"MacAndrews," Benedict rasped, his head throbbing so violently that his vision blurred with each beat. "They must have noted our vector. They'll be coming after us. Shift vector—"

But MacAndrews was already responding. The ship pivoted on its gyros and began accelerating. Benedict rapped out orders to the rest of the fleet, at the same time giving Kirsten a set of coordinates.

He had just finished when Bestial ships sprang from nothingness, hurling missiles and laser fire at them.

Jump!

*   *   *

Thirty light cruisers were arrayed on the vector line defined by the *Gryffon's Pride* when it had entered Space$_2$. On any command screen they would appear identical.

The Bestials leapt into existence—and paused, momentarily uncertain of their target. In that instant, the Centauran ships on every side of them unleashed a barrage.

Younger was cursing happily, glad to be dealing out punishment instead of running from it. Benedict shared that savage exultation, even as a Bestial ship that had been closing on them detonated, converting itself to energy with such fury that he could feel the heat radiate in from the hull.

The cruisers closed interval, disappearing from instrument readings within the clouds of ionized gas that were all that remained of the attackers. Inside the clouds, they shifted vectors and jumped again into Space$_2$, surfacing throughout the fleet.

"Damage report," MacAndrews commanded.

"Quantum drive is partially destabilized," de Toledano replied. "We have lost Space$_3$ and Space$_4$ capability."

"We weren't going to use that, anyway," MacAndrews commented. "What about Space$_2$?"

"Still available. And we have full maneuverability in Space$_1$."

"Good enough. Gunners."

Benedict peered at the screen, striving to control the shivering and nausea that had nearly blotted out every other reality. He inhaled just one breath of painkiller, hoping it would dull at least some of the pain without appreciably blunting his alertness.

The Bestial fleet still hovered above Chiron. Something was wrong. They should have launched an all-out attack as soon as their attempt to get him had failed.

". . . good, except that aiming response on the lasers is slow," Younger was saying. "Some laser fire must have splashed in the gunport and overheated the universal joints."

"Navigation."

It was almost, Benedict decided, as if they were being distracted, kept off balance. Something seemed to flicker at the far range of his instruments, but he was suffering such extensive retinal feedback that it might have been illusory.

". . . so far," Kirsten was saying, "but a few times the needles tried to smash through the red end of the dials. If we get many more hits that close, our superconductors will flash over and turn into insulators."

"I'd like to promise that won't happen," MacAndrews said, "but I don't know how the hell they picked on us to begin with."

My fault, my fault, my most grievous fault . . .

He had told them himself, Benedict realized bitterly. When he had assembled the fleet after the first jump, he had ordered each contingent into position as it surfaced. Between the ships' appearance and the time they altered vectors there had been a gap: the time it took light from them to reach Benedict, and then the time for his orders to reach them. Since the ships had surfaced at different distances from the *Gryffon's Pride*, the gap had been reflected in the different lengths of time it took each ship to take up position. Some smart computer technician in the Clans' fleet must have extrapolated those gaps to get the position of the *Gryffon's Pride*. And just to make things easy for him, she *had* been in the obvious place, the very center of her fleet.

From now on, he thought, I'll put a pause on some of my commands so that their program will give spurious emana—

Suddenly the Bestials exploded into activity. Then the battlestars appeared on Benedict's screen. Evenly spaced along the diameter of the Bestial fleet, they accelerated into the center of the Bestial formation. Fusion lasers swept out across the sky, vaporizing every Bestial ship they touched. In a second, nearly two hundred flared and disappeared.

The rest of the Bestial fleet vanished. Another three seconds and they commenced attack runs on the battlestars. The battlestars, zigzagging at twelve gees acceleration, were not the easiest of targets. Nonetheless, one after another erupted in fiery brilliance. Benedict pressed a series of buttons, sending fighters off after the attacking Bestials.

And then, shimmering into reality like a mirage, an entire fleet appeared above Benedict, tier after tier extending upward in diminishing perspective.

Ishige's face appeared on his screen. "It appears that battlestars do have some uses, after all. Especially once one has abandoned them and sent them in under the guidance of their programming. You may now show us the same is true for Multi-Neural Capacitants."

It took an instant for Benedict to realize the extent of the invitation. Taking command, he hurled Ishige's fleet at the Bestials.

It was a strange, almost ghostly battle. Were one drifting through the battlespace in a ship too badly damaged to take part in the conflict, the first thing one might notice would be the quiet. The Bestials' screamers had been turned off after their numbers had been so depleted as to render them ineffective. Still, most ships continued to communicate by narrow beams for security reasons. There was, therefore, almost complete radio silence.

Nor was there much of anything to see. Hundreds of ships were loosing energies at each other that would have been unimaginable a generation earlier, yet in the volume of space in which they were fighting, it would be only coincidence if one saw either the Cerenkov wake of a vessel surfacing from quantum space or the pinpoint glare of a missile detonating.

One could float in one's coffinlike craft across the length of the battlespace and imagine that there was not another living being for light-years.

Even to Benedict, the battle had an abstract air. He hunched over his console, his face illuminated by the glow of the viewscreen. The rest of the cabin was nearly lightless. Here and there in the dark, a face would be silhouetted by the green glow of an instrument panel. The *Gryffon's Pride* drifted with a slight roll, a weak distress signal spiraling out from it, as it sought to evade notice by imitating war debris.

Brother Timothy had once compared Benedict's skill with a computer to that of Johann Sebastian Bach at the organ. As his fingers whisked over the keyboard, Benedict felt for the first time the justness of the comparison. Engagements in different sections of space formed polyphonal counterpoint with each other. Wave after wave of ships attacked, retreated, and attacked again in bewildering *fugato* complexity.

Bach, however, had never played an organ that fought back. As the Bestials counterattacked, the image in Benedict's mind altered, and he saw himself as Liszt, pounding one of the latter's more intricate and darker compositions, expending all his passion and energy to bring order to an ever wilder cataract of notes.

These images flitted quickly around the edges of his thoughts like half-forgotten dreams. His main attention was focused on the viewscreen, watching multicolored dots race and swirl through three dimensions, throw themselves viciously against each other—and disappear as if swept from the board by an invisible games master.

He noted with distant gratification that he had judged rightly the relative strengths of the two fleets. Ship for ship the Bestials were faster, more maneuverable, quicker responding, and more aggressive. Yet that very aggressiveness could be used against them. A slow-moving, disorganized Allied squadron would always draw an attack. And as long as Benedict kept the Allied fleet in retreat, giving the Bestials the illusion of continued victories, he could hope they would ignore the fact that their losses were substantially greater than those of the Allies.

In the upper left-hand corner of his screen, the ratio flickered under the computer's continual adjustment, the upper figure jaggedly increasing and decreasing but generally growing larger as the bottom figure shrank correspondingly. He expected it to reach unity in less than ten minutes—at which point it would be impossible for the Bestials to turn the tide of the battle.

"Sky Marshal Rénard." Ishige's face appeared on the communication screen. Transmission data displayed at the base of the screen indicated that the message was being received in code as part of a general, nondirectional transmission.

"I regret that I must withdraw all Terrestrial Commonwealth units from this battle. My orders state that I must disengage and return to the Solar System in the event my casualties exceed sixty percent. That has now occurred. I am giving you ninety seconds' warning before jump. Good luck."

Benedict felt the shock spread through the ship like a physical impact.

"'Good luck'!" MacAndrews exclaimed. "Why, that cowardly, cocksucking—"

"Cut it off!" Benedict ordered. "Ishige has given us time. I intend to use it."

His fingers flew frantically across the keys. Centauran units coalesced into groups of three and jumped to individual Bestial units scattered around the circumference of the battle, enveloping them in cocoons of high-energy violence.

Ishige's fleet disappeared. The Bestial commander seemed to hesitate, as if expecting the Terrestrial fleet to reappear at any moment, countering any move he might make.

The Centauran triads continued eating their way into the Bestial fleet, jumping, striking, and jumping again too quickly for the Bestials to organize effective resistance.

The Bestial vessels vanished abruptly, reappearing seconds later—reformed in a more densely packed sphere, closely resembling Benedict's initial formation for the Centauran fleet. He nodded appreciatively. His generals were probably wondering why the Bestials, now that they had numerical superiority, had retreated to a defensive position.

In the next few minutes, they would realize that it made excellent sense. A sphere protected the maximum number of vessels while exposing the minimum number to attack. To be sure, Benedict could jump ships right into the midst of the Bestials, but then his ships would come under fire from all sides. The best he would be able to hope for under those conditions would be a one-for-one trade-off. Under present conditions, that meant Bestial victory.

The alternative tactic, attacking the surface of the Bestial fleet and destroying it layer by layer, would increase the favorability of the trade-off. But not enough. The Bestial commander, whether Gubbio Lupus or someone totally unknown to Benedict, was inviting the Centauran fleet to break itself on the Bestial formation.

His opponent had learned quickly. He was adopting not only Benedict's formation but also the strategy that went with it. He would not be as quick as a Multi-Neural Capacitant to see openings for attack, but he would not have to be to maintain a static defensive position.

"Still, my commanders have military discipline ingrained in them," Benedict said softly, "while you people of the Clans have fought most of this war in small packs, relying largely on individual flexibility and initiative. And to assemble a fleet this large, many of you must be young. Hardly beyond *testrarch*."

His fingers moved lightly over the keys. Centauran fighters flickered around the circumference of the Bestial fleet, surfacing and jumping too quickly to be fired upon, too quickly even to fire accurately themselves. Nonetheless, a few Bestial dots disappeared from the screen.

Within the sphere, there was quick, convulsive movement—which abruptly stilled. Benedict smiled.

He touched another series of keys. The pace of attacks stepped up. They were still doing little visible damage. Psychologically it should be another matter. To be inside the sphere, able to do nothing as an enemy attacked at will, to foresee the erosion of the sphere and the necessity of having to fight without being able to maneuver freely...

At Benedict's direction, a volume of space a third of a light-second from the Bestials began to fill with Centauran ships, which paused only briefly before jumping again. The intensity of the attacks increased. The Bestials would realize quickly that from their advance staging point the Centaurans were able to jump with devastating precision. Benedict could almost feel the pressure building on them.

Holes appeared inside the Bestial sphere as small packs broke formation, jumping to the staging point to engage the Centaurans. Even though Benedict had been waiting for this, it now seemed to him that his body moved too slowly, that he could not force his fingers to respond quickly enough to the data that were pouring across the screen.

Three keys depressed, and the ships that had been shuttling into the staging point were shunted around it, directly into the gaps left by the packs. Quickly, quickly, he thought, before they adjust their formation and flow into those spaces. He hit four more keys. Centauran cruisers and dreadnoughts jumped to areas of the sphere above the gaps. Missile salvos exploded in circles of harsh radiance as the ships blasted their way through the perimeter.

Now! Benedict thought. Hit them inside and outside and crack them like a nut before their commander realizes the extent of his peril and retreats.

Again the commands went out from his keyboard, hurling reinforcements into the fray. His fingers swept across the keyboard in a quickening staccato—

—and paused. In his haste, he had neglected to put delays on his commands.

"Evasive action," he called.

The *Gryffon's Pride* came about immediately under MacAndrews's expert handling. Five gees' acceleration thrust the craft onto a new vector.

Lasers lanced through the space they had just occupied. Bestial vessels crowded his screen into incoherence. Younger and Dalton released the rest of their missiles, knowing they could hardly help finding enemy targets, and immediately began firing laser bursts at the nearest vessels. From the corner of his eye, Benedict saw Kirsten hit a red button, transferring a set of coordinates from her readout to MacAndrews's.

Restraining straps bit into his ribs and thighs as the ship dodged laterally. A futile maneuver against lasers at this distance, he thought irritably.

Coolant roared through the hull.

Jump!

—screamed. Or thought he did. For a second the shock banished the ability to feel anything. His screen showed them surrounded by friendly blue dots: Centauran vessels. MacAndrews and Kirsten were talking to each other. The tones were clear: terse, excited, with a tightly reined hint of fear. Yet somehow, the words failed to carry any meaning.

His left hand was clenching and unclenching, totally without his volition.

Red dots peppered the screen, jumping in recklessly close to the Centaurans and to each other. He was looking at his death, Benedict thought with an instant, dreadful certainty. They could neither fight nor evade so many craft willing to sacrifice themselves to destroy him.

Then, even as the dots began to connect themselves with lines of searing energy, yet more Bestials poured in and—

—jumped into Space, coordinates already occupied by other vessels.

Quantum drives disrupted, forming halos of total mass-energy conversion. The universe became a ravening white negative of itself. For an instant, Benedict knew what it must be like to be within a supernova.

Jump.

Thus we pay the final price of stupidity, the Rénard thought.

Heat flowed from all sides of the cabin, scorching the air. Somewhere behind him was a hissing. The air was sickly sweet with the smell of coolant.

You don't understand the stakes, Brother Benedict responded. *We are dealing with souls here, not mere empires.*

"We have company," Kirsten said. "Three Bestials made that jump with us. I think they're still suffering overload from the blowup, but that'll probably clear in a second."

"Give me jump coordinates," MacAndrews demanded.

"Negative that," de Toledano interjected. "This drive is on the edge of destabilization. Give me some time to bleed off the excess energy."

The Rénard is correct, Valentino said. *I told you long ago that you must master your enemies, not fly from them. Too late have you realized this. Your attempt to hide from them was as futile as your attempt to hide from yourself.*

But then Valentino grew silent under Allele's watchful gaze.

The three Bestials began closing on them. MacAndrews brought the *Gryffon's Pride* along a tangent, letting the first vessel within range as it eclipsed the second.

"Dark area on the bottom," Younger said to Dalton. "Aim for it." A warship's almost perfectly reflective surface was its first line of defense, able to throw back into space ninety-five percent of any laser pulse. This vessel, however, had seen uncomfortably close action, and part of the hull had been seared black. The captain had rotated his vessel to keep most of the blackened area away from the *Gryffon's Pride*.

But not quite far enough. Younger and Dalton fired. The abdomen of the craft ruptured, spewing air and debris into space. Some of the pieces were human shaped.

The wreckage hurtled on past them. The other two were drawing quickly within range. They would have about ten seconds to fire before they, too, shot on past.

Laser beams converged on the *Gryffon's Pride*. Alarms shrilled.
Jump.

The engines groaned, thrusting them into a new vector. *Jump.*

The boy was crying. He tried to choke back the sobs, knowing the penalty for weakness. But fear and desperation overwhelmed him, erupted into a wail spiraling upward in pitch and intensity.

De Toledano shut down the drive, cutting off the alarm.

"Quantum drive is down," he reported, only the slightest tremor in his voice disclosing how near they had been to total disruption. "I can still give you three gees acceleration. For a while."

"Port batteries are inoperative," Dalton said.

"Starboard batteries just barely operational," Younger stated.

Benedict saw the child staring up at him from the console, crying quietly now. A teardrop slipped from his cheek to splash on the clear plastic.

It was in this transparent case, the boy explained, eyes distant with remembered horror. *Half the head was cut away. I could see the smooth, white bone of the cheek, the dark hollow of the eye socket....And above that, even the skull had been cut away, and I could see the folds of the brain case, wrinkled up like worms crawling over each other*.

And the other half was my face!

"Rénard," Kirsten said. "Get us some cover, quick!"

MacAndrews gave him only a brief glance. "I can't even tell if he's alive in this light. Space$_2$ jumps, even with damping fields, cause surges of synaptic overload. I may have killed him with that last series of jumps.

"We're on our own. I'm programming our computer to flip our starboard side to face any attacker. I also intend to close in the event of attack, since we can't really run. That way we'll be in range for a shorter period of time. Maybe get to take one or more of the bastards with us."

There was silence. Shadows moved fitfully, given form as they blotted out the red warning lights on the consoles. He felt the boy try to huddle aside as a new presence entered. Valentino and the Rénard ceased their background murmuring to watch the approach with trepidation. The newcomer was tall, with snow-white hair swept back from advanced widow's peaks. Pale, almost translucent skin sheathed a dome-shaped skull and fine, oddly angular bones. The eyes were a mild, light blue yet were disconcerting: They focused not on the listener but rather six inches behind him.

He looked at—through—Benedict. *So you, too, have failed me. I had such hopes once. Pity. Still, there may be something salvageable: a ligament, a length of bone, an interesting cluster of neurons, perhaps.*

His image blocked the console screen. Benedict strained to see through Snowden's ghostly presence, to discern the color of the dots dancing slowly across the screen.

Get out of the way! Benedict commanded. *If I can't call for help, the Clans will kill us all.*

The Clans, Snowden mused. *Yes, I was much more successful at creating lions than I was at making foxes. Hear them roaring, now! They were created for strength, and they are perfect at it.*

His hand reached out as if to seize Benedict. *Whereas you were made for calculation but have been good only for deceit. And finally, in your rebellion against me you have deceived yourself into believing that there is One greater than I am and that you are a holy man serving Him. Well, back into the vats—*

He stopped, surprised, as his right eye began to wink on and off. Greenly. All the voices within Benedict stilled themselves. Snowden faded into nothingness. The green square continued to blink. Only Centauran vessels showed on the screen.

"Kirsten, get me General Turner-Smith. Or if he has been killed, whoever is next in line," Benedict snapped.

From the way she started at his voice, it might have seemed that he had come back from the dead. Nonetheless, she soon had Turner-Smith's image on his screen. Sweat had plastered the General's hair to his skull, and his eyes looked slightly wild—signs that his own vessel had not escaped unscathed.

"General, the *Gryffon's Pride* suffered heavy damage during the last engagement. I am directing Captain MacAndrews to return us to Pierpont. I am relinquishing command of the fleet to you. Be sure to post pickets in case the Clans are lurking just outsystem for another attack."

He turned off the screen, hardly waiting for Turner-Smith's reply. His last thought was of the instructions he must now give MacAndrews.

And then everything slipped away from him.

XVIII

SLEEP WAS DEEP AND DREAMLESS . . . UNTIL THAT PARA-doxical moment when he became just conscious enough to know that he was still sleeping. And then he thought/dreamed of sleep as a deep, cold lake and himself as swimming in the shadowy depths. As he swam, the cold seemed to penetrate every cell, cleansing each capillary until it was as pure and clean as crystal, stilling his mind until it was almost transparent, infusing his spirit with refreshment and strength.

He could continue in this silent, twilit realm. Or he could rise to the light of day. He considered and then let himself float to the surface.

He opened his eyes. Wind buffeted the glass door to the terrace. The slant of the sun told him it was early afternoon.

He sat up. An MPR unit, much like the one Chiang had put at his disposal on Neoptolemus, glided over to him.

"Good day, sir," the robot said. "May I do a health check on you?"

"Yes," he said, holding out his arm so that the robot could slip over it the cuff that would take his blood pressure as well as monitor all his other bodily functions. He felt a soreness on his upper arm and at the same time saw the jet-injector in one of the robot's other appendages.

The cuff deflated in bursts, releasing him.

"You are doing well, sir," the robot announced. "Dr. Russell has been in to see you twice and is pleased at your progress. He is on call if you need him. He wishes you to take these every four hours." The robot handed him a box of pills. "These are mild tranquilizers supplemented with calcium and lithium to ensure that your synapses maintain their proper timing."

He took the box and, under the robot's watchful lenses, obediently took a pill.

"Mrs. Chiang has also checked on your condition," the robot continued. "She thought you would like to have this." The robot uncoiled a tentacle, allowing him to take the cassette it held.

"Do you have any instructions, sir?"

"Breakfast. A waffle with maple syrup. Bacon. A large orange juice. A pot of coffee." The Stewards served such breakfasts only on feasts as major as Christmas or Easter. And even then the syrup would be imitation.

"Yes, sir."

The MPR unit moved off to the kitchen area. Benedict stood, found his habit newly cleaned, and dressed himself, marveling once again at the simple utilitarianism of this sturdy garment with its belted sleeves and heat vents, retractable hood and dust mask. He turned to the mirror.

"I am Brother Benedict of the Order of Stewards." He licked his lips, half expecting the image to challenge that statement. "Once I was Paul Niccolo Rénard. In too many ways, I suppose, I still am. But for the most part that *has* been put behind me."

As he began to turn away, another face overshadowed his own. Benedict felt a chill of recognition.

"You were wrong. It was not to spite you that I joined the Order. And even if that had been the reason—sometimes we do the right thing despite flawed motives."

The MPR unit came back with his brunch.

Well, he thought, settling himself down to eat. "It may not be sanity, but it will have to do.

As he ate, he punched himself into the TRANSCENDA-TRAN index and ordered hard copy on several war-related items. Most of it he already knew firsthand; in several minor respects it was inaccurate. He skimmed quickly through the material, reading for tone rather than content. Most of the reports noted, at least in passing, that the attacking Bestial forces had been numerically inferior to the combined Centauran fleet and Solar Expeditionary Force.

Turner-Smith, at his press conference, had commented on the daring of the Bestial attack and on the bravery and expertise of the Bestial fighters. This was at least as self-serving as it was gallant: It was the best face that could be put on getting no more than a draw from engaging an enemy force of half his strength.

Give him his due, though. When asked to name the most important factor in their "victory," he had answered without hesitation: "Sky Marshal Rénard. If he had not taken command when he did, forced us to retreat and regroup, we would have been hacked apart piecemeal."

Overall, the news coverage treated the Bestials as feared but respected adversaries. No such respect was shown to the Solar Expeditionary Force. Columnists and editorial writers universally condemned the "cowardice," "disloyalty," and even "narcissism" of the Terrestrials and their dependents. A flood of resolutions in the General Council called for severing diplomatic relations with Earth. Rascavia had been able to defeat these in the

Inner Council and would probably continue to do so. But the Alliance was shattered.

Benedict finished his meal. He picked up the cassette Bobbi had delivered to him and inserted it in a viewer.

A holographic ghost sprang up. Nearly six feet tall, his wide, athletic shoulders amply filled the white cassock in which he was dressed. Gravely humorous blue eyes gazed from a round, dark-skinned face. Australasian population shifts had made any classic racial classification impossible.

"Ex semine Adam," he began. "The seed of Adam..." The voice was soft yet clear. A slight, almost musical quaver in the intonation betrayed a Chinese cultural influence.

On the surface it was like listening to a legal brief being argued orally. The groundwork was laid with a recitation of facts, in this case a history of practical genetics beginning with Gregor Mendel and continuing up through the previous generation's disastrous wave of experimentation. Paired against these snippets of history were selected excerpts from Scripture, the Church Fathers, and previous encyclicals.

Benedict closed his eyes, listening intently. Beneath the overly fine distinctions and the dry recitations, a tremendous battle raged. Words were woven into a net to catch and guide the most powerful forces of hatred and fear the century had produced. Save for its utter necessity, it was a foolishly audacious enterprise. Nor could it proceed without compromise, for this document must not merely state the truth—it must convince, it must change actions. An excess of unpalatable truth would relegate it to academic oblivion, often quoted, never followed. Thus, "novel theologies that would recognize the personhood of chimpanzees, dolphins, and certain self-programming computers are matters that need not be resolved at this time."

That done, the speaker brought his exposition to its

climax. "Therefore, I, Leo XV, servant of the servants of God, do hereby declare and define as human all those who partake of Adam's seed, to whatever degree, and who can call upon God as Father. All such shall be acknowledged as His children. Among these are all so-called Bestials, Multi-Neural Capacitants—"

The room seemed to roar and recede. Benedict gripped the arms of his chair to steady himself.

"—Satyrs, Savants, and Succubae. This list is only partial. It shall be expanded according to the principles enunciated above, for we have only begun to fathom these mysteries. Nonetheless, we can say that we are all God's children now; what we shall be later has not yet come to light."

The storm swept across the placid, early afternoon sky with little warning. A sharply defined line of clouds raced in from the west, cutting off the sunlight like a cosmic curtain. Rain began to fall, lightly at first, then with increasing violence as gusts from the hills drove the rain almost horizontally along the streets of Pierpont.

Benedict stepped off the hovertrain. Even in the station he could smell traces of ammonia and other, more exotic gases, all witness to the millions of years the ice had traveled the depths of space before being blasted from orbit. He took the underground tunnel to the chancery. The foyer was crowded with cots. Families talked together in low tones. Benedict glimpsed the sheen of plastiflesh on many of them. He made his way to the secretary's desk and asked for Archbishop Kourdakov, only to learn that he was out at one of the blast sites, helping direct emergency relief. Father Barbet had been in and out all day. If he was still in, he would most likely be back in the Archbishop's office.

The hallway was crowded. People slept or tried to sleep in some of the offices. Others rooms were piled high with food and medical and sanitary supplies. The doorway to Kourdakov's office was jammed with people waiting to get in. Looking past shoulders, Benedict could see Barbet seated at a large desk, speaking peremptorily at a holoscreen. Assistants were dealing with most of the visitors, giving them orders, receiving information, directing them to other parts of the chancery.

Benedict suddenly saw again the matrix he had envisioned while waiting to see Gubbio Lupus. It had been under tension, each piece resolutely seeking a nonoptimal position. That tension had increased—Benedict gasped silently, abruptly gaining access to a repressed memory—almost to the point of explosion during the battle of Allied and Bestial fleets.

Even here, the matrix was under tension. But now it functioned like a powerful motor under load. Information was received and processed, orders issued, adjustments made. For now the pieces of the matrix were set not against each other, as they had been, but in harmony. And with the combined and subtle pressure of all the pieces, reality itself was beginning to flow and shift.

Barbet was clearly deluged with work. Benedict turned to leave.

"Benedict! Don't go," Barbet called. "Thomas, please take the desk. The Sky Marshal and I will be in conference."

He motioned Benedict down the corridor into a small, bare sleeping chamber. Barbet's face was gray with fatigue. His dark-ringed eyes shone with a feverish brightness. There was a tremor in his breathing.

"Stimutabs aren't advised for use over twenty-four hours," Benedict observed. "The heart is strained, blood pressure raised. Judgment becomes faulty."

Barbet shrugged. "Sleep has been an unaffordable luxury the last few days. We have all been busy with relief work. Too often the only thing we could really give was the last rites. Thank God the military's passion for security made them construct their bases out in the desert. If the Clans had bombed closer to Pierpont . . ." He shuddered, thinking of what civilian casualities would have been then.

"As it was, half the bodies were unrecognizable. They were bulldozing mass graves when I was sent back here. There was no sufficient ground defense. Protection was supposed to come from the fleet. I understand it was withdrawn." Exhaustion blurred the challenge in his voice.

Benedict's eyes remained mild and unwavering. "The ground-level attacks were a feint. If I had countered them, our fleet would have been destroyed."

"Instead, those who relied on you were destroyed." Barbet dropped his gaze, suddenly having no appetite for continued argument. "Well, I suppose those are the decisions a Sky Marshal must make."

"They are," Benedict agreed. "And Turner-Smith is welcome to them. I submitted my resignation to First Councilor Rascavia this morning. He has accepted it."

Barbet looked up, surprised. "You have had a change of heart since we last talked."

Benedict shook his head. "My usefulness was not finished then. It is now."

Barbet considered this. "Then what are your plans?"

"I have none. By God's grace, I shall soon be free to be a Steward again, at the disposal of my superiors."

"That I will believe when I see it. Come back when it happens."

Barbet turned to leave. Benedict hesitated.

"I have a favor to ask," he said then.

"Yes?"

Benedict produced his specie card. "When you command a battle fleet, it is easy to become lost in abstractions. Your ships, the men and women in them, become dots on a video arcade screen. You think of positions, vectors, throw weights. When your ships are destroyed, you don't feel the horror of your pilots who are breathing blood into vacuum or your gunners whose flesh has melted from their bones. Instead, you curse the luck that has put you fifty points behind in the game."

He shut his eyes, fighting a distasteful inner vision. "Perhaps that is necessary. Too much of such reality would almost certainly drive one mad. Not that I was troubled by excessive sanity while Sky Marshal.

"But it was different at Pearl. After all the fighting there was a time when I listened to the radio as the Clans tried to rescue their Pack Members from the radioactive wreckage of their battlestars. That was when they stopped being dots, stopped being Bestials, and became human beings suffering the most agonizing deaths imaginable."

"You are telling me you have a conscience," Barbet said flatly.

"Perhaps. I understand your doubt. Guilt is rather pointless when you would do exactly the same thing over again. But I would be reconciled with their ghosts, if nothing else. And now the Pope has made that lawful."

He held out the specie card to Barbet. Barbet took it and inserted it in a thin metal case he had extracted from his wallet. He punched buttons indicating the KDT amount. Benedict pressed the thumb plate, entering the transaction.

"The first Mass will be said tomorrow," Barbet said. "It will undoubtedly cause scandal among the Defender-oriented of the congregation. But best that they see some effect of *Ex semine Adam* immediately. They will like the other changes even less. If they complain about funeral masses for Bestials, I will emphasize to them that a Multi-Neural Capacitant has been fully admitted to holy orders. And let them chew on it."

For the first time that Benedict could remember, he saw a hint of comradeship and acceptance in Barbet's eyes. He found himself irrationally pleased.

"Before I go, I have one other errand. Rascavia has

declared a victory celebration tonight. He has invited
you and the Primate."

"I doubt that either of us will be able to attend." Barbet's smile was bitter. His eyes looked beyond the walls,
through the rooms temporarily crammed with emergency
supplies, the offices swarming with volunteer workers,
and out beyond to where the desert had been melted into
black glass. "We have no victory to celebrate yet."

Benedict entered the ballroom unobserved at first.
The highly polished floor spread out before him, large
enough for three athletic events to take place simultaneously. Space Force officers in their dress whites, dark
blue half-cloaks off their left shoulders, were prominent
in the crowd. The dining areas rose up along the wall,
one on top of another, like terraced mountains.

Then someone recognized him and called out. The
call became a chant and then a thunder:

"SKY MARSHAL! SKY MAR-SHAL! SKY MAR-SHAL!"

The mass of people around him took on a life of its
own, turning into a river that propelled him to a podium.
For an instant he let himself savor the exultation of
power. More than ever before, he understood why
Valentino had forsaken caution, staking everything on a
bid for power.

Valentino! It was gone like a lightning flash, leaving
only the ghostly afterimage of piercing dark eyes set in a
sardonically amused face. Benedict scanned all the faces
turned toward him, many shouting. His brother was not
among them.

A halluncination, then. An aftereffect of the stress of
so many jumps through quantum space. But even so, it
had served its purpose, sobering him. Lust for power
had brought Valentino only death.

He mounted the steps and positioned himself before
the wafer-mike. Caught in the throng below him, pressed
into impotence, Rascavia, Cowan, and Esptein looked

up at him with expressions of fear, anger, and doubt. Benedict tried to smile reassuringly at them.

He held up his hands for silence. "You must restrain yourselves from such adulation," he said when the roar had subsided to a murmur. "Else I shall be forced to launch into 'Toad's Last Song.'" Scattered startled laughter shot through the general incomprehension. "Ah, some of you do still read the classics. There is hope for us yet!

"You have acclaimed your Sky Marshal. Well you should. Earlier today I presented my resignation to the First Councilor, who accepted it. Let me present to you your new Sky Marshal, General Nathan Turner-Smith."

The applause rose again, surprised but no less enthusiastic. Turner-Smith looked uncomfortable as he was urged forward to the podium. From the corner of his eye, Benedict could see the relief on Rascavia's face.

Once again he held up his hands for silence. "Archbishop Kourdakov would have liked to be here with us this evening. Unfortunately, his presence is required with the relief crews. We have won a mighty victory; we have paid a mighty price. Therefore, as my last official act among you, let me do as the Primate would do if he were here and ask for a moment of silent prayer for all those who have fallen."

Benedict bowed his head over his hands. An acute realization of his own vulnerability distracted him from thoughts of the war dead. Dear God, he found himself praying, please let all potential assassins be put off balance enough by my resignation that they will wait for new instructions before pulling any triggers.

He started at a movement at his elbow. Chiang had climbed up beside him.

"I think we would agree that the former Sky Marshal has been far too modest," Chiang said, speaking into the microphone. "I have just been informed that the Bestials have proposed a truce. They wish to send an embassy to bring peace negotiations."

There was a moment of almost disbelieving silence. Then the applause and cheering began again, swelling in an almost explosive crescendo. Chiang let it continue for more than a minute before calling for silence.

"I think, therefore, it is only fitting that the people of Centaurus grant Brother Benedict a fitting reward of his choosing."

The irony was appealing. There was only one thing he really wanted, only one thing the Inner Council was likely to grant him, and only one reason why it would be Chiang rather than Rascavia who would make the offer for the Council. Still, that part of him that was still Rénard was tempted to ask for something absurd, such as being made First Councilor for life.

Firmly repressing that impulse and stepping back to his ordained place in the matrix, he turned his eyes to Chiang. "Councilor, I would have my freedom."

"Done," Chiang said with the barest hint of a smile. "The bond of indenture between us is dissolved. As witnessed." He turned to their audience with a rare smile.

During the ovation that followed, Chiang bent away from the microphone and murmured, "Please come to my table. I would like to talk to you."

Benedict descended from the podium. Van ter Haals and others he didn't recognize pounded him on the back, shouting congratulations and good wishes. Eventually he and Chiang came to the room's edge. With Chiang, Benedict crowded his way onto the small lifting disk and was whisked upward.

He stepped out on Chiang's dining platform.

Bobbi rose to greet him. "I'm pleased to see you again," she said, planting a light kiss on his cheek. He had never before felt so confirmed in his vow of celibacy as he did at the brush of that chaste kiss. He nearly said as much but held back, fearing that she might misunderstand and feel hurt.

There was a cascade of applause, curiously muted. Benedict had to guess that it had been triggered by Turner-Smith's speech, for everything outside their dining platform was blurred as if by heat shimmer.

"Sonic bubble," Chiang explained. "It gives us privacy. Mr. Sun, or course, cleared this area of all eavesdropping devices."

Tension began to coil in the pit of Benedict's stomach. There should be nothing between them now that called for such elaborate precautions.

"Dr. Russell reports that you are fully recovered," Bobbi said. "He was quite concerned for a while. None of us understood the strain quantum shifts put on you."

Benedict smiled. It was part of her art that made her almost totally transparent. Her concern for him was simple and genuine. Yet her lightness of tone was forced. She knew at least something of her husband's intentions and feared them. Chiang stood at the nexus of suddenly disturbing possibilities.

"You said you wished to talk to me," Benedict said, trying to force whatever danger there was into the open.

Yet Chiang looked down at his clasped hands almost shyly. "When we first met, you warned me of the dangers of employing a Multi-Neural Capacitant such as yourself, that you could be useful precisely because you would be able to see...potentialities...beyond my range of vision. And that if I followed your advice in such an instance, I would have to proceed by faith in your goodwill. Which my own actions had done much to destroy. Herter gave me much the same warning, advising me to drop any plan of using you. My wife said the same thing from her perspective, that there could be no honesty between master and slave."

Chiang looked up, slightly defiant yet with a tangle of other emotions Benedict could not read. "I ignored them all. Without you I was finished. You could hardly devise a doom worse or more certain than that I already faced.

"By luck—grace, Bobbi would say—you were faithful in your forced service. More than faithful. I asked only for a return of the status quo, for mere existence. In return, you have made me the second most important member of the Inner Council. I hear that I am now called Warlord and that some say that I have not used the refugees as a private space force to force a coup only because it does not suit my present whim. I am more feared, more respected, more powerful than ever before.

"That, however, is not what I desired. No, do not protest! You assured and strengthened my position on the Council, as you were instructed. Yet I wanted that position only to ensure the continued growth of Chiang Biosynthetics. And I wanted that not as a power base but so that I could do what I really wanted to do as a scientist. To explore. To discover. To see the interrelationships of living things and how those could be modified to be more useful or pleasing.

"So. I am Councilor, I am Master of Chiang Biosynthetics. Perhaps I am even Warlord. But I am these only because I am first of all a scientist. I wish to know. I wish to know about you."

Benedict sighed, his expression wistful. "I cannot fully explain myself to myself, much less to you."

"I do not request a full analysis. I wish the answer to one question. I have given you freedom before asking it, in the hope that that may allow honesty. Perhaps you will fear to give the truth now. If so, say nothing. But later, when you feel yourself far away or well enough hidden, send me a message with the truth.

"Tell me, Benedict, why you destroyed the alliance between Centaurus and the Terrestrial Confederation, why you took what would have been a certain victory and turned it into a stalemate."

Strains of music drifted through the sonic bubble. The

speeches had ended, and dancers had taken to the floor. They moved with slow grace, impressionistically conceived flowers floating in a stream.

"That would be a terrible thing," Benedict said softly. "Worse than being a traitor for the Bestials. Then, at least, I would be true to something, would be attempting to end this war with a victory. What you accuse me of is creating a stalemate at the cost of thousands of lives, to no purpose at all."

Tell him nothing, the Rénard urged within him. It is much too dangerous. Even if he intends to keep confidence, Sun may have missed a bug, intentionally or otherwise. And even if this area is secure . . . Possibilities branched off to infinity. He had been wrong. Chiang was not the center of danger. He was himself the source of his own fear.

"As you have interpreted it, it would be terrible," Chiang said. "And it would be entirely inconsistent with what I know of you. Even Valentino was not so arbitrary. So there must be another reason."

Still Benedict said nothing. "You are testing me," Chiang said at length. "You are not sure if I know enough to be trusted. Perhaps you even think that I am merely guessing your responsibility.

"Benedict, I *know*. Find a flaw in my reasoning if you can.

"It started with anger. When I heard that Ishige had withdrawn his fleet at the height of the battle, I was outraged. My anger even spread to you. If you were such a clever fox, why had you not foreseen this treachery?

"That thought gave me pause. Perhaps you had foreseen it. I thought back to our meeting with Ishige. I remembered how much he had stressed that self-interest, not honor, motivated the Terrestrial Commonwealth. He shook his head when you suggested that he had brought his battlestars into Centauran space last because he recognized their vulnerability. But if that wasn't the reason, what was? Could it be that he was under orders to return immediately if he ran into hostile fire?

"Terrestrials are notorious for considering themselves the center of the universe, for thinking that the well-being of their garden planet and the safety of its genetic stock is the be-all and end-all.

"Ishige wasn't allowed to tell us that under certain circumstances he was ordered to cut and run; the Terrestrial Commissioners realized what a furor that would cause. But his own sense of honor impelled him to give us sufficient clues to deduce the limitations under which he was working."

Benedict sat absolutely still. Chiang's voice became more confident. "So much was obvious in hindsight. So obvious that I felt you must have understood it at once. Yet you had obviously been powerless to prevent it.

"Normally, I would have confronted you at once. I tried to, in fact, but Dr. Russell informed me that you had not yet regained consciousness. So I went instead to the Defense Ministry, where I was able to obtain taped copies of what they call the battle history. The verbal communications weren't very enlightening. But when I ran an analysis of the actual ship movements, it all became clear."

Chiang sat back in his chair, not taking his eyes from Benedict for an instant. "The first thing I noted was that Ishige was far from the coward TRANSCENDATRAN is calling him. His losses passed the critical point as soon as his battlestars were destroyed. He can have justified his continued participation in the battle only by adopting your rationale that battlestars are a net liability, and therefore their destruction was not a 'real' loss.

"The second observation I made was more subtle but even more important. As soon as Ishige put his fleet under your command, his ships bore the brunt of the combat. They were exposed to Bestial fire fifty percent more often than were our Centauran vessels. And when

Centauran and Terrestrial vessels attacked together, the Terrestrial vessels were almost always the vanguard; the Centaurans were almost always the secondary or reserve units. As a result, the Terrestrial fleet began to take two casualties for every one of ours.

"Orders were coming so quickly and in such complex bundles from your console that I am sure even Ishige did not realize what was happening. And doubtless you believed that if any Centauran official ever noticed the pattern, he would decide that you were just resting our forces, which had until then borne the brunt of the battle.

"I am not so simple. Neither are you. Your strategy forced Ishige to withdraw his fleet. That withdrawal shattered the Alliance. You planned it. Only I don't know why."

The bass notes of the orchestra penetrated the sonic bubble, more regular than a heartbeat. Dancers, following that beat, swirled about the floor in complex orbits. It would be very pleasant to sit half mesmerized by music and movement.

And it would certainly be safer than answering Chiang. Yet suddenly Benedict knew that he would answer and would do so truthfully. Too long, he had been exiled from a human race that valued his talent while considering him loathsome. Even on Ariel, his superiors had only provisionally accepted him. The brothers, who had had no idea that he was a Multi-Neural Capacitant, had accepted him personally and had been delighted with the results of his work, but none of them had really understood it. Chiang and Bobbi might well understand this masterwork. They might even approve.

"You won't disappoint me, will you?" the tall, pale figure had asked. And deeper even than the horror at seeing himself flayed open, floating in a plastic case, Benedict had ached from trying to earn affection from a man who had stifled all human emotions except curiosity.

"Yes, I did just as you have said." Benedict took a deep breath, surprised at how freely it came.

His gaze locked with Chiang's. "I served you well because of my oath of indenture. But I took that oath to prevent you from destroying, in a fit of temporary insanity, everything the Stewards had accomplished on Ariel. My first oath, my main loyalty, has always been to the Order of Stewards and the Church.

"My superiors were distressed that you had forced me from Ariel, but faced with the accomplishment, they looked for some way to use me to influence you."

"That possibility had occurred to me," Chiang said evenly.

"They did not wish you misfortune," Benedict said quickly. "Quite the contrary. But they were perturbed by your switch from the peace to the war faction in the Inner Council."

"It is all very well to wish for peace," Chiang said. "But once war has started, the only way to get peace is with a decisive victory."

Benedict nodded. "It *is* a misfortune that Church leaders look at peace as a 'natural' condition that can best be achieved by exhorting the populace to trust and goodness. In my experience, trust and goodness will be one-sided at best. From which it follows that achieving peace for any duration is a process as subtle and mysterious as balancing a quantum drive. Being totally correct about ends is almost useless if one is incoherent about means."

He looked over at Bobbi, his eyes wide. "Perhaps all clerics should read a chapter of *The Prince* for every chapter of, say, John's Gospel. I don't suppose such a suggestion would get very far, though.

"Not that I should pat myself on the back for being so discerning. I originally thought, like you, that a decisive victory was necessary to end the war. Only after some thought did I realize that would be disastrous."

"How so?" Chiang asked, obviously irritated. "The alternative is a war of attrition, bleeding both sides for years to come."

Benedict shook his head. "A decisive victory such as you imagine was impossible in this war. First of all, the sides were too evenly matched. The Allies had more and better armament, but the Clans had better fighters and more aggressive tactics. The various advantages pretty much evened out.

"Beyond that, no victory in battle could be translated into a durable peace! Suppose the Clans totally destroyed the Allied fleet. Then what? There aren't enough of them for an army of occupation. If they tried to enforce direct control, they would be bled to death in guerrilla skirmishes. Within a matter of years, they would be faced with widespread revolt.

"Well, then, suppose the Allies won. That would pose a different problem. In the past, a victorious power could establish control over a defeated country by disbanding the army, occupying the capital, and controlling the main access routes and frontiers.

"But space is infinite. Access roads and frontiers don't exist! The Allied fleet would reduce planet after planet, at great cost in lives and material, and when the Clans decided they had had enough, they would simply move on out until they were too far away to make continued military operations practical. And there they would grow and flourish, nourishing hatred for the parent race that had tried to destroy them. Within a generation the war would start again. But because of it trade would stagnate, exploration would cease, and hatreds would be bred on both sides that could be sated only by genocide. It would be a new Dark Age, on an interstellar scale."

"So neither alternative would work," Chiang said

slowly. "Yet despite that, you believed that there was a solution."

"I did. I asked myself why the war had started in the first place. My analysis disclosed three major interests behind the war. Each one of them has supported war because they fundamentally have misconceived the reality with which they are faced.

"First of all, there are the large corporations, the First Families and their Terrestrial counterparts. They wanted cheap, highly skilled labor that could perform in extremely unpleasant environments, without union problems or labor laws. Snowden Associates filled this want by creating the Bestials. There was some resistance on the part of the Defenders of Humanity, but that was actually an advantage: It reinforced the popular conception that Bestials were inhuman and therefore could be treated only as a capital investment, the same way you treat a robot or an animal. A lie, of course. Any company official who honestly considered the amount of human genetic material in the Bestials or the amount of intelligence and initiative needed to perform their tasks would have to conclude that they *were* human. But all the incentives were with dishonesty. The result of this dishonesty was that the corporations could not seriously consider opposition from their creatures. Even when it appeared, their mental image of the Clans as subhumans prevented them from understanding that they would fight if pressed.

"Then there were the Defenders of Humanity. They were threatened in two ways by Snowden's simulacra. First of all, being mainly lower-class, they were being displaced from the job market. Less immediately but perhaps even more importantly, their entire self-identity was threatened.

"Note this: As is not unusual with common folk, their instincts were quite sound. As the line between human and animal was progressively blurred, there has been an increasing tendency on the part of society to treat the two the same, not by raising the dignity of animals but by considering people to be fungible biological products. If you are on the lower end of the power spectrum, such a tendency creates a very reasonable uneasiness. Graeme Williams understood the basis of that uneasiness so successfully that the Defenders of Humanity grew from their original fundamentalist base to embrace Catholics, Jews, and not a few agnostics.

"They have two weaknesses, though. They are largely anti-intellectual, so that they are as likely to strike out at potential allies as at their enemies. And despite Williams's pervasive influence, they are largely undisciplined. The combination means that they are easily manipulated. My sister, Allele, was able to set their own violence against them. The result was a widespread reaction against them.

"When the Bestials attacked, it seemed to the Defenders that God was vindicating them. No wonder that they had no incentive to seriously study the question of whether the Bestials were really human or who was really responsible for the war.

"Finally, there were the Bestials, or the Clans, as they prefer to call themselves. The same intelligence that made them useful to their owners let them know that they were being exploited. It also created the strategy of easing normal humans out of lower-level positions of responsibility, ostensibly to save the corporations money, but actually to make themselves effectively self-governing.

"Yet despite this intelligence, the Clans suffered from two nearly fatal misperceptions. The first was that the Defenders of Humanity were as powerful as they were vocal. When the corporations realized that their slaves were in rebellion and so began to tighten the screws, the Clans interpreted this as the first stages of a genocide campaign. That was why they launched their initial attack.

"The other misperception was of themselves. One of the unlooked-for side effects of the genetic tampering that created them was *testrarch*, a period of emotional violence during the onset of puberty. It is the formative fact of Clan society. The Clans have evolved rigid codes of self-discipline and ritual honor to deal with it.

"They have been only partially successful. Deep within each of them is a fear that the Defenders are correct, that they are only savage beasts. And so they have made war not only for survival but also from despair, thinking that nothing better is possible."

Benedict paused as if contemplating the full extent of the scene he had described. "Nobody wanted war. All were acting in what they perceived to be their best interests. Yet their perceptions were so warped by their sins —you don't like that word, Chiang. Most of us don't. Perhaps I should date my conversion from the instant I realized that moral theology gave a more accurate account of human conduct than any school of psychology, because it understood that the basis of evil is intentional self-delusion.

"As I was saying, their perceptions were so warped by avarice, fear, and despair that they simply blundered into war without intending it, and having done so, they had no idea how to restore peace. In fact, they were so confused that they weren't even sure they wanted to."

Chiang leaned forward, intently interested. "And this analysis suggested to you a course of action."

"Reality. What other cure is there for delusion? Allele was my model for dealing with the Defenders of Humanity. Broadcasting her own murder rubbed the faces of the Defenders and their sympathizers in their own violence. They never fully recovered from that blow.

"I chose to show another reality. Until now, for most of the populace, this war has been as clear and distant as

a fireworks display. Military censorship has helped rein-
force that impression.

"I recorded all of the battle of Pearl and arranged for
the tapes to be leaked to TRANSCENDATRAN. For the first
time, the public heard soldiers describing the horror of
finding their brother soldiers charred by blast heat, torn
apart by explosive decompression. They saw soldiers
cutting their way through half-melted radioactive wreckage, taking the most reckless chances to save their
comrades. They didn't see their Bestial forms, and even
though they knew intellectually that these soldiers were
Bestials, the label became abstract. Hardly anyone could
listen to those tapes and fail to realize that our opponent
was brave, compassionate, and most definitely human."

"That may have been your intended effect," Chiang
objected, "but the actual effect was to show that the
Bestials could be beaten decisively. There was never
such enthusiasm for the war effort as when we returned."

"I planted a seed," Benedict said. "It took time to
mature. The enthusiasm you noted was sparked by the
demonstration that the war might be ended, and at a relatively low cost. And that enthusiasm was needed if I
could move to the second part of my plan."

"Becoming Sky Marshal of the Allied fleet," Chiang
said flatly.

"Yes. I have already explained how the contemporary
stalemate promised interminable attrition while a victory
by either side would be disastrous. The only choice left,
then, was simultaneous defeat!"

"Which you accomplished," Chiang said slowly as the
rest of the answer unfolded in his mind, "by destroying
the Bestial fleet and the Alliance."

"Yes," Benedict said, pleased. "The Clans will now
ask for peace terms because their losses were so severe
that they have no choice. Centaurus and Terra will be
willing to negotiate because neither, separately, has

strength sufficient to protect itself *and* send a fleet out to all the Periphery."

Bobbi frowned. "That doesn't make sense. If both sides have been hurt equally, they can continue the war on equal terms."

"They could, but they won't. Each is properly more concerned with his own wounds than those of his opponent. And as I have shown, the primary motivations have been lessened. Many of those once sympathetic to the Defenders of Humanity, including some of their leaders, like Epstein, have come to realize that the Clans are composed of humans with justified grievances. As the Clans perceive this change, their own fears diminish. And the corporations, which triggered the war by trying to maintain the Clans as slave labor, have found the war unprofitable from the beginning. They have plenty of room to make reasonable contracts with the Clans, because the Clans can still exploit the Periphery at less cost than human labor. And the Clans will deal with the corporations because they need the resources that only the corporations can provide."

Chiang mulled this over, sipping his drink. "Very neat."

"But not perfect," Benedict admitted. "Still, it was not my task to bring forth the millennium. I was charged with aiding you and with ending a war. It may be a mark of spiritual pride, but I must confess myself content with the results."

"What will you do now?" Bobbi asked.

"I really don't know," Benedict answered. He laughed at their looks of incredulity. "Oh, I would like to go back to Ariel, but I understand that everything has proceeded quite nicely without me. Perhaps the Stewards will establish houses on planets in the Periphery. From what I have seen, the Clans could use our terraforming expertise. But it all depends on what my superiors direct.

"Or perhaps I shall devote my time merely to being

human now that I have papal dispensation to do so. I have been both fox and lion: Humanity may prove more challenging."

He let his glance fall to the dancers on the floor below. His expression darkened. "It may also depend on what capacities remain to me. Dr. Russell is wrong: I am not quite fully recovered. My neurons occasionally misfire in the most curious way, and then I see before me, if just for an instant, people who have been dead for years.

"But that is hardly a great handicap," he said briskly. "I have been sane for years, and it is much less than it is cracked up to be. Nor is it unfair that I should suffer some emotional discomfort when so many under my command were killed."

BOMB DEMOLISHES STARLINER STATEROOM

Chiang ripped the TRANSCENDATRAN release from the printer and handed it to Bobbi. "Some people are just poor losers," he said.

"'A stateroom in the starliner *Pegasus* was destroyed today by a miniature gamma ray device,'" Bobbie read. "'The device was apparently planted by professionals, since it was, by means not yet discovered, smuggled in despite the starliner's stringent security precautions and set to go off less than a minute before the first jump into quantum space. At that time, it would be certain that the occupant would be immobilized within the room in his cold-sleep capsule.

"'The stateroom had been booked by Paul Niccolo Rénard, recently Sky Marshal of the Centauran Fleet.'" She sat down quickly. All of Neoptolemus seemed to tilt crazily around her.

"Only three days ago—" she began, and faltered. "I guess he'd become almost mythical to me. I didn't think he could be killed."

"You stopped reading too soon," Chiang said. "The stateroom was empty."

ABOUT THE AUTHOR

Born in Massachusetts in 1948, Robert Chase was educated at Phillips Exeter Academy, Dartmouth College, and the Duke School of Law. He presently lives in Maryland, working as an attorney for the U.S. Army, with his wife, two children, dog, and cat.